Judge Sheffey looked at the Court Clerk. **"What is the longest sentence that has ever been handed down in this court?"**

She looked up. "Your Honor, I believe it was ninety-nine years –by you."

The judge looked down at me and a wide smile covered his face. "Mr. Erler, I sentence you to ninety-nine years and six months at Florida State Prison at hard labor." His words didn't really sink in. "Remember something, Mr. Erler, it's not how long you make it, it's how you make it long." The words were from a popular cigarette commercial, and he started laughing at his own joke.

They Called Me The
CATCH ME KILLER

BOB ERLER
John C. Souter

INTERNATIONAL ROCK MINISTRIES, INC.
Bob Erler, President
P.O. Box 901907
Dallas, Texas 75390-1907
a division of the Bob Erler Evangelistic Association

First printing: August, 1981
Second printing: July, 1982
Third printing: December, 1986
Library of Congress Catalog Card No.: 80-50666
ISBN: 0-8423-0213-1, cloth
ISBN: 0-8423-0214-X, paper

CONTENTS

ONE
THE CATCH ME KILLER

It was a beautiful August day. I drove my green-and-white police cruiser out of the city garage and quickly rolled down the windows to let the salt air blow through. The warm Florida sun was already peeking over the neatly trimmed palm trees lining the highway as I drove through Hollywood. It was 7:00 a.m. and I had just come on duty. I pulled into a gas station to grab a quick sandwich.

Before I had reached the sandwich machine, a late model blue Falcon drove up. The driver honked his horn noisily to get my attention. I stooped at the passenger side of the car and looked in at an older couple. The man leaned past the woman to tell me they had just spotted a body lying by the road in the industrial park sector.

I returned to my vehicle and called in. "One forty-seven to headquarters at Sheridan Road Interchange and I-95. I'll be 10-8 investigating a complaint of someone lying in the road in the industrial park sector."

Headquarters acknowledged and my car engine roared to life. I quickly traveled the half mile to the business park. Once in the area I drove slowly, searching for what the people had seen. Up ahead, someone was lying by the side of the road. Pulling my car up, I realized I had discovered a heavyset white female who had been shot numerous times in the head.

"One forty-seven to headquarters. Be advised of a homicide, a white female, who has received multiple gunshot wounds in the head. Send an ambulance and homicide detectives out here immediately."

"Ten-four, 147. Homicide detectives and ambulance en route. Check the scene and keep us informed. 10-4."

The victim was wearing a plaid blouse and the bottom of a two-piece bathing suit. Her blonde hair was matted with dried blood. By the time I pulled my car around to block off the area, police sirens were screaming in from several directions.

Units from the Broward County Sheriff's Department, the Highway Patrol, the Fort Lauderdale Police, and the Hollywood Department all converged on the scene at the same moment. The Hollywood detectives immediately took charge. After a few moments, one of them asked me what I had seen. I explained how I had discovered the body and the detective wrote down everything on his pad.

We formed a human chain and searched the area inch by inch, walking over it in every direction looking for clues. We hoped to find spent shell casings, signs of a struggle, or perhaps a murder weapon. We searched thoroughly but found nothing.

An off-duty Deputy Sheriff from the Broward County office drove up in a white Mustang. He told me his office had received two phone calls from the killer. The caller claimed he had killed three people and told where to find the bodies. (As it turned out, there were only two victims.)

"They just found another victim over at the airport; a white woman, about forty years old. She's still alive—they took her to Broward General. That makes two. There's supposed to be another one in the water somewhere. The guy who did this is really sick."

It didn't take long after my report went over the radio for the area to become inundated with curiosity seekers and reporters. Cameras were flashing everywhere. Because of the calls from the killer, the murders were considered front-page news. A Coast Guard helicopter suddenly whirled overhead and began to follow a nearby irrigation ditch, searching for a third victim. Before long many helicopters were involved searching all the county waterways.

An ambulance arrived, but the detectives wouldn't allow the attendants to remove the body until all the photographs and other evidence had been gathered. The Broward County Medical Exam-

iner arrived and began a preliminary examination. Body temperature and the lack of bleeding on location seemed to indicate the
wounds had been inflicted elsewhere at approximately 5 a.m.

Once the ambulance took off, my sergeant asked if I could
remember seeing anything unusual or any vehicles in the area.
When I explained how I discovered the body, he advised me to
return to headquarters and write out a thorough report.

When I arrived at the Hollywood Police Department, several
officers were milling around the station, anxious for information
about the case. I explained what I knew, then made my way
through the crowd to the detective bureau.

I wrote out my report, exactly as it had happened, and turned it
in. The detective sergeant went over the report and told me if I
remembered anything else, to let him know. My sergeant called in
and told me to come back on road patrol because traffic was
backing up in the area as a result of the radio news coverage. They
had played the two tapes from the killer over public radio.

Returning to my area, I helped move the traffic around the site
where the girl had been found. Crowds of morbidly curious people
surrounded several divers who were searching the nearby canal
under the direction of some detectives.

The patrolman in the adjoining district called me on his radio
and asked to meet for a cup of coffee at a restaurant bordering our
two sections.

When we sat down he said, "What's going on, Bob? I've never seen
so much action on one case. What do you think the motive is?"

"I really don't know, Bill. Medical reports say neither of the
women has been sexually molested, but they think they might
have picked up a hitchhiker."

"Phew!" Bill said simply, nodding his head.

"I guess it just goes to show you that you never know who you're
talking to anymore."

"Boy, you said that right."

After several hours of directing traffic I was recalled to headquarters to assist the investigating detectives. They had obtained a
copy of the two phone calls by the unknown male.

The first tape had been recorded at 6:18 a.m. Deputy James Rice
had answered: "Broward Sheriff's Department, Complaint Desk,
Deputy Rice speaking," he said in a monotone.

"Who is this?" the caller asked.

"Rice," the officer answered simply.

"Ah—sir. Ah—I'd like to report a murder."

"A what?"

"Murder."

"A murder?"

"I just killed three people.."

"You just killed three people?" Rice asked.

"Right."

"Are you serious?" asked the deputy.

"I'm serious. Please catch me. Please."

"Where are you, son?" Rice asked while the caller kept repeating, "Please, please, please."

"I ju—please." the voice said.

"Where are you?" Rice asked again.

"I'm gonna kill' em tonight, too. Please."

"Where are you?" Rice insisted.

The caller hung up. At exactly 6:30 a.m. the complaint phone rang again. Deputy Hal Lemore answered it this time.

"Sheriff's Department."

"Rice, is this Rice?"

"He's in the other room. What do you want?"

If you want to find those bodies, go down to the airport."

"Down to the airport?"

"Right."

"Lauderdale Airport?" the Deputy asked.

"I don't know what it is, but it's an airport, and then there's one in the water and one on a side street."

"Wait" Lemore demanded.

"I'm at this race . . . the main highway here."

"Route 1?" Lemore asked.

"Sh-She—the Shell gas station. Hurry up, please."

"Okay."

The caller hung up again.

Listening to that strained voice gave me an eerie feeling. It belonged to a troubled man. The detectives from several different police departments were present as we listened to the tape several times and discussed the many possibilities of the case.

Everybody had a different opinion as to what type of person we were dealing with. Some felt he must be a multiple killer, or an escaped convict, or perhaps someone from the nearby insane asylum. Everyone also had different ideas concerning how and when the murders had taken place.

The phone calls seemed completely authentic. The caller stated he had killed three. So far we had found the girl's body and the woman had been discovered near the Hollywood-Fort Lauderdale Airport. She was found in a bloody parked car and was in critical condition at Broward General Hospital. As yet, a third victim had not been found.

During the day, over fifty people were detained as possible suspects in the murder. Most of these were released when they were able to prove they were not in the area at the time of the murders.

Several departments were working simultaneously on the case. The investigation was soon turned over to the Broward County Sheriff's Office and the Fort Lauderdale Police Department because the woman had been found in that city. But we continued to assist in the case.

When it was time for me to go off duty, the shift lieutenant asked me to play the tape for the on-coming officers. There were many reactions to it.

"That guy is really flipped out," one officer remarked.

"You can tell from the strain on that voice," the lieutenant said, "that guy is really in deep trouble." He looked at me and I nodded agreement.

"I feel sorry for that person," another added. "He's really lost."

After I played the tape at least a dozen times, the lieutenant said, "That voice sounds familiar."

"When you listen to it over and over it seems familiar," said a sergeant, "but you've probably never heard it before."

I returned the tape to the detective bureau and walked to the Assistant Chief's office. I knocked and he called me in. A number of people were already in his office and several phone calls were on hold. "Chief, I've got to talk to you. There's something really important I want to tell you."

"Officer Erler, I've got too many important things going now. Why don't you come back later."

"Well . . . okay, Chief."

"You've done a good job, Erler. I appreciate your staying over."

"Can I stick around and talk to you in a little while?"

"No. Best you catch me tomorrow. I'll be working overtime."

I walked out of the Chief's office. My head was throbbing. It had been a confusing day and I felt so bad because of that poor girl. I was overwhelmed with depression and could have cried at that moment.

The banner headline on the August 12, 1968 edition of the *Hollywood Sun-Tattler* that evening read: "TEENAGE GIRL MURDERED, WOMAN SHOT, POLICE SEARCH FOR POSSIBLE 3RD VICTIM."

That night, an eighteen-year-old man was arrested at the Hollywood-Fort Lauderdale International Airport. He had tried to buy a ticket on the first flight to anywhere. After interrogation it was determined that he could not be the killer and was booked only on petty larceny.

The next day, documents found in the interior of the car where the older woman was found indicated she was Dorothy Clark from Clarkston, Georgia. Identification was confirmed later in the day. Mrs. Clark was described as a multiple divorcee who had left her job at Emory University in Atlanta in May. The dead girl was believed to be Mrs. Clark's twelve-year-old daughter Merilyn.

Fort Lauderdale police had located a witness who said he saw the two women on Sunday. Also in the car were another young woman and a youth described as being five feet eleven and about 160 pounds. He was between eighteen and twenty years old, with blond hair combed straight back and was wearing a blue shirt with white polka dots and Bermuda shorts.

An attendant at an all-night Shell service station told of seeing a stockily built blond with a crew cut. The man was in his early twenties and had obtained change from him around 6:00 a.m. He made a call from the pay phone outside, then returned to his car. He said the man sat in his auto a while, then made a second call before driving off.

A tavern keeper said he had served a woman and child of the victims' description Sunday afternoon. They were accompanied by a sandy-haired young man in his early twenties. He was of stocky build and wore khaki slacks and a polka dot sport shirt.

From these descriptions a composite drawing was made. I was assigned to take copies of these drawings to every post office and supermarket in the area. The artist's conception was published in Tuesday's papers and shown over television.

Each of the police departments involved was receiving hundreds of phone calls on possible leads in the case. The tape recordings were broadcast statewide and Florida residents were greatly upset by the murders. Radio and TV stations carried bulletins at regular intervals, warning motorists not to pick up hitchhikers. After hearing the tapes, thousands of people contacted Broward authorities claiming they could identify the voice of the killer.

The investigating officers were surprised by the public reaction of fright. Hounded by reporters and public officials demanding action, all police officers were expressly forbidden to discuss the case with anyone. All information made public about the "Catch Me Killer" began to be issued in carefully prepared press releases.

Over the next few days there were many arrests of people who fit the suspect's description. I was on patrol one night when headquarters called. "Car 147, be advised of a 'Catch Me Killer' suspect in the Tiger Tail Lounge. The barmaid is convinced this is the suspect. Take all precautions; a backup is en route."

When I arrived at the lounge the barmaid came up and nodded toward a man sitting by himself. "Look at that man with the suitcase. He fits the killer's description perfectly. When I talked to him he was shaky and nervous and he keeps looking around like somebody is after him."

The suspect saw me staring and turned away. I walked to his booth, pulled my revolver, and informed him he was under arrest. He was extremely nervous.

I made him lean against the wall, then searched and handcuffed him. Not only did he fit the description, he was from out-of-state and that made him an even better suspect. The backup officer arrived and we transported him to headquarters where the detectives began interrogation.

The man had run out on his family in Michigan, which explained some of his nervousness. He could not have been in the area at the time of the shootings and was released.

For the next few days, our detectives interviewed suspects and collaborated with the other agencies involved on the case to painstakingly compile all available evidence. Mrs. Clark and her daughter had barhopped all day Sunday and the sandy-haired, crew-cut young man had been their companion during this time.

The woman's car became the object of intense scrutiny. There were no fingerprints inside the vehicle except those of the woman and her child. The crime lab reported that no traces of the dead girl's blood were found in the blood-splattered car. This indicated the daughter had not been shot while in the vehicle.

The coroner's office reported that Merilyn was killed with a .22-caliber weapon, and X-rays of the mother indicated she had also been shot with a .22-caliber gun.

The mother remained in a coma. She spoke occasionally, but was incoherent. If she did not recover, detectives feared the case would never be solved. With nationwide publicity, there was tremendous pressure on them to make a solid arrest.

Later in the week, I received a call to check out a prowler in the North Hollywood area. It was midnight when I arrived at the house and rang the doorbell.

"Who's out there?" a woman called from inside.

"Police. You called us, didn't you?"

She peeked out the window, then came to the door and opened it a crack. She peered out at me over several door chains and locks.

"Oh, officer. I'm so glad it's you. I'm so afraid of this 'Catch Me Killer' I wouldn't let anybody in here but you."

"Yes, ma'am. What seems to be the trouble?"

She unlocked the door and let me in. There were several children inside.

"My husband is on a business trip and I've heard lots of noises outside. I've been listening to the newscasts about this killer and I'm terrified."

"I wouldn't worry. This person, whoever he is and wherever he is, is not interested in hurting you. He'd have no reason to hurt you."

She calmed down and I searched around her house to make certain no one was lurking nearby. "I'll be in the area most of the night," I assured her. "If you hear any other noises, just call the station and I'll be right over."

I was phoning my family on a regular basis as my mother had gone into the hospital for cancer observation and I was fearful my family was keeping the truth from me about her condition. I was spending a great deal of money, which I didn't have, on those calls. I finally got in to see the Chief and told him I needed a leave of absence because of my personal problems.

"Bob, you're one of the investigating officers on the Clark case. This is a crucial time and we need all the help we can get."

"Sir, this is an emergency. My mother is very close to me and I love her very much. I'm not going to put my job above my mother.

If it means I have to resign, then I will. I have to go to Phoenix."

"Listen, Bob, you're a good officer and we'll bend over backwards to keep you. How about a two-week leave of absence?"

"I'd appreciate that very much, Chief."

I filled out the paperwork and left the following day for Arizona. Mother seemed to be doing better and that was great news. Right after I arrived in Phoenix all the cash from my last pay check was stolen by someone who broke into the apartment. I had to borrow money two weeks later to fly back to Florida.

No new leads had turned up on the "Catch Me Killer" case while I had been away. The mother-in-law of a fellow police officer and a good friend was the nurse attending Mrs. Clark. No one was supposed to know where Mrs. Clark was being hospitalized because it was feared the killer might make another attempt on her life. But because I was a police officer and had worked on the case, she told me what room Mrs. Clark was in at Broward General, how she was doing, and what the doctors were saying about her chances for survival.

On a night off, I decided to go to the hospital to see how she was. When I arrived at her hospital room, I was greeted by two officers who were friends of mine.

"What are the chances of my getting in to see the victim?"

"Listen, Bob, we've got direct orders. Nobody is to go in there. But you being an officer, and one of the investigators on this thing, I guess we could let you in to see how she's doing."

They took me into the hospital room where there were two more officers, a doctor and a nurse. Mrs. Clark had tubes coming out everywhere.

"Doctor, what are the chances this woman will live?"

"A million to one that she won't. If she does live, she'll never be anything but a vegetable for the rest of her life."

"A million to one?"

"That's right," he said matter-of-factly.

While I stood looking at the victim, one of the officers turned to me and suggested I leave. "The lieutenant's going to come back. It would look bad for us if somebody came in and saw you here, even though you're an officer."

"Yeah. I can understand your position. Thanks for letting me see her."

While driving home that night, I thought out my personal

situation and all the problems I had had with my wife who had recently left me. I really didn't know what I wanted to do. I couldn't decide if I should continue police work or go home and be with my family. But as I reflected on my problems, the decision came to me. There were just too many bad memories in Florida.

"Chief," I said to Carl King the next day, "I've decided to resign from the force effective September 5."

"You're not serious, Bob!"

"I'm very serious. I'm going home to Arizona."

He tried to talk me out of the decision, reminding me there was a $100 raise coming soon. He made several other suggestions, hoping to keep me but my mind was made up. I knew it was time to leave. I sold my trailer to Donald Parton, the Dania Chief of Police, and quickly peddled most of my other possessions, including one of my cars and drove my Volkswagen back to Arizona.

TWO
"COME OUT
WITH YOUR HANDS UP!"

A few days after I arrived in Phoenix, my mother was released from the hospital and was told she didn't need another cancer operation. We were all quite happy and relieved with the news.

Having driven straight through from Florida, I was physically exhausted and still recovering from the strain of my personal problems. I was staying with my sister De De and her roommate, Judy, who had a little boy of her own. For a few days I loafed around the house with no real plans for the future.

On Monday morning, September 15, I awoke with a slight headache—what was left of the migraine I'd had the night before. After dressing I walked through the living room, flipped on the TV, and continued into the kitchen.

"Judy, can I get you to make me something to eat?"

"Sure, Bob. No problem."

A television program began to chatter in the other room only to be interrupted by a special news announcement: "We interrupt this program to bring you a special law enforcement bulletin. Police and FBI agents have begun an intensive nationwide search for an ex-Green Beret killer who vows never to be taken alive."

When I heard the newscaster say "Green Beret" I was drawn from the kitchen like a magnet. I had been in Special Forces, which is such a small elite group there was a good possibility I might know this man. I walked to the set and turned up the volume.

"An intensive search is being conducted by several law enforcement agencies for a Phoenix man, Robert John Erler, in connection with the slaying of a twelve-year-old girl in Florida. The authorities believe Erler, a former police officer, is heavily armed with an automatic rifle, at least three handguns, and several grenades. He is believed to be extremely dangerous and has vowed never to be taken alive . . . "

For some reason, the name didn't register. Judy looked at me. "Didn't he say, 'Robert John Erler'?"

"Yeah. I think he did say that," I replied, a little dazed. As the interrupted program resumed its chatter, I picked up the telephone and dialed the station. I couldn't get through to the news announcer, so I called the Maricopa County Sheriff's Office.

When the booking desk answered I asked, "Are you looking for a Robert John Erler?"

"We sure are!"

For the first time, fear splashed over me like someone had dumped a bucket of cold water over my head. I abruptly hung up.

Judy walked back in from the kitchen and asked what was going on.

"Oh, man. This is wiping me out. They're really looking for me! What can I do?"

"Hey, listen. I've got a bunch of drugs here. You wanna take some?"

"What are they?"

"Don't worry about it. It will just do you in. It will take care of any problems you're having." Judy produced a bottle of pills and selected a handful to give to me. I downed them with one quick swallow. I needed relief.

After a few moments I decided to call the police department again to see if I could talk to Dave Koelsch, an officer I had known for several years—but I couldn't reach him.

I dialed my mother's house but was startled when she practically began to scream. "Butch! They're standing outside with machine guns. They're hiding behind the fences and the cars. There must be a hundred police officers out here. Oh, Butch, they're gonna kill you! What have you done?"

I hung up. Now panic was really flooding my brain. My body began to shake uncontrollably. I had never been so unnerved or scared in my life. I didn't know what was going on. My mind was totally confused and disoriented.

When Judy saw how I was reacting, she offered me more pills.

"Judy, aren't you afraid? You heard what they said about me on television."

"Why should I be afraid? I've known you all my life. I'd trust you with my son as well as with my own life."

"Man, I just can't figure out what's going on."

I downed another handful of Judy's pills and called the Sheriff's Department again. I identified myself and said I wanted to speak to Dave Koelsch. The officer kept asking me where I was.

"I'll let you know where I'm at if you get Koelsch for me. I know he won't shoot me on sight like most of the rest of the Phoenix police."

"I'll reach Koelsch by two-way radio," he said. "Give me your number and I'll have him call you."

"No—I'll call you back."

I was on the phone constantly. Groping for someone to help me in my dilemma, I made several phone calls to Claire Kaufman, a friend in Florida whom I'd met about the time I started with the Hollywood Police department.

"Claire?"

"Yes . . . Bob? Oh, Bob! Where are you?"

"I'm in Phoenix, Claire. What's going on back there?"

"Bob, they said you killed that little girl."

"Claire, everybody's laughing at me."

"No they're not, Bob. I'm not. My husband isn't. Bob, you have to give up and face this. You know we'll stick by you."

We talked briefly then I hung up. On my fourth try, I reached Koelsch at the Sheriff's Department.

"Dave, I can't figure out what's going on. I trust you. I know you won't shoot me if you get the chance."

"Let me come talk to you, Butch."

I gave him my address and sat down to wait. I stared blankly at the television screen for a few minutes before it suddenly dawned on me I was looking at a picture of the house *I was sitting in!* Right there on the screen was our house—and it was surrounded by police! They were hiding behind unmarked police cars, armed with rifles, shotguns, and anti-riot gear!

I jumped up and ran to the front window and peered out. Sure enough, our house was surrounded. In a moment an officer spoke to me through a bull horn.

"Attention in the house! Robert John Erler, you have one minute to come out with your hands up or we will force you out with tear gas!"

I yelled back I wasn't coming out. I was sure they'd cut me down when they got a clear shot.

The officer on the bullhorn asked if there was anyone else in the house. I yelled that there was a woman and child with me. I was standing in the doorway and they could have shot me but I'm certain they were afraid of hitting Judy and her son.

By now I was really goofy on drugs. I was having difficulty thinking straight and was soaring higher and higher. It was like living in a dream; it was too unreal to be true. I strapped on my police revolver so nobody would come near the house.

"Judy, if you want to take Mike and leave, go ahead, 'cause I don't know what's gonna happen here."

"No, I'm not leaving. If I leave, they'll kill you. With that bulletin they had on TV, there's no doubt in my mind they'll kill you."

The police let my brother Danny come into the house. We talked about what I should do. I was so frightened, I kept looking at my revolver. Maybe that was the only way out.

The phone rang. Danny picked it up. It was Dave Koelsch.

"Dave, I don't want to hurt anybody. I've decided to end it all and just commit suicide."

"Come on, Butch. That's a bad way out. That won't solve anything. Why don't you let me come up to the house and talk to you in person. I'll come unarmed."

Dave Koelsch arrived and Danny let him in. He immediately questioned me to find out what was going on—but I didn't know any more than he did.

I kept fingering my revolver and cocking it. I was thinking seriously about taking my life. "Dave, I don't want to hurt anybody. I just wish everyone would leave me alone. What are they doing to me?"

"Bob, why don't you just give me your revolver and give up? Let's get this whole mess straightened out."

"No, I'm not going to give up. I'll kill myself first. Man, I don't want this kind of smear on my record. What good can come of this? If I give up and go back to Florida how could I ever get a fair trial with all this publicity they've given me? I think the only way out is to kill myself."

Danny spoke up. "Butch, if you kill yourself, what will the family do? Bob, think of us. You've got to give yourself up."

The police let De De and my mother come into the house. The pressure from so many people telling me to give up finally cut through my drug haze. I decided to surrender. Because I was afraid to walk outside into that mess, Koelsch volunteered to drive me to the station.

"Dave, I'm not going to give up my weapon until we get to the station. I'd be afraid to walk out of here without it."

"That's okay. Just give me your word you won't shoot me or anybody else."

"You've got my word—as long as they don't try to come shoot me."

Dave, Danny, and I all walked cautiously out of the house and down to Dave's unmarked police car. My revolver was still in its holster as I nervously slid into the front seat next to Dave.

He pulled out and we began the twelve-mile journey to the station. Before long, I realized we were surrounded by unmarked police cars. It made me uncomfortable.

"Dave, get those cars away from us; they're bugging me." He got on his radio and they backed off.

In a few moments we reached the Maricopa County Sheriff's Station and once we passed into the center compound, the gate came down. Before we stepped out of the car, I turned my revolver over to Dave.

A moment later, a half dozen officers raced to the car, opened the door, and dragged me out. A number of rifles and pistols were pointed in my direction and a shotgun was placed at my head.

"Leave him alone," Koelsch commanded. "I'll take care of him."

They backed off and Dave took me inside. All sorts of reporters were waiting for us. Several TV cameras followed our progress; a number of cameramen jumped up and shot flashbulbs at me.

After we arrived at the booking desk a police major came up to me. "Listen, would you mind going back outside to walk in again? Channel 12 wasn't here in time to get pictures of you."

I made an obscene gesture and cursed him. I was going through a terrifying experience and he wanted me to relive it. Already I felt like an animal the way people were treating me.

I was stripped naked, searched, and made to take a shower. It was difficult to stand because I was so loaded on drugs. They finally gave me some clothes and led me upstairs to a cell where I quickly passed out.

The next thing I remember someone was shaking me. Groggily, I looked up into an officer's face. "Wake up. You've got to be arraigned."

I had slept for twenty-four hours but still my head was foggy. Two officers escorted me from my cell down to the elevator. When we entered the hallway downstairs, it was packed with reporters, floodlights, and camera equipment. My appearance caused an instant commotion. The photographers began to shoot picture after picture—flashing bulbs in my eyes. Reporters yelled over each other trying to get me to make a statement. They were treating me like some kind of animal. I turned away from the cameras as much as I could.

We had to cross a busy street in downtown Phoenix to reach the courthouse. As the officers took me across, the newsmen surrounded us and formed a giant circle, stopping traffic. We fought our way through the crowd.

One cameraman stood in my path, badgering me to start an incident. "Come on Erler, give us some action for the camera. *Give us some action!*"

He pushed me too far. I kicked him in the groin and stomped on his camera before the officers could stop me. They subdued me and quickly ran me back to my cell.

A few hours later they came again and handcuffed me. They also put a restraining leash around my waist but removed it when I promised not to cause trouble.

Again, we marched across the street through a large crowd of heckling reporters. This time there were more officers to make the mob stand back and we were able to reach the courthouse. Inside, the walls of the corridor were lined with camera equipment and news people. I was still quite high and the noise and confusion really pressed in on me.

"Hey," I said to one of the officers, "please get these people away from me, man. They're really bugging me. I'm too high."

"You're tough, Erler," one of them mocked. "You're a Special Forces man. Those tattoos on your arms show what a tough guy you are. You can take it."

We finally arrived in the narrow hallway leading to the judge's chambers. The words on the frosted glass door panel read: "Judge Coppock, Superior Court of Arizona." The door was locked and the officers kept knocking on it.

While we stood there waiting, the newsmen continued to hound me for pictures and a statement. The tension was building in my head. A photographer stepped forward and taunted me.

"You flipped a gear, didn't you, cop? Yeah, you must have flipped a gear when you killed that kid."

"Hey, man, get these people back," I asked again. But my guards just stood there.

We couldn't get into the courtroom. Finally, in desperation, I said, "I'll get in for you." I reached back and slammed both fists through the frosted glass window, shattering it. Most of the people in the hallway fled in panic. Some screamed.

I looked in at the judge and his secretary who glared back in stunned surprise. The glass had shattered all over his office. My wrist had suffered a deep gash and blood was squirting out.

The officers forced me to the floor. One wrapped my wrist with a handkerchief, then they picked me up and carried me on a run to a squad car. I was rushed to the County Hospital where they sewed up an artery and closed the wound with seven stitches.

Later that day, Judge Charles F. Coppock placed me under an $82,500 bond on a fugitive-from-justice charge in preparation for possible extradition proceedings.

In a day or two, after the effects of the drugs had worn off, I received a long-distance phone call from Joseph Varon, a prominent Florida lawyer. He offered to take my case and instructed me to waive extradition. I agreed to do as he asked.

On September 17, Claire Kaufman called me at the jail.

"The only thing that's important now is to get this thing squared away, right?" she began. "They're going to bring you back anyway. It might take a while and . . . they're going to make fun of you . . . "

"I told them to bring me back," I said.

"Just tell them you want to waive extradition and you're coming home . . . We'll stick by you all we can, you know that."

"Thank you, Claire, I know that. What does Jim think?"

"Why? Don't you think he's on your side?"

"Not anymore. I feel just like an animal now. I don't feel like I'm the police officer anymore."

"Look, Bob, there are certain things, no matter what people say ... you can't take them away ... Do you remember those people at all? Don't be afraid of me, Bob. Do you remember this little girl?"

"I don't want to talk about that on the phone, Claire."

"Do you remember anything about this murder, Bob?"

"I don't even know what's going on right now, Claire."

As soon as I waived extradition, two officers came immediately from Florida to get me. The deputies had been instructed not to take me by air so we traveled by car. By the time we reached El Paso, the officers were convinced I wasn't dangerous. We enjoyed good conversations all the way.

"Bob, you don't look crazy to me," one of them said.

"I'm not. Everything you heard about me causing problems happened while I was high on drugs. When I broke the window and jumped on that photographer I was high and scared."

"Let's stop in El Paso and call the Sheriff's Office. I'll tell him there's no problem with you and we'll see if we can all fly back."

I stayed in the El Paso City Jail that night. The next day we were going to fly to Miami. While being transported I reflected on my brief career as a police officer. Only a short time earlier I had been considered a model officer. I was hopeful that those who knew me could see this crime was out of character with my recent police history.

THREE
"ME! A COP?!"

I was born into a large family with eight kids. Because I was the oldest son, my father gave me his name and pushed me to be as tough as he was. After unsuccessful surgery performed on my dad, he became semi-invalided and we moved to Phoenix for his health. He began to put increased pressure on me to live out his life for him.

Because of my struggle to get along with dad, I decided to join the Army as a cook. Later I went to Special Forces school and became a Green Beret. News that dad was dying brought me home on emergency leave, and later ended my military career.

Back in Phoenix I became involved with a dancer named Pat. When she told me she was pregnant, I decided to get married because I had always wanted a son. But our problems went from bad to worse, so we moved to southern Florida in hopes that the change in environment would help our young marriage.

After living in the city of Dania for three weeks, I drove my car up to a stop light next to a police cruiser one day. The officer sounded his horn and I looked over to see the smiling face of an old friend. We pulled over together.

"Jim! What are you doing as a police officer?"

"Do you want to be an officer?"

I laughed. "Hey, man, you must be joking."

He noticed my Special Forces tattoos. "I heard you were a Green Beret. We can use guys like you, Bob." It got me interested.

We drove to the Dania Police Department where I filled out an application. Several weeks later the Chief of Police called. "Erler, your FBI record came back and you have an outstanding military record. We'd like to have you on the force. We can't put you on this minute but we'd like you to start riding around with the other officers as soon as you can."

I was then working for the North American Boat Corporation, testing racing boats. I decided to play "cop" on my day off. I was given a uniform and placed with a black cop who went by the nickname June Bug. He was assigned to the black area of Dania and we drove into that section of town where we were summoned to a disturbance of the peace.

After several other routine calls, June Bug tried to break up a fistfight between his fifteen-year-old brother and a young cousin. One of them pulled a gun, and evidently June Bug was trying to take it away from them. In the struggle that followed, the gun, a .22-caliber pistol, went off. The bullet entered his abdomen, deflected off his hip bone and cut into several organs. He was rushed to the hospital but it was too late. He died very quickly of massive internal hemorrhaging.

When I found out he was dead, a terrible sick feeling came over me. I couldn't believe how fast death could come to a police officer. I never even got to know June Bug's real name.

The next day I was sworn in as a regular officer on the Dania Police Department to fill the vacancy the black cop's death had created. I was determined, right from the beginning, that I was not going to die as the victim of my own stupidity.

I was assigned to stand watch over June Bug's casket for two days at the funeral parlor. Staring at him, dead in that casket, with his uniform on, had quite an effect on me.

The chief of police took me aside and said, "Bob, Dania is a small town and we don't have the funds to send you to police academy right now. If something looks wrong, make an arrest. We'll find something to charge them with when you bring them in."

Another officer took me out and showed me how to work the siren, the lights, and the radio. I received a clipboard with a list of the police signals and what they meant. My tutor had me pull over a few vehicles and give warnings, but after three hours I was on my own.

I was a bona fide police officer. I had never had any training, but now with a quick three-hour pep talk, I had become one of the city's finest. Somehow I felt a little unprepared as I drove into the community.

Dania is located on the Gold Coast between Fort Lauderdale and Hollywood. I would be patrolling approximately two miles of the main highway plus a mile of public beach.

I drove into the gas station on U.S. 1 in front of the police station. As I stepped out of the vehicle, several guys I knew pulled into the station and we began to talk. While we were standing there, a truck ran the red light on U.S. 1. "Hey, man, get that guy, he just ran the light!"

I sprinted to my car. Dania had just purchased three high-performance 360-horsepower cars and it had been some time since I had driven a car with so much power. I punched the gas pedal to the floor but instead of going forward, the car burned rubber— sideways —on the slick surface between the pumps. I panicked, but fortunately the car cleared the pumps before the tires caught and I swerved out of the gas station.

I was so flustered by the close call in the service station my heart was really pounding. The truck pulled over and I chewed the driver out telling him what a hazard he was. He gave me his driver's license and I walked back to get my ticket book. When I opened it and saw the complicated form, I realized I couldn't fill it out. I didn't even know what statute to put on the ticket.

"You're lucky," I told the driver. "I'm just going to give you a warning this time." He thanked me graciously several times. If he had only known, I couldn't have given him a ticket if I had wanted to.

When I returned to the gas station to sign for the gas I had received, I noticed the black marks where I had burned rubber out of the station. My friends ran to my car and said, "Boy, you really know how to drive that thing. I've never seen *anything* like that before!"

"Ah . . . there was nothing to it," I lied.

Dania was divided into two areas for every shift. I was assigned the white area and one of the black officers took the black section of town. Our sergeant drove a third car which overlooked both areas and acted as a backup for either officer. In addition to the three officers on the road, there was one dispatcher at headquarters. I really enjoyed the work and spent my free hours learning the state statutes and everything else I was supposed to know.

On the night shift one of my duties was to take a key and change the red light on U.S. 1 to a flashing yellow at midnight. One night while I was changing the light, a Greyhound bus came through town doing at least 60 miles an hour. Because the speed limit was only 30, I jumped in my cruiser and gave pursuit. I shined my spotlight up in the driver's mirror but he just looked down at me and waved. When I hit my siren he pulled over.

"Headquarters, this is car two. I'll be out with a signal 54 (which is a traffic violation)."

A little gray-haired man came walking back to my car. He had a patch on his arm that said "Twenty-two Years Accident Free."

"What's the trouble, officer?" he asked politely.

"You were doing 60 in a 30-mile zone."

"I know that. But I've been doing that for the last two years here. Nobody's ever bothered us before."

"Well, I'm a new police officer here and nobody's told me any different. I think 60 miles an hour is much too fast for our city."

"Yes, sir, officer. I'll obey the speed limit if you say so. I'd really appreciate it if you wouldn't give me a ticket. If we get a ticket, we lose our regular route."

"I won't give you a ticket, but just make certain you slow it down coming through my city."

"Yes sir, officer. Thank you."

When I came back to my car, headquarters was trying to reach me. "Car two, what's the tag number on that vehicle?" I had failed to give the license number.

"Which one do you want, headquarters? It's got fifty plates on it. This thing's a Greyhound bus."

"Ten-nine?" (Repeat your last transmission).

"I said, this is a Greyhound bus and it has about fifty license tags on it."

My sergeant got on the air. "Headquarters to car two. Don't be messing with any Greyhound bus. That's interstate commerce."

"Car two to headquarters. Don't worry about it. I'll be 10-19 (enroute to headquarters) and I'll be 10-15 (with prisoners) with 59 people on a signal 54."

In the still night air I could hear two police cars squeal out of headquarters two miles away. In a moment they came screaming up the road, made a U-turn and pulled up beside me. I was laughing so hard I could hardly see.

"Did you really stop that bus?" my sergeant asked.

"Yeah, I stopped him. I just gave him a warning."

"We never bother those buses in here."

"Well, if the speed limit is 30 miles an hour it's good enough for them, just like everybody else." The sergeant and I quickly came to an understanding that if a law was on the books I was going to enforce it.

After we had been in Dania about one month, my wife Patty gave birth to a beautiful baby boy whom we named Bobby. I had always wanted a son and desperately desired the kind of relationship with him that I had never had with my father.

But Patty and I were still having constant marital problems. She wanted me to buy a new trailer, so I overextended myself and purchased a three-bedroom mobile home. I also purchased a new air-conditioned Dodge Dart, and a new wardrobe for Pat in an effort to satisfy her.

One night two of the black officers asked me to meet them at the Paradise Club in the black section of town just before we all got off shift. They had me guard the back door while they went in the front. I kept everyone from fleeing at gunpoint, then entered the bar to see the two officers shaking down all the males. They collected sixteen or seventeen pistols and several switchblades but made no arrests.

When we left I asked what was going on. "Don't worry," one officer said, "you'll get your cut later."

"A cut of what?" I asked naively.

"A split of the money, man. Don't you understand?" I discovered the officers would raid different black bars and collect every illegal weapon, then they would "sell" them back to their original owners at twenty to thirty dollars each. When I realized what they were doing, I told them I wanted no part of it.

On another evening, I pulled over a car with two occupants that had been weaving erratically. The dispatcher backed me up. As I searched the intoxicated offenders, a big Buick swished by at an excessive speed and just missed me.

"Put them in the car, they're clean. I'm going after that guy in the Buick."

The driver of the Buick was slow to pull over. Instead of giving me his license, he flashed a detective's badge and said, "I'm one of you guys."

He was Detective Sergeant Jim Weaver from the Hollywood Police Department and he was drunk.

"That's very nice, sir, now let me see your driver's license."

"Look, punk, I've been doing this kind of stuff for years, and you're not even wet behind the ears."

"Well, in the first place I'm not a punk. In the second place you almost killed me back there, and in the third place—you're under arrest."

"You've got to be kiddin!" He started his car.

"You are under arrest, mister. Now turn that engine off," I repeated firmly.

"Are you for real?" he said in obvious exasperation.

"You better believe I'm for real. Now step out of that vehicle." He just looked at me in disbelief. I opened his door and ordered him out of his car.

"I'm gonna have your job tomorrow," he threatened.

"Well you may have it tomorrow, but you don't have it tonight and you're still under arrest."

He started cursing, so I pulled my revolver. "Now I'm telling you for the last time, get out of that car."

He looked at me in amazement. "Hey, *you're serious!*"

He got out of his car and I took his revolver from him, then shook him down for other weapons. "Hey, brother, don't you understand, I'm one of you?"

"Yeah, I understand. I also understand you almost killed me."

"Hey, man, is Kelly on duty? Call him on the radio."

"I'm not going to call him, you're going to go see him."

"Buddy, you don't know who you're messing with."

When we walked into the station, Sergeant Kelly looked up at his friend. "Jim! What are you doing here?"

"Super cop here just arrested me," he said pointing at me.

"Erler, what's the problem?" Kelly asked. "This is a good friend of mine."

"Sarge, I don't care if he is your friend. This man almost ran me down. On top of that, he called me a punk and said he was gonna have my job. He might have this job, but as it is right now, he's under arrest."

Kelly took the detective into the back room and I began to write out citations. In a few moments they both came out.

"Bob, I know I already owe you some favors," Kelly began, "but I've known Detective Weaver for years. How 'bout cutting him some slack and considering it a favor to me?"

"Look, Sarge, this guy isn't gonna pull that with me. I don't care what his rank is. He's in my area and this is my job. He's not gonna threaten me.".

"You've got a point. But as a personal favor to me, please don't give him a ticket. You'll ruin his career."

Weaver walked up and stuck out his hand. "Hey, I've been drinking heavy, I've got a lot of personal problems, and I apologize."

I thought for a moment. "If you're man enough to apologize, I'll be man enough to let you off. But only if you sit in the back room and drink six cups of coffee." He agreed.

A week later, I was patrolling late in the morning and drove behind a closed nightclub. I inspected the building and surrounding area with my spotlight. But as I drove away, I had a strange feeling something was wrong. I turned out my lights and drove back slowly. In fifteen minutes I reached the building and shined my spotlight on the window. The screen had been ripped off; someone was inside.

"Car 2 to headquarters," I called quietly. "A burglary in progress at the Show Club. Suspect or suspects still inside. Send backup units."

I left the spotlight aimed at the window so whoever had crawled in would not come out that way. As I stepped out of the car, a black male rounded the building and fired at me. The bullet whizzed past my head and struck the squad car.

The man turned and ran. I aimed my revolver right between his shoulder blades—but I knew if I pulled the trigger, I would kill him for certain. Raising the barrel I fired a warning shot and yelled, "Halt! Police!"

The suspect continued to flee still within range—but he was running toward the Hollywood airport. He would be easy to find when the backup units arrived. Right then I heard the bushes rustle on the other side of the club. I ran to the back and searched the bushes with my flashlight.

Backup units arrived from Hollywood and Fort Lauderdale along with my sergeant. We checked inside and discovered all suspects had fled. I informed the backup units which way they ran. They put police dogs on the trail of the man who had fired at me and immediately surrounded the airport area.

I was certain the man would elude the ring of officers. "Sarge, I just don't feel that man will keep going towards the airport. He's black and he won't run into the white section of town. He'll double-back and crawl down toward the canal and try to slip into the black section."

"No, he's here. We've got him surrounded. We'll have him in a few minutes."

"Sarge, the man isn't here. I just have a feeling I know where he is. You've got twenty officers here, let me go check out my hunch."

My sergeant said okay, so I drove toward the canal and parked where I felt the suspect would attempt to cross the highway. Within minutes the man ran out of the bushes.

I jumped out of my car, pointed my pistol at him and yelled, "Halt!" Again, he turned and ran. I could easily have shot and killed him again. Instead, I holstered my weapon and ran down the street to cut him off. I waited behind a building until he came running by, then tackled him.

We wrestled for several minutes before I finally snapped the handcuffs onto his wrists and forced him into my car. The man I had captured turned out to be a nineteen-year-old black named Garrett, a well-known burglar the Dania police had been trying to catch for some time.

When one of the black officers realized whom I had caught, he said, "Why didn't you kill that nigger? We've been trying to kill him for years and you had a perfect chance to do it."

"My job isn't to kill 'em."

"Well, he shot at you."

"Yeah, but when I pulled out my weapon he was fleeing. He was no longer a threat to me."

I was surprised to receive so much criticism from the Chief on down for not shooting Garrett. But I wasn't going to kill anyone if I didn't have to.

Three days later, Garrett was released on bail. He found out where I lived and came to our trailer. He told Patty if I knew what was good for me I wouldn't testify against him. He scared her to death. I told the other officers what Garrett had done and they said not to worry. I was certain they would arrest him. But two days later, he was found on the beach with a broken neck.

"It looks like Garrett got what he deserved," I said to the officers the next day. They implied I now owed them a favor. "You mean you guys actually killed that man?"

They looked at each other, then back at me like I was a naive schoolboy. "No, we're only kidding. Forget it."

I tried to do everything a policeman was supposed to do. I would get out of my vehicle to check the doors of businesses after hours. I cruised dark streets with my lights off looking for violators. Because I hunted for things that were wrong, I was getting many solid arrests—usually two or three a night. Many of the other officers began to give me a hard time because I was making them look bad.

I pulled up to a red light at 11:00 one night next to a Chevrolet with three white males in it. The license plate indicated the car was from the Miami area and the occupants looked over at me uneasily. Something was wrong.

"Pull it over," I called to the driver. They drove into a closed gas station. I drew my revolver and made the occupants get out of the car. As it turned out, the car was stolen and the three men had just committed an armed robbery.

Often when I made out my reports, my sergeant would tell me to put his name on it. Almost everytime I made an arrest or did something that looked good, he would ask me to include his name. I began to get disgusted with him. The other officers told me he was not backing me up. Whenever I'd rush to cover some complaint, he seldom showed up until after the danger was past. I was really on my own and it began to bother me.

I decided to transfer to another police department. Jim Walsh, a friend on the Hollywood Department, encouraged me to transfer to his city. They had 150 officers and sent new men to the police academy. They also paid twice as much as Dania.

I quit abruptly and the next day went into the Hollywood Police Department. They seemed to know a lot about me and wanted me to go to work immediately. Because it would be three or four weeks before they could get me into the academy, I would ride with a senior officer. Two days after I quit Dania, I was out on patrol with an officer named Ed.

"So you're the 'super cop' I've been hearing about," Ed said as we pulled out of the station.

"I'm not any kind of a super cop. I just want to be a good officer, and I'd appreciate it if you wouldn't call me that."

Ed smiled. "You better get used to it because that's what everybody's calling you. I feel it's a privilege just to ride around with you." I didn't know if he was trying to be funny or if he really meant it.

We drove around for two or three hours with no major incidents. As we pulled back on the main highway, we came up behind a four-door Impala with five white occupants. The two men in the back seat turned and looked at us strangely.

"Ed, that's a stolen car in front of us."

He started laughing. "Okay, 'super cop' so we've got a stolen car." But he didn't believe me.

"Let's pull them over. If it's not stolen, there's something wrong."

"Hey, man, this isn't Batman and Robin. Let's just cool it. We'll pull over a car later. What do you say we get something to eat now?"

"No, I want you to pull that car over!"

Ed shook his head. "Okay, so we'll pull them over." He put on his red light and all five occupants turned around and looked at us. As they slowly began to pull over, Ed looked over to me as if to say "I told you so."

The moment the car stopped all four doors flew open and everyone ran. Ed called headquarters while I ran after them. All five suspects fled toward the swamp. I fired a round into the air and four of them stopped. I took them back to the patrol car and we put them into the back of the car. They had all escaped from a state institution and their car was stolen.

The boy who escaped was only sixteen. They gave me his name, so I walked out to the swamp and yelled to him that we were going to get the police dogs. He soon slogged out with his hands up.

After this incident many of my fellow officers really began to call me "super cop." Again, as at Dania, there seemed to be a lot of jealousy on the part of the other officers. The only real friend I had on the force was Jim Walsh.

I was soon enrolled in the police academy. After the training I received in Special Forces, the academy was almost a joke to me. The biggest problem I faced was with my wife. She refused to take care of Bobby or change him in the middle of the night. After a hard day at the academy, I would sometimes have to spend half the night up with my son. We fought constantly.

After graduating from the academy, I was assigned a regular patrol car of my own. During line-up one day, we were warned to watch the liquor stores closely because several had been robbed. Later, while driving down Dixie Highway, I saw a black male run out of a liquor store, throw a bag in the back seat of a Buick Riviera and burn rubber out of the parking lot. I fell in behind him and when he saw me he floored it.

"Car 145 to headquarters. Be advised I'm in pursuit of a fleeing black Buick Riviera," then I gave his license number and our location.

We were quickly up to 100 miles an hour. The suspect cut in and out of traffic, but I stayed right on his tail. He slowed to make a right turn. I was going so fast I had to cut through a gas station on the corner and slid sideways onto the next road. He made a quick left onto another street and looked over his shoulder to discover I was right behind him. He accelerated and we both went back up to 100 miles an hour right into Hallandale.

We were in the heart of the black section. People were everywhere. The buildings which were right up to the street whizzed by, making it impossible to see cross traffic. We ran numerous stop signs and the opposing traffic had the right-of-way. One of us had to get unlucky and hit something.

The suspect ran a stop sign and in a fraction of a second a Chevrolet drove into that intersection. There was no way I could miss it. I jammed on my brakes and slid fifty-six feet before hitting it dead center. The impact slammed the vehicle off the street and into a corner building, which was the funeral hall where June Bug's coffin had been.

The collision thrust my head through the window and knocked me into a stupor. My squad car spun around like a top and continued down the road for almost a block. While it was spinning,

I saw myself in that same funeral hall, lying in a casket just where June Bug had been. The car came to a stop, fortunately missing the many pedestrians.

My head cleared momentarily and I reached through the window to pick up my microphone. "Car 145 to headquarters. Be advised of a signal 314" (a car accident with injuries). Then I passed out.

I vaguely remember people dragging me out of the car and someone yelling into my microphone, "You got a policeman hurt here! You got a policeman hurt here!"

When I was wheeled into the hospital, I regained consciousness. I tried to get off the table but the doctor restrained me. He informed me I had a severe brain concussion and bandaged me up. Although I was still dizzy and couldn't maintain my equilibrium too well, concern for the people I had hit motivated me to walk into the next room to see them. All three were injured, but they would be okay.

Pat and several of the Hollywood officers soon arrived at the hospital. Carl King, the Assistant Chief of Police, asked me how I was feeling. By this time my head was feeling a little more stable and I managed to convince both him and the doctor I should be released. I simply couldn't afford being off work for any length of time and gave the impression I felt well.

The very next day I was given a new car and put back on the job. But I continued to have stomach sickness, severe headaches, dizziness and blackouts for the next month.

Shortly after this, while Pat and I drove to work, we became involved in a heated argument over finances. She was spending far more than I was earning.

While we argued, eleven-month-old Bobby playfully pulled the green ribbon from Pat's hair. Because she was upset at me, she grabbed his hand and slapped it hard. Bobby's face turned red and he cried in anguish. I pulled over and slapped Pat in the face with the back of my hand.

"Don't you ever hit Bobby like that!" It was the first and only time I ever laid a hand on her, but I couldn't bear to see my son slapped for no reason.

That night Pat didn't come to pick me up. I quickly discovered she had left with Bobby. Pat had left me before, so I wasn't surprised. But in a few days I started receiving phone calls from the bank that our checks were bouncing. She had withdrawn all the money from our joint account, then had written several checks before leaving. Every day I received news of new debts. She had also forged my name on two loan applications for $1200. I was financially wiped out.

I went to each of the creditors, explained my situation, and offered to pay $10 a month until the debts were paid. But new charges kept coming in. Several of the creditors called the department. I offered to resign, but Assistant Chief King told me they would stick by me. He gave me all the extra work I could handle. I began working seven days a week at the department, plus six nights.

This demanding schedule quickly exhausted me physically. And to make matters worse, I was still battling migraine headaches, dizziness, and nausea from the concussion I had received. Without Pat and Bobby, I lived alone for over a month, mechanically performing my police duties with no social life at all until I resigned.

Now, they were returning me to Florida and the other side of the bars. I just couldn't believe this was happening to me.

FOUR
BROWARD COUNTY JAIL

We flew in from El Paso and I was immediately taken to Broward County Jail. When we arrived, as in Phoenix, there were reporters and curosity seekers everywhere.

At the booking desk, they removed my handcuffs and rolled my fingers in the fingerprinting process just as I had done to so many others. They stripped and searched me, checking everywhere for drugs or other contraband.

The room was filled with police officers—all glaring at me. As I looked around, the unmistakable emotion in every pair of eyes was fear. They seemed to fear me like some kind of monster. Their expressions startled me. What kind of transition had taken place? Only a few days earlier I had been the super cop; now they saw me as a maniac.

They gave me a pair of coveralls and led me upstairs to the maximum security section. The noise of iron doors opening and slamming was terrifying. My nostrils were immediately assaulted by the stench of rank urine, as I walked into that hellhole.

The other prisoners began to call out to one another. "They just brought in that cop!" "Erler's here!" They whistled, yelled, and rattled their doors. Several made threats.

I was placed in a one-man cell. The mattress was badly torn and stained with blood and urine. The floor was filthy; it was covered with newspapers and toilet paper wrappers. The place had a musty sick stench to it. It was hot and stuffy.

There wasn't any pillow so I asked the guard for one. He told me I had to use the blanket. Because it reeked of human waste, I folded my arms underneath my throbbing head, lay down on the filthy but cool floor, and attempted to shut out the world.

I stayed in that cell for five days and didn't eat a thing. My mind blanked out most feelings and emotions in an attempt to escape the terrible hostility around me. I felt stranded on an asteroid in outer space. Nobody knew me or understood my situation. I felt completely helpless.

"Hey, I can't stand this cell," I told the guard posted outside. "Can't you put me in with the other prisoners?"

"Everybody knows you were a police officer. We're afraid they'll kill you."

They hadn't given me any newspapers because almost everyday the headlines were filled with the developments in my case. But all the other prisoners were reading about me.

"Why do they want to hurt me?" I asked the lieutenant. "I haven't hurt any of them. To my knowledge, I haven't put any of them in here."

"Erler, you were a cop and you represent authority, an authority they can reach. With all the publicity you've received, these guys will kill you just for a reputation."

The seriousness in the lieutenant's voice was startling, but even terror dissipated in the isolation of that bleak cell. I began to crave other people to talk to even if it meant some risks. I couldn't survive alone. I pleaded with the guards to move me in with other prisoners.

"Look, Erler, do you think you could get along with prisoners who are in jail for minor offenses?"

"Yes," I answered eagerly. "I just need somebody to talk to." They asked if I would be responsible if they moved me. "I can handle anything you give me. Don't worry about it."

Most of the officers were hostile towards me. I was a police officer who had fallen and they despised me. It reminded me of a group of sharks swimming together; one scrapes his belly and draws blood and in an instant the others jump on the injured predator to finish the job.

They took me to another cellblock. When I walked in, everyone stared. I tried to read their faces; it appeared they were staring more out of curiosity than hatred. I was locked in my cell while the others were free to roam the cellblock. The first day no one even said "hi," so I lay down and slept.

The next day the men began to communicate with me and the guards let me out of my cell so I could walk around. The other prisoners showed me the newspaper clippings they had saved about my case. I couldn't believe the articles. They weren't talking about me. They were talking about some monster—a figment of someone's imagination.

The articles claimed Special Forces had made me a killer and I had gone berserk. They claimed I had gone off the deep end. They even quoted my wife as saying the army had made me a killer and sadist.

In our cellblock was a twenty-three-year-old mentally retarded kid named Danny Jensen who had the mind of a seven-year-old. One morning he ran through the block screaming. He woke me up and I came out of my cell and told him to be quiet.

Jack Griffith, who was in jail for an incident called the Whiskey Creek slayings, also came out of his cubicle. Thinking I had been making the noise, he told me to shut up.

Griffith was in his forties and was supposed to be a karate expert. When I was stationed in Korea I had been wiped out in a fight with a small Korean who knew karate and I was a bit leery. But I knew I had to prove myself. I told him where he could go.

Griffith didn't answer, he just stood sideways and looked at me. Because everyone else was watching, I began to push him with my finger. I was over my head, but I had to play the role in front of the other inmates. "Old man, I'm gonna give you a break, and you better take it, 'cause if you say or do anything to me, I'm gonna crack your jaw." He didn't say or do anything and the incident ended.

After I had been in jail a week, I wanted to call my family in Phoenix. To do that, I had to walk past some of the other cellblocks to a large cage called the bullpen. When I walked through, one prisoner called out to me.

I approached his cell cautiously and said, "What is it?"

"Here!" he cried, and flung a cup of urine in my face. Everyone laughed and banged on their bars. There was no way I could get to the guy. The lieutenant quickly led me to the bullpen.

When I entered, four prisoners were also in the pen, all leering at me. Everyone looked away when I glared back. I was given a dime to call the operator. No sooner had the coin dropped into the phone than I was knocked to the floor. One of the other prisoners had come up behind me and hit me on the back of the head.

I jumped up and we wrestled for a few seconds before the guards separated us. I had an egg-sized knot behind my ear, so they took me to the nurse downstairs.

She was extremely icy towards me. She had been reading the papers and made several caustic comments. She didn't give me much for pain and told me not to come back unless my head was cut off.

An inmate in our cellblock named Steve had stringy carrot-red hair. His brown eyes were often glazed and he stared blankly. He had escaped from the Hollywood insane asylum.

"Yeah," he said to me, "when they were bringing you across the street in Phoenix, we were watching you on TV. I saw you kick that photographer and fight the cops." I couldn't remember the incidents he was talking about, so they showed me pictures that appeared in the newspapers.

"When we saw you break out the window in the courthouse, everyone at the state hospital said, 'We've got another one coming to be with us.'" He said the guys were all betting I would come to the state hospital and never be tried.

Steve had strangled a girl named Bess. He had been dubbed in the papers as "the Daytona strangler." He had found his girl friend in bed with another man and killed her. He would sit in his cell all day and torment himself by repeating, "Man, I killed her, I killed Bess," over and over.

A new guy was moved into our cellblock. He wouldn't talk to me so I ignored him. Later, as I was standing with my back toward his cell, he came up behind me and struck my head viciously with the mop handle. The blow opened a four-inch gash in my scalp and blood spurted everywhere.

My assailant dropped the mop, ran back into his cell and climbed under his bunk. I followed and dragged him out. I began to pound on his face with my fists until the guards appeared.

My head was swimming because of the blow I'd received. They

rushed me to Broward General. My skull had been fractured and it took a number of stitches to close the wound.

When the guards asked what happened, I told them I slipped in the shower. If I had told the truth they would have sent me to "the hole" (solitary confinement) for fighting. Apparently my assailant was from another part of the jail and other prisoners had put him up to clobbering me.

Everyone was impressed that I fought back after receiving such a blow. Several of the older cons told me if I went to prison, fighting back was the only way I could survive.

Another escapee from the mental hospital came in. His name was John. There was also an Italian named Pete in our section who had been arrested for nine armed robberies. Pete was supposed to go for arraignment and he asked John for advice on how to play crazy.

John dressed him up in a sweat shirt and used silver gum wrappers to make lieutenant's bars for his shoulders. They covered his sweat shirt with various medals and other junk to make him appear mentally imbalanced. He came back smiling because his public defender was going to file a motion for a psychiatric evaluation.

The next day they brought another escapee from the state hospital and locked him into the cell on the other side of me. He was a skinny six-foot-nine fellow who kept walking back and forth in front of my cell, glaring at me through the bars.

"Are you a cop?" he asked.

"No, I'm an ex-cop."

"I don't like you," he said simply.

"Well, I don't like you either."

"I'm gonna kill you," he threatened. He picked up a gallon can which was being used for cigarette butts and took it into his cell and began to smash it flat. He was sitting on the floor pounding and bending it to form a sharp blade.

"What are you doing?" I asked.

"I'm making a knife," he said matter of factly without looking up, "cause I'm gonna kill a cop in here."

"Kill a cop?" I asked.

"Yeah, I'm gonna kill you."

I took a dixie cup full of mustard left over from lunch and flung it at him, catching him in the face. I grabbed the broom and threw it through the bars, jamming him in the stomach. He jumped back against the wall and his personality instantly changed from a would-be killer to a little boy.

In a childlike voice he whimpered, "Bob, you're mad at me. I wanna be your friend. I wanna be your friend."

The transformation was so complete it took me by surprise. I felt guilty for picking on him. "What's your name?"

"My name's Tim."

"Tim, you can be my friend."

Jim Strong, a hardened convict from the Florida State Prison at Railford was in our section. His conviction had been overturned and he was waiting for a new trial. Walking around with just his shorts on, he was a terrible sight. Strong was scarred from head to foot from knife wounds.

I asked what prison was like. He said, "Bob, I hope you don't go to Railford, because they'll stick you good up there. You're an ex-cop and they'll never forget that. Sooner or later they'll get you. You'll never be able to live there."

The more we talked about prison, the more I became fearful of what might happen if I was convicted. He told of stabbings and killings and how life didn't mean too much. He also described what had happened to other ex-cops.

I felt totally alienated. I was no longer a police officer—they hated me because they thought I had fallen. Neither could I be accepted as a convict because I had once been a cop. I was in the twilight zone—a no man's land filled with intense hatred.

Some officers did try to be friendly with me. At first, I welcomed their interest. But the other prisoners advised me not to communicate with the guards in any way.

Every time I was taken downstairs, whether it was for arraignment, phone calls, or visits with my lawyer, I had to walk past other cells. The other prisoners would boo or swear at me. Sometimes they threw things through the bars. They always made threats.

I was taken out for a line-up in front of Mrs. Clark. They marched me and five other guys up onto a stage with bright lights blaring. I was told she could not identify me from the others. I was relieved.

In the jail we never knew what kind of person we were rubbing shoulders with or what terrible crimes he had committed. There were so many diverse personalities; one person might want to fight if we talked to him, another might fight if we didn't.

Jack "Murph the Surf" Murphy was placed in our cellblock. He and Griffith were charged with the Whiskey Creek slayings. Murphy turned out to be a friendly, likable guy. He was intelligent and we immediately became good friends.

After two weeks in jail, I began to smell something burning. It was a sickening odor, like flesh burning. I came out to discover a roaring fire in the cell next to mine. Steve had created a bonfire with several days worth of newspapers and was sitting on the edge of his bunk casually roasting his hands.

I ran into his cell and stomped out the flames. "Steve! What are you doing? You're burning up your hands!"

"I know," he said in a daze. "The devil told me to burn my hands off because I killed Bess with them." His skin was completely cooked, yet he was oblivious to the pain.

"Steve! What's the matter with you!" It terrified all of us. Everyone began to yell and rattle the bars in an attempt to get a guard into the block. I wrapped his hands in a wet towel. The officers came and took him to the hospital. He was really tormented. He ended up back in the state hospital.

Because Pete had been to the "joint" (state prison), he began to teach us how to adjust to prison life. He started ingraining the "chain-gang code of ethics" in us. We were never to talk to guards or let ourselves be caught alone with them as other prisoners might think we were snitching. We were never to carry any valuables or accumulate any possessions that would cause others to rob us.

Pete had already done seven years and was facing a lot more prison time. He constantly talked about how to beat his sentences. Everyday when he came back from his trial he gave us a blow-by-blow description of what was happening in the courtroom.

He was convinced the DA and his public defender had conspired to convict him. Every time the district attorney looked at his lawyer, they would wink at each other. We laughed at the ridiculousness of his situation, but he obviously didn't think it was funny. When he tried to read a motion to fire his attorney, the judge wouldn't let him talk. He came back completely frustrated.

"What you need is a mistrial," somebody suggested.

"Well, how can I get one?"

"Just punch your attorney in front of the jury," said another.

"Do you really think that would work?"

"Of course it will work. Anything like that would prejudice the jury against you. They'll have to give you a mistrial."

Pete went down to his trial the next day, and sure enough, we heard the results on the cellblock TV. When he was refused another motion, he hit his attorney. He was extremely happy when he returned because he had received a mistrial. Pete was later sent to the state hospital and eventually all charges against him were dropped.

One of the few things I looked forward to were visits. But the conditions were ridiculous. We could have only one visit a week, for only fifteen minutes, and it had to be a family member. If that wasn't bad enough, we had to look at our relative through bullet-proof glass and if we wanted to talk we had to shout through a small screened hole. If we looked, we couldn't talk and if we talked we couldn't look. Because conditions were so bad, and my relatives lived so far away, I didn't receive too many visits.

Danny Jensen, the mentally retarded kid, was placed in the bullpen ouside our area. He would yell over to our block, "Hey, Bob Erler! Catch me killer! I told my mother all about you!" Sometimes he would wake up in the middle of the night and shout, "Bob Erler! Catch me killer! I told my mother you were my friend!" He was like a parrot, repeating those phrases over and over.

While in the county jail, I ran into several people whom I had given breaks as a police officer. When I needed friends most, several of these people were put in my cellblock.

There was one prisoner, however, I had arrested several times who ended up in the block. He was a wino named Ronnie Davis. He had been to prison and delighted in talking about how police officers were killed in the joint. I wanted to hear everything possible about what prison life was like—just in case. But Ronnie's words had a drastic effect on my outlook.

Patty had gone to live with her mother in Kansas City. She had filed for divorce, but I didn't hear about it until it was granted in November. When I learned of the court's decision, my only regret was that I had lost custody of my son.

I looked forward to my trial, believing I would be acquitted and could go home. Joe Varon, my attorney, had said he would walk me out of the courtroom. "Bob, they have nothing on you. They have no motive, no weapon, no bloodstains, no fingerprints, and no witnesses. They've created such a fervor in the newspapers I expect them to try some form of entrapment to squeeze hard evidence out of you. I wouldn't be a bit surprised if they plant evidence against you."

My attorney told me he was going to have a psychiatrist examine me to determine whether I was mentally competent to stand trial. Before long, I was called from my cell to see a man who claimed to be a psychiatrist.

He began to ask questions about my case. I told him I didn't know anything. He claimed he had news from my family—he had been out to see them.

"Hey, you're not a psychiatrist. Who are you?"

The man admitted he was Detective Sergeant Jerry Meltzer of the Fort Lauderdale Police Department, but he wanted to talk to me anyway. I remembered what my attorney had said and refused to say anything.

A lieutenant named Sullivan also called me out of my cell. He attempted to get me to incriminate myself by asking, "Why don't you tell me where the gun is?"

"Listen, I don't know anything about any gun and I don't appreciate you bugging me like this. You want me to tell my attorney you're questioning me without his presence?"

Varon came up to see me later that day and I told him what Sullivan had done. Joe made a big issue out of it and almost got the lieutenant fired. He filed a motion to prohibit the prosecution from "harassing, molesting, or interrogating" me or subjecting me to tests or experiments of any kind. But the judge denied the motion. Varon's psychiatrist finally examined me and I was found perfectly sane.

Just before my trial, a news bulletin broke on television and in the newspaper. The authorities claimed they had found a hair band in my car that Mrs. Clark identified as belonging to her daughter.

My attorney immediately came to see me. I explained the band belonged to my wife. I even told him what color it was. It had fallen between the seats of the car when I slapped Pat for spanking Bobby. Varon questioned me at length until he was satisfied I was telling the truth.

The newspapers claimed the band definitely belonged to the victim. They exhumed her body, clipped a lock of her hair, and sent it to the FBI lab. They were trying to prove the hair of the victim matched that on the band.

My attorney was fearful they would "create" some evidence by putting some of the victim's hair on the band. They needed evidence and we both knew strange things sometimes happen in cases where the authorities don't have enough. Just prior to my trial they held a news conference about the FBI test.

Lieutenant Irvin Goetz, the detective in charge answered the reporter's questions by saying, "I can't tell you, Erler's defense attorney would scream if I gave out the information." The actual results were that the hair was my wife's, but the way they slanted the information to the public gave a different impression.

I had received so much adverse publicity, I began to wonder if I could ever expect to receive a fair trial. But I was anxious to get it over as I knew there simply was no case against me.

FIVE
FRAMED!

It was Monday, January 27, 1969, the first day of my trial. I was marched through the corridor between the other cells. Everyone knew I was going to trial and the inmates reached out through the bars as far as they could trying to grab at me. They would jeer, call me "pig," and "oink" as I walked by.

"Hey, Erler!" one yelled out. "Tell them you'll plead guilty if they reduce the charge to police brutality." Everybody roared.

"No, Erler," another chimed in, "tell 'em you'll plead guilty if they drop it to discharging a firearm in the city limits!" Another roar of laughter filled the cellblock.

I kept walking, but it was hard not to listen. They transferred me to the Broward County Courthouse and escorted me into the crowded courtroom of Circuit Judge E. Summers Sheffey. They had reserved a complete section for the news media.

Somebody yelled at me so I turned around. *Everyone* was staring at me. Again, I detected both fear and curiosity in each pair of eyes. Their gazes caused me to feel like a bug under a microscope. I caught sight of my mother, brother Danny, and my two sisters. I waved and they waved back. Their presence was reassuring.

Judge Sheffey first addressed the newsmen in the courtroom. "In the event it comes to my attention that any of you people print any motions for a mistrial made by the defense counsel, I will bar you from the courtroom. Do I make myself clear?"

"Yes, your Honor," they said together.

The reporters were ordered not to discuss the case with the prosecutor, defense attorney, or any witnesses; they were not to publish any evidence which had been suppressed, nor any extraneous material. "This defendant is not going to be tried in the newspapers, nor is the state," Sheffey said.

A little later, Varon stood and addressed the judge . "Your Honor, I have reviewed the evidence the prosecution intends to present and I respectfully request the court to consider a motion to suppress a certain tape recording of a telephone conversation between one Claire Kaufman and Robert Erler made on September 17th of last year."

"On what grounds?"

"It was recorded without the knowledge of either of the people mentioned. It is an attempt at entrapment. It is a clear case of psychological coercion and as such might be incriminating to my client. The law is clear on this. The transcript in question is the most deliberate device I have ever seen."

Judge Sheffey denied the motion, but told Varon he could renew it when the tape was brought up in testimony later.

The lengthy procedure of selecting a jury began. Out of thirty-two people questioned, most were eliminated by either the prosecution or my lawyer until six men—all fathers—were selected. One was held in reserve.

Court recessed and I was placed in a little cell between the two courtrooms. I was only in the room fifteen minutes when the judge's secretary walked in. She was twenty-five years old and quite attractive. I had met her earlier, during my arraignment.

"Bob, can I come in and talk to you?"

She didn't seem to have the animosity everyone else was showing towards me. "Sure, if you're not afraid."

She laughed and the guard opened up the cage and let her in. "I've got some very important things to say to you. I don't want to get myself in trouble, but this Judge Sheffey is wacky. He has been meeting with the prosecutor the last three months and they have conspired to convict you. They have even talked about what your sentence would be.

"I heard him tell the prosecutor that you would be found guilty. That all the motions of your attorney would be denied, and that regardless of what happens, you are going to prison for the first five or six years and you could probably beat the conviction on appeal."

"Wow! Will you tell all that to my attorney?"

"Well. . .you tell him what I said." She had to leave, so she wished me luck and started to go. "Oh, there's one other thing, the judge said 'you are nothing but a keystone cop.' Before he got on the bench, the police department arrested and roughed him up. Now he's going to get even with you."

She left and when I was taken back into the courtroom I leaned over and whispered what she said about the conspiracy into my lawyer's ear.

He looked at me strangely. "Don't worry about any of that. They don't have any evidence against you. There's absolutely nothing here. You're gonna walk out that courtroom door." I took his word. I believed him, because I wanted to believe him.

Dan Futch, the prosecuting attorney, gave his opening statement. He told the jury he would show "lust and greed" was the motive in the shooting of the mother and daughter. He proceeded to summarize the case against me, stating, "The state of Florida intends to prove that Robert Erler killed Merilyn Clark!" He then offered a list of more than twenty witnesses he had subpoenaed.

One of the first witnesses was Mrs. Dorothy Clark. She testified she came to South Florida on a job-hunting vacation until her money ran low. Then she decided to sleep on the beach. On the morning of August 12, she said a policeman or guard approached the car and invited her to his air-conditioned trailer where he said his wife would give them something to eat and a place to sleep. She claimed the man said to Merilyn, "Your mother has got to go out to the car and take care of me." Both she and Merilyn left the trailer and got into their car to leave when the man slipped into the passenger seat in front. "I commented on his gun, and he said, "We'll get to that later. All I want now is your money." That was the last thing she remembered.

When my attorney cross-examined her, Mrs. Clark balked at admitting how many times she had been married. Varon attacked her character, trying to show that she had been married many times, spent many nights in bars and slept on the beach. She became hostile and at one point compared the trial proceedings to "another Perry Mason show."

My lawyer asked Mrs. Clark how many times she had met with prosecutor Futch. She stated she had talked with him just before her testimony. He asked if he had shown her any pictures. She admitted to having seen over a dozen photographs of policemen and had picked up my picture "out of the crowd." But she also admitted she had not been able to identify me at the line-up.

On Tuesday morning, the first witness was Assistant Broward Medical Examiner, Dr. Jack Mickley. He was asked by prosecutor Dan Futch if he could identify the person in a color photograph taken of the victim. Varon objected that the photograph was highly prejudicial, so the six-man jury was taken from the court-room and a long argument began over its admission. Varon claimed the photo did not establish identity and that as a color morgue photograph of the deceased it was designed to inflame.

The judge ruled that he would allow the photograph into evidence because it could be relevant to the chain of identity. He felt that Mrs. Clark may have received the same number of wounds in the same part of the body and therefore the photograph could be relevant.

The jury was brought back in and Dr. Mickley admitted the photograph was a "little more reddish than the actual subject." Mickley said the cause of death was shock and hemorrhage from five gunshot wounds to the brain. He estimated the time of Merilyn's death at 6:30 a.m. on August 12, 1968. He also stated the place of her death was not known.

Hollywood policeman Larry Lallance was called to the witness stand. He said he noticed a woman and a young girl resting in a car at Taylor Street near the beach at 2:30 a.m. and told the woman she would have to move and suggested the Dania beach area. He said they had moved on when he returned to the area after about forty-five minutes.

Helen Jones, a waitress in the Royal Castle Restaurant on Dania Beach Boulevard, testified she saw me in the restaurant around 11 p.m. and again at 5 a.m. the following morning. Both times, she said I was wearing the same plaid Bermudas and white tee shirt.

James Rice and Harold Lamore, the two sheriff's deputies who had received the telephone calls at the Broward County office were called to the stand. They said the calls came in at 6:18 and 6:30 a.m.

Lieutenant Wayne Madole came to the stand and testified how the two tapes were made. He also said I had attempted to distort my facial appearance when I was brought in for the line-up in front of Mrs. Clark. He said I puffed my cheeks, dropped my chin, and closed my eyes. He also said Mrs. Clark had not appeared well at the line-up.

Hollywood officer, Robert Davis said he was called at 7 a.m. on August 12 and told to photograph the death scene at the 2800 block of Pershing Avenue where Merilyn's body was discovered. He was then ordered to the corner of the Ft. Lauderdale-Hollywood International Airport where he photographed the car that had been occupied by wounded Mrs. Clark.

Davis said he made the connection between the two incidents when he saw the murder victim wearing a bathing suit and saw the top part of the suit in the car. He estimated the distance between the two bodies as from five to eight miles and said it took him ten to fifteen minutes to travel it by car.

Dania police chief Donald Parton, who bought my trailer, took the stand and claimed he found a number of spent .22-caliber shells in the trailer, as well as some old khaki-colored Dania police shirts. Under cross-examination, Parton told the court, from his experience in police work, that he believed .22-caliber ammunition to be quite popular.

At the end of the day's testimony, the jury was dismissed and the judge, prosecution, several witnesses, and some members of the press were crowded with me into the Sheriff's Department communications room where we listened to the two "catch me" tapes.

On Wednesday morning, the third day of my trial, Joseph Portelli, detective sergeant on the Dania Police Department, claimed it was my voice on the tapes. Under cross-examination he stated that I "had a polite way of speaking and that's the way it came on the tape . . . He always used the word 'sir' and I did recognize the tone of his voice also—a young, high voice." Portelli also stated I had a western accent.

Then Dania police Lieutenant Peter Dalziel took the stand and said he believed the voice on the tape was mine. Under cross-examination he was asked if there were any characteristics in my voice which he used for identification. "Just that I know his voice. That's the only answer I can give you." Dalziel stated that I had no accent but that my voice was soft.

Former Dania policeman Fred Caldwell took the stand and identified the voice on the tapes as being mine. Under cross-examination he admitted that he had discussed the possibility I might be the man on the tapes with the Hollywood Police *before* listening to the tapes the first time. He also admitted that he could not say the voice was positively mine.

Dania patrolman William White took the stand and said I had asked, after the shootings, for the Dania department to say that they had received an emergency phone call from my mother. He also claimed that we were the best of friends— which was not true.

Jim Walsh took the stand and said that the voice "sounded like Bob Erler's." Under cross-examination, he admitted that he could not positively state to the jury that the tape was made by me.

Detective William Roberts testified that he had photographed and taken fingerprints from the green 1960 Falcon two-door that Mrs. Clark had been driving. He found only fingerprints of Mrs. Dorothy Clark and her daughter Merilyn. He pointed out to the jury that the Falcon was found approximately one-half mile from my former trailer. Then Robert Cowart, the airport security officer, described how he discovered Mrs. Clark in the Falcon on the airport property.

Roy Mitchell, a mechanic, testified that I had tried to sell him a .22-caliber pistol that was not registered. Detective Sergeant Jerry Meltzer then took the stand and told how Mrs. Clark had picked my photo out of a "photo line-up" of twenty-one pictures.

Assistant Hollywood Chief of Police Carl King explained to the jury about his four telephone conversations with me on the day of my arrest. He felt he had advised me, somewhat, of my rights in one of those conversations. A big point was made that I was very suicidal when the police had surrounded our apartment in Phoenix. He quoted me as saying, "If I show myself in the door they'll kill me and I'll have to take some of them with me." Under cross-examination King discussed my financial problems and my asking for a leave of absence.

On Thursday morning, the fourth day of my trial, Claire Kaufman was brought to the stand. She was questioned about the two phone conversations she had with me and how she knew the second one was being taped by the police, but because she had not doubt about my innocence, she did not tell them not to tape us. My lawyer asked if I had ever admitted any involvement in the homicide and Claire said, "No, sir."

Next, Prosecutor Futch brought Hollywood Detective John Cox to the stand to play the tape recording the police made of the conversation between Claire Kaufman and myself on September

17, 1968 while I was still in the Phoenix jail. My attorney argued the tape should not be admitted into evidence because neither Claire nor I gave our permission for the taping. My lawyer felt the police had used Mrs. Kaufman, unwittingly, as their agent.

Judge Sheffey, however, ruled the tape would be admitted into evidence because Mrs. Kaufman had been unable to recollect the entire conversation, because she was aware of the taping at the time of the call and had not objected to it, and finally, because he felt that I had been advised of my right to remain silent on the day of my arrest by Chief King.

Detective Cox then described the morning of August 12th at the site where Merilyn Clark's body was found. He explained that I had arrived at the station at 6:34 a.m. and after I had gassed up at the city garage, two people stopped me to tell of the presence of the body. While I called headquarters on my radio, the people left.

Apparently the fact I failed to get their names and license number was one of the "clues" that led detectives to suspect me for the crime. They felt that I was too good an officer to forget to get some evidence like that unless I had created the incidents so I could "discover" the body.

Then the tape of my conversation with Claire was played for the jury. The most damaging part of it was when she asked me if I did the crime, and in my confusion at that time I said, "I don't know."

Next a Phoenix deputy sheriff named Harold White took the stand. He was one of the officers who had escorted me across the street in Phoenix for my arraignment. He built up the details about my kicking the photographer and breaking the window to make me look like a real animal. He claimed I said, "I'm an animal. I should be put away." He also stated I had bragged about having some explosives in my room.

Dave Koelsch than took the stand and told how I was arrested. Koelsch told of coming in to see me in the jail the next day and how we talked about my past. He said I had gone out on a prowler call shortly after the shooting and the woman was frightened of the "Catch Me Killer." He quoted me as saying, "And all the time it was me."

When he said that, I lost my composure. I stood and cried through clenched teeth, "You're a liar! You're a liar!"

My attorney had the jury removed. "Your Honor, the Defendant moves for a mistrial. This statement, Your Honor, under the circumstances in which it was made, even if true, would have to be subject to Miranda rights, and this man was in custody, and there is no reason why an officer voluntarily goes to make a visitation upon an accused in custody. The real error here is this should have been proffered first out of the presence of the jury. This is highly prejudicial to the accused. It prevents him from receiving a fair trial, and no amount of explanation by the Court could remedy or eradicate the irreparable damage that has been done."

The judge denied the motion for mistrial and the jury was brought out again. Koelsch then testified that I had contemplated destroying the part of the hospital where Mrs. Clark had been kept.

Varon quickly stood and objected. "I am going to reiterate my objection for a mistrial. This is absolutely improper. This should be done out of the presence of the jury. I submit this is improper." But the motion was again denied by Judge Sheffey.

Koelsch continued, "He didn't feel that woman would regain consciousness. He didn't feel she could say anything—that she couldn't hurt him any."

Varon stopped him again. "Same objection. It's absolutely improper, compounding the prejudice." Again he was overruled.

When Varon cross-examined Koelsch he admitted that there was tremendous publicity over my arrest. Koelsch's picture had appeared in the paper and he had actually appeared on an NBC television broadcast. He came to see me out of "curiosity" but was allowed into the jail because he was an officer.

The prosecution rested its case at noon on Thursday. Joe Varon began his defense by asking for a directed verdict of not guilty because the state had not maintained the burden of proof required by law. "The case is fraught with vagaries in the form of circumstantial evidence which is tainted and improper because we are pyramiding one assumption on another . . . You can't place one assumption upon another assumption, Your Honor, where there has been no proof of fingerprints, no weapons, no witnesses, no overt act." He also pointed out that the location of the actual crime had not been proven and according to many previous law cases this was absolutely necessary. But again, the judge denied Varon's motion.

Leon Gagliardo, a photographer and state-licensed investigator, was called to the stand by my lawyer. He discussed the police line-up and said that Mrs. Clark could not identify me. She said, "He's just not there." He also stated that none of those in the line-up, including me, had attempted to distort their faces.

On Friday morning closing arguments from the prosecution and the defense were given. Daniel Futch stood and summarized the evidence against me and claimed that fingerprints in my old trailer and the victim's car apparently had been smudged to cover up the crime. He went over all the evidence, giving his analysis of its meaning.

Joe Varon then began his defense summation. "Remember, gentlemen, it's not my obligation to prove innocence. His guilt must be proven beyond a reasonable doubt."

He stated it was an impossibility for me to appear at the restaurant where Helen Jones worked, go home, change my clothes, meet Mrs. Clark and her daughter, have a talk, take them to my trailer, do what was necessary to eliminate them, deposit the bodies five miles apart and call the police all in one hour and eighteen minutes. "The point of time is something you cannot ignore."

"Reasonable doubt, gentlemen. There is no motive . . . no fingerprints, no blood stains, no witnesses; there are no logical possibilities, so we cannot guess, we cannot conjecture, and we cannot speculate . . . I know your verdict will be true and a just one if you follow the law, as I know you have followed the facts. And I *know* you will come back quickly with a verdict of *not guilty.*"

Mr. Futch came back to complete the second half of his summation. He stated there was no room for sympathy, bias, or prejudice. "Gentlemen, if you're going to feel sorry for Bob Erler, feel sorry for Merilyn Clark. What did Merilyn Clark do wrong?

"Gentlemen, he can't get the death penalty. We talked about that. What kind of penalty did Merilyn Clark get? Merilyn Clark got the death penalty. She didn't even have a trial. She was just executed."

After instructions from Judge Sheffey, the jury went out to begin deliberation. The alternate juror turned to my family and said, "Not guilty! I thought they had a case, but there's no evidence. I'd have to rule not guilty."

Because it soon became obvious the jury was not going to return in twenty minutes, I was taken back to my cell. After about two and a half hours they called and told me the jury was coming in. As I walked through the cellblock, I was so confident I would be acquitted, even the hecklers didn't bother me.

In the courtroom everyone was instructed to rise as the jury returned to the room. I looked at the six men as they walked in. None was looking in my direction. I kept my eyes fixed on them until finally one looked my way. He glanced at me then quickly turned away. Instantly I knew the verdict; I felt sick at my stomach.

The judge addressed them. "Has the jury reached a verdict?"

"Yes, we have, your Honor. We, the jury, find the defendant guilty of murder in the second degree." The courtroom exploded. Reporters ran from the room. I sat down—numbed. My attorney made me stand.

The judge looked down at me, smiling. "Will the defendant approach the bench with his counsel," he commanded.

We walked to the bench and I looked up at the judge. "Do you have anything to say for yourself?" he asked.

"I just don't know what to say," I responded in a daze.

Judge Sheffey looked at the Court Clerk. "What is the longest sentence that has ever been handed down in this court?"

She looked up. "Your Honor, I believe it was ninety-nine years—by you."

The judge looked down at me and a wide smile covered his face. "Mr. Erler, I sentence you to ninety-nine years *and* six months at Florida State Prison at hard labor." His words didn't really sink in. "Remember something, Mr. Erler, it's not how long you make it, it's how you make it long." The words were from a popular cigarette commercial, and he started laughing at his own joke.

I was fingerprinted in front of the judge. My mind still had not accepted the verdict. I looked back at my family; everyone was crying. I just shook my head "no." I was marched back to my cell in a stupor.

When I arrived, everyone asked what happened.

"They found me guilty," I replied blankly, but my friends didn't believe me.

"What was your sentence, if they found you guilty?" Griffith asked.

"They sentenced me to ninety-nine years and six months at hard labor at Florida State Prison."

Griffith started laughing. "Who ever heard of a sentence like that? That's ridiculous. They found you 'not guilty,' didn't they?"

"If they'd found me 'not guilty' I wouldn't be standing here. I'd be free." As the truth of my words sank in, all the expressions changed. In a moment the verdict came on the television newscast and everyone turned to watch it.

I walked to my cell in shock. I felt estranged from the world. My mind began to fabricate what prison life would be like; I pictured myself stepping off the bus and walking into prison—the hardened convicts began to club and stab me.

SIX
HARD TIME

One of the many front page headlines that night read "CATCH ME KILLER GETS 99 YEARS." Several inmates tried to show me the paper but I wanted no part of it.

My second trial was due soon. I was charged with the attempted murder of Mrs. Clark. But my lawyer reasoned it would never come to trial because they could never get a jury to convict me on a first-degree charge—with the death penalty—on so little evidence.

A lot of mail started coming from religious people who wanted to convert me. I gave it to other prisoners. I had no interest in God after receiving such a grossly unfair sentence. I told the guards not to bring any mail unless it was from my family.

After several months, the second charges were dropped, just as my lawyer had predicted. The guards came and told me to pack my belongings. All I had was a toothbrush and a couple of pictures.

I was shackled with twelve other prisoners into a long leg chain and we were marched outside and onto a gray bus to begin the ride to the prison 300 miles away. As we pulled out of Fort Lauderdale, I looked at the world for the last time through the wire-mesh covered windows. Everyone was quiet on the bus. It was like we were being taken to an execution. We were going to the big house.

After several hours we arrived at Lake Butler Reception Center where we were marched into a room with a small set of bleachers.

We were ordered to strip. It was threatening to be completely naked with so many people staring in contempt. They marched us into the barber shop and shaved off our hair, then we were herded into the shower. The guards kept up a steady harassment; if we didn't move fast enough they would lock us in a cage.

We were searched thoroughly for contraband. A white disinfectant powder was dumped on us and we were commanded to rub it in. Some of the convicts assisting the guards began to whisper among themselves and point in my direction. Finally we were allowed to put our shorts back on. We were then fingerprinted.

When they took our photos, the convict taking pictures adjusted his lense, leaned in my direction and whispered, "They're gonna make an attempt on your life, so be cool."

Fear exploded in my head. "Who?" I whispered back frantically. But he ignored me and walked away.

I immediately became wary of anyone who came too close. Someone would probably try to creep up and stab me from behind. I tried not to turn my back toward anyone within range.

We were marched into the yard. Convicts were everywhere; some yelled and whistled at guys they knew. I walked by myself at the end of the group. Several guys were talking and nodding in my direction as if they knew who I was. They marched us to a cellblock and locked us in individual cells. We would be here for several days while all our records were processed.

Other convicts yelled back and forth, "Erler is in number five." Several yelled down asking if it was me. I answered a voice that sounded familiar, and immediately everyone on the tier began to breathe threats; they all said they'd get me when I came out. I didn't know what I was going to do.

One of the guys in the block, the "run around" who swept up the tier, came to my cell. "Listen, I'm not supposed to talk to you, but you wanna get in the sun? A new guard is coming in who'll take a forged medical pass. He'll let you go 'cause lots of us get medical shots. You want me to give it to ya?"

"Yeah, give it to me." I hadn't been in the sun for eight months. He gave me the pass and I wrote my name on it. When the shift changed, I stuck my arm through the bars and handed it to the guard as he walked by. After he made his count, he pulled my cell door open and I walked out. He pointed downstairs and told me I had to be back in two hours.

I walked down into the yard. I noticed a few prisoners staring in my direction but just ignored them. I hiked out to a baseball diamond where several cons were playing a game.

I sat down on an empty bench. Nobody seemed to be paying much attention to me and the sun felt so good and warm I decided to lay down and soak it up. I closed my eyes.

In a moment a shadow crossed my face and I opened my eyes to see a gang of blacks peering down at me. In the same instant I saw something flying toward my head. My hands shot up, but I wasn't fast enough.

A bone-crunching blow from a three-foot long two-by-four caught me full in the face. The pain was incredible. I jumped to my feet and spit out a handful of teeth. I could feel and taste the blood running down my throat. My nose had been smashed to one side and blood was everywhere. Nine blacks began punching and kicking me. One of them beat on me with an empty five-gallon metal bucket.

All the fear, rage, and hostility I had suffered over the months exploded in my pounding head. I went berserk. Fear completely took over. I started hitting and kicking anyone within reach. I was oblivious to my own pain. I was determined to hurt those who were hurting me.

"He's a devil! He's a devil!" one of my assailants cried as we struggled. Blood was everywhere. I punched one man in the jaw and knocked him to the ground. He didn't get up.

I was getting hit all over, but I could only feel the pressure of the blows—I was numb to the pain. In a moment I knocked another down, then another. The rest of my assailants began to run. I chased the man who had been beating me with the bucket and tackled him.

By now, several hundred inmates had gathered and formed a giant circle. I wrestled the man until I was on top, then smashed my fists into his face until he was a bloody pulp. Somebody yelled, "The cops are coming! The cops are coming!"

I jumped up and tried to disappear in the crowd. But my shirt had been ripped off and I was covered with blood. My face felt like hamburger. I couldn't breathe through my nose. Every time I took a breath through my mouth, the cold air sent pain knifing into my jaw. Many of my teeth had been broken off and the nerves were exposed.

The officers ran out and yelled, "Hey, you!" They handcuffed and returned me to my cell. Most of my assailants had fled, but three were carried off the field on stretchers.

The sergeant came down and looked at me. "We've got to get this man to the hospital—immediately!" They took me to the clinic and everyone was yelling and screaming at me.

There was no dentist on duty and my teeth were mangled. The doctor washed me up and called the dentist. In about thirty minutes he arrived. He injected a shot in the gum and gave me something I could apply to help deaden the nerves. Then they took me back to my cell.

The pain was incredible. It felt like someone was hitting my jaw with a hammer. In a few hours, they took me to be examined again. The doctor told me they were going to have to x-ray my head, but the machine was broken and they didn't know how long it would be before they could use it.

"Is there anything bothering you real bad?" he asked.

"I hurt all over," I mumbled. I could hardly talk because all my front teeth were gone and my jaw popped every time I opened or closed my mouth. They put me back in my cell and gave me some pain pills.

When I was back in my cell that night the blacks who had attacked me yelled from the other levels. They threatened to kill me for what I had done. The next day, the prison authorities held a meeting in the laundryroom.

When I entered the room, the warden, the captain, and another big-wig were waiting. All the blacks who had attacked me were lined up on one side. Their threats through the night had filled me with hate and rage. I was determined to get them before they got me.

I walked calmly over as if to join them, but suddenly sucker-punched the first man in the stomach, sending him doubled-up to the floor. As I went after the second man, everyone scattered. I grabbed him and we fell into a pile of clothes and began to swing wildly at each other.

The officers quickly restrained us and led me away. Once the blacks had been removed, they brought me back downstairs. Captain McMullen, a short stocky man with triple chins, was sitting behind the table puffing on a cigar. As soon as I walked through the door he jumped to his feet, pointed his finger in my chest, and began to badger me arrogantly.

"Let me tell you something, Erler!" he ranted, "you're in prison! You're in *my* prison! And you're not a tough guy! You're not gonna go around doing this type of thing! Is that understood?!"

I tried to talk, but with no front teeth and my popping jaw, I couldn't pronounce my words well.

"Listen, Erler!" he continued, not giving me a chance to explain, "if someone in this prison hits you, you come and tell me or an officer and we'll take care of it. Is that understood?"

I blew it when he said that. I jumped to my feet and began screaming. In an instant he and the warden had their backs to the wall. "Let me tell you something, *you punk!* I'm doing *ninety-nine years!* Do you understand that? I am doing this number! And I've got to live here! Nobody is gonna jump on me and knock my teeth out! Nobody! Do you understand?" I was pointing my finger in the captain's face. Tears were streaming down my cheeks. I had completely flipped out.

"Calm down, Erler," said the captain, "calm down. We know you've had a terrible experience. Just calm down—you've lost it."

I kept my finger in his face. "You're gonna lose it if you keep telling me that. These guys are gonna make no punk out of me! I've got to live here! I've got to be here!"

The "goon squad" had been called but they were afraid to come in. Finally I calmed down and they handcuffed and returned me upstairs. Once in my cell, tears streamed down my face. I just didn't know what to do. Everyone was against me. While I was sitting there, several blacks who had witnessed the fight but who hadn't been involved yelled that I would have to contend with them as well.

In an hour, the guards came and got me. I was placed in a truck by myself and transported ten miles to the maximum security section of Florida State Prison at Railford. They backed the truck up to a loading ramp and a lieutenant asked for my number. I told him I couldn't remember it.

"Let me tell you something, punk! You better remember your number, because that's all you are in here—a number."

I made an obscene gesture and told him what I thought of him. He slammed the door and told the driver to put me in the hole. The prison emergency squad was standing by when they opened the door. They were huge men, dressed in combat gear.

I was a complete mess when I came out of the truck. My eyes were almost swollen shut; I had no front teeth; my lips looked like hamburger; my nose was smashed to one side; and I was covered with dried blood.

They led me down a long corridor and locked me in a cage in front of the control room. All the wings of the prison were off this main corridor and prisoners continually walked by. Many looked at me and asked what happened.

Before I could answer, someone would call, "That's the pig from Fort Lauderdale," and everyone would just walk away.

After three or four hours, I was shackled and led down the hallway. They took me to N Wing which was maximum security, and placed me in a cell by myself. When the door was closed, the guy who took care of the tier asked, "What happened to you?"

"I had trouble at Lake Butler."

"Are you Erler?"

"Yeah, why?" He just shook his head and walked away. He spread the word I was on the wing and several of the other prisoners yelled threats. Apparently, everyone already knew about the incident at the reception center. The cons seemed both to fear and respect me. They thought I was fighting back out of courage. In reality, I was fighting out of fear—for my very life.

One of the officers who had witnessed the fight came on the wing and told the inmates I had whipped nine men at one time. That baffled me. I was the one who had been hurt—but because I stood and fought and broke several jaws and ribs, they respected me.

They told me the classification team was trying to determine where to put me. It was recommended I be put in protective custody so nobody could get to me.

In two days, the warden and Captain J. C. Combs came to my cell. He ran a stick on the bars. "Hit the floor, Erler." I jumped off the bed and came to the bars.

"What do you think we ought to do with you?"

"Captain, I want to go out to population."

Combs looked at me in disbelief. He shot a glance at the warden, then back at me. "Are you serious?"

"Yes, sir. I don't want to cause any trouble captain, but I've got ninety-nine years and I can't make it if I live back here." I was having an extremely difficult time talking without my front teeth. "The guys will think I'm afraid and they'll want to kill me for sure."

Combs stared right through me. "Erler, I'm gonna come back and talk to you tomorrow. If you still want to go to population, you tell me then."

I had a migraine headache and a half. I couldn't eat anything because my jaw kept popping. They called me out to the dentist, but he told me he had 200 men on his waiting list and couldn't do anything for me unless it was an emergency.

"Man, what do I have to do?! All my teeth are knocked out and the nerves are exposed. Isn't that an emergency?"

"Well you're just gonna have to wait like everybody else. You're not a privileged character." It was a full week before they did any work on my teeth, and that was only because the captain ordered them to.

The next day, Captain Combs and the warden returned. "Do you still feel you want to go into population?"

"Yes, I do, sir."

"You realize you could be killed in population?"

"Yes, sir, I do." I handed him a note which said I would accept all responsibility if the administration put me in population. Combs looked at the note, then at me.

"Erler, if you really want to go out there, I'm gonna give you a chance—against my better judgment. But I want you to be careful. There are people out there who will kill you."

"Thank you, sir, I appreciate the chance."

In a few hours, my door popped open and the loudspeaker told me to pack up my sheet and blankets and carry everything up front. Then I was marched down the corridor to J Wing where I was given an empty cell.

The inmates on the wing stared at me. I said "hello" to a few, but they ignored me and turned away. I surveyed my new home and found it extremely sickening. The mattress was turned upside down on the floor and was soaked with blood. The floor had pools of blood on it.

The wing officer said, "You're gonna have to clean this up."

"What happened?" I asked, a little sick to my stomach.

"The guy before you decided he wanted to check out early." He gave me a cynical **grin** and started to walk off. Over his shoulder he called, "When you finish, go down to the supply room and get your linen and a new mattress."

After cleaning the cell as best I could, I walked down to supply and asked the convict attendant for some linen.

He glared back at me arrogantly. "Do you have a carton of cigarettes?"

"No, I don't smoke, thank you."

"I'm not gonna give you any; you're gonna give 'em to me."

"Give them to you for what?"

"You want your linen supplies, don't you? Give me a carton of cigarettes and you can have them."

"I didn't know I had to buy them," I offered innocently.

"Well, you know now." The other cons in the supply room laughed.

"Is this standard procedure?"

"*It is for a pig!*" he replied sarcastically.

"Listen. I just came out of max. I don't have any store. I just got—"

"That's your problem," he cut me off. One of the men behind him added, "That's right, cop!"

I'd taken enough. I smashed my fist into the man's face, then jumped over the counter and started beating the arrogance out of him. All the others backed up. Grabbing him by the shirt, I cried in a rage, "Let me tell you something, I'm coming back in fifteen minutes—and you better have my stuff ready!" I was so mad I was shaking.

I returned to my cell, but marched back in fifteen minutes. A number of cons were standing around. All my clothes and laundry were sitting on the counter.

"I need a pillow." Someone threw me a pillow and I walked away. Nobody said anything.

I finished cleaning everything up and made my bed. Chow call came so I got in line, but no one would be my partner, so I had to go to the back of the line. When I entered the mess hall, all the inmates stared at me. When I got my food and sat down, everyone made a big deal about moving away from me.

I couldn't eat; it was impossible to chew my food without my front teeth. I couldn't even drink; my nerves were extremely sensitive to the cold liquid. After a few moments of utter frustration, I picked up my tray and threw all the food away.

There was a commotion outside. Smoke was curling out of J Wing. Once on the wing I realized it was my cell that was burning. I ran downstairs and found it surrounded by convicts and officers. Someone had made a Molotov cocktail with lighter fluid and a mayonnaise jar and had thoroughly incinerated everything. All my bedding, clothes, and personal belongings were going up in smoke.

Once the flames were out, I entered the cell and began sifting through the remains. Captain Combs pushed through the crowd and asked what had happened. All the cons looked at me.

"Well, sir . . . I guess I was smoking in bed."

"You don't smoke, do you Erler?" he asked in knowing tones.

"Well, no sir, but I guess this was a special case."

Combs looked at me then at the other cons standing around. "Would you like to go to max?"

"No sir. I'd like to clean this mess up and get some new supplies."

The captain addressed the wing officer and said, "Give this man the things he needs to clean up and let him have more supplies." He nodded at me and walked off.

Much of the black soot would not come up. The fire had burned the paint right off the walls. I put all the ashes in a laundry bag and threw it in the trash, then went to supply and got a new set of prison clothes and linen.

Just before evening chow, someone threw a note in my cell. It told me to check out or I would be killed; they didn't want a pig on the wing. I ignored the note and flushed it down the toilet.

When I went to evening chow my cell was burned out again. This time they really torched it. Everything was consumed. Another cell was empty on the wing so I asked to be moved into it. The lieutenant agreed, but said I was probably making a mistake because it was out of view of the officer on the second floor. I moved into the new cell and took a third pile of linen.

At night, after the count is taken, everyone's door is opened. A prisoner has the choice of locking himself in his cell or coming out and going to the day room. I had received so many threats, I decided it was time to bring things to a head. I left my door open and went into the day room.

There were fifty cons sitting in the room watching one television set. I walked to the front of the room and switched the TV off.

Picking up an iron folding chair, I slammed it on the floor. Instantly everyone jumped up and retreated to the back of the room.

"Listen, you guys! I was a cop! Now I'm a convict and I don't care if you like me living here or not! I will not be threatened! I'm staying in this wing! If you want a hunk of me, you don't have to rattle my cage. Fall out and get it right now!"

Nobody moved. Every eye stared right back at me but nobody said a thing. I was enraged. I had taken so much abuse I was anxious to fight back. I kicked a few chairs around but still nobody stepped out.

"Listen, I am going down on the bottom floor, and if anybody wants a hunk of me, they can get it right now."

I walked out of the day room and for the first time, no one made any remarks about what they were going to do to me. I went downstairs and waited for fifteen minutes but nobody came. Returning to my cell, I locked myself in for the night.

After that incident, several of the guys started talking to me. The guy working in the supply room walked by my cell and said, "Hey, Erler, you're all right."

The next morning they served grits for breakfast. A con on the serving line slapped a spoonful down on my tray and they shot all over, burning me.

I reacted by flinging my tray back at the man, catching him right above the eye. He quickly backed off and fled across the room. I jumped on the serving line to pursue him, but accidentally stepped into the pot of grits. I fell off the counter but couldn't get that hot pot off my foot. I was dancing like an Indian, shaking and kicking, trying to dislodge it from my shoe.

Several cons started laughing guardedly. In a moment everyone was roaring. I must have looked pretty comical trying to shake off that pot. I sat on the floor with my burned foot and laughed with them. The laughter seemed to break some of the tension and it appeared the men were starting to accept me.

I returned to the chow line and the other inmates backed off—not knowing what I was going to do next. I was given extra portions of food and when I sat down to eat I noticed everyone was staring at me. The guards soon came over and asked what had happened.

"Don't ask me, ask the other guy," I told them.

I was called to the control room and informed I was being sent to the Rock, the medical section of the Florida prison system. What I didn't know was that inmates put people on call-outs, read the records, and generally ran the day-to-day prison activities. Word of my presence had spread and several brothers and friends of the cons I had had that fight with at Lake Butler worked at the Rock.

I was handcuffed along with some other prisoners and taken in a panel truck over to the hospital section. I was escorted to the second floor of the hospital and told to sit. I assumed I was there to get some kind of physical or examination of my recent injuries.

An inmate walked into the waiting room carrying my medical records. "Erler?" he asked, looking around.

"Right here," I answered, standing up.

"Follow me."

He led down a long hallway. When we reached the end, he stopped and handed me my records. Pointing to a door, he said, "You have an examination. They're waiting for you in there."

The door was actually the door to a bathroom. When I rounded the corner I was smashed in the eye. Three guys jumped me with broken broom handles.

I went absolutely crazy. I lost it. I started punching and screaming and fighting like a maniac. I knocked one of my assailants to the floor and the other two fled.

The man on the floor managed to pull away so I ran after him and made a shoe-string tackle right in front of a seventy-year-old guard. I began to pound the con's head against the radiator while the terrified old guard watched in shock.

In a moment several guards pulled me off the man. They quickly whisked me to the cage in front of the control room. Some of the other inmates volunteered that I had been bushwhacked and assaulted. But I refused to say anything to the guards because inmates worked in the office and word would get around if I stooled. I found out later the brother of one of the guys whose jaw I had broken worked in the hospital. He had set me up to get even.

Back at Railford, they decided to have me work in the medical clinic to keep me away from most of the other inmates. The warden went to the trusties working in the clinic and asked if they would mind working with me. They knew I hadn't finked on anybody so they agreed.

I went to work in the clinic, taking care of records. The first day on the job, several old-time, hard-core convicts gave me a quick tour. They showed me a still which they used to convert tincture of benzine into pure liquor. They also showed me a big shank—a terrifying knife with a twelve-inch blade which they had taped under the counter.

I didn't realize it at the time, but they were testing me to see if I would squeal. When no shakedown inspection occurred, I had passed the first of several loyalty tests. Gradually they started to accept me and I was told I had earned their respect by the way I had been fighting back.

SEVEN
THE WAY OF
THE WARRIOR

After about three months, my teeth were finally fixed. They performed root canals to deaden all the exposed nerves, then gave me some false teeth. But soon I was involved in another fight and all my bridgework was knocked out. For a long time the prison dentist refused to fix it up again.

I found out later my jaw had been broken, but they never gave me any treatment for that. It simply healed by itself.

My nose was still a mess. I looked like Henry Chickenhawk, the cartoon character. One entire nasal passage was blocked by bone. It was determined I needed extensive work, so they decided to send me to the plastic surgeons who were coming in from Gainesville.

I was transported back to the Rock. Returning to that place induced a strong fear. Not only had I been attacked there, but several had made threats against my life.

I was checked into the plastic surgery ward. The inmates who were in charge of the operating room had me lie down on the operating table, then they cinched me down with several three-inch straps. While the doctor was out putting on his gloves and preparing for the operation, they were to inject my nose with six shots of pain killer—three on each side.

One of the cons inserted a hypodermic needle but instead of

pain-killer, he injected water into my nose. It burned like an iron and I screamed in pain.

The inmate looked down with a sadistic grin. "We've got you now, cop! You belong to us!" They had read my record jacket and knew I had been a police officer.

The surgeon entered the room and prepared to operate.

"Doctor," I said. "Whatever you gave me hasn't taken effect. It didn't kill the pain. It's burning like crazy." I was afraid to squeal on the cons and was careful in what I said.

He grabbed my nose and started squeezing it. "No, it will take effect in a minute."

"No. I didn't get any pain killer. I'm telling you, I didn't get any pain killer."

"I can see where they injected it right here. It will get numb in just a moment."

My nose kept burning. They were supposed to swab out both nostrils with cocaine. But the cons had stolen the cocaine and there was nothing on the swab. The doctor was sure I was numb. He placed a utensil up my nose to spread the nostrils.

"Doctor, I'm in tremendous pain!"

"No, you just think you are. It's purely psychological. You'll feel a little pressure but nothing else."

He took a small scalpel and made two incisions in my nose. I could smell the blood and feel the cuts. I told the surgeon I could feel it, but he was convinced I was imagining everything.

I couldn't see what he was going to do next, but he had placed a chisel way up into my nose. "Now you're going to feel some pressure on this so don't be alarmed." Then he hit the chisel with a wooden mallet.

My nose exploded in the most intense pain I have ever felt. It was as if he had used a sledge hammer. I screamed in absolute agony. The doctor looked at me in amazement.

"This man isn't under sedation!" he said in surprise.

I cursed and screamed and tried to break out of those big three-inch straps. But I was totally helpless. I couldn't move.

"Give me some pain killer quick!" the doctor called to his assistants.

"Don't let them give me a shot!" I cried. "They're trying to kill me! They've already stolen all the pain killer. Listen, I'm an ex-cop and they're trying to get me!"

The doctor was not a prison doctor and had no idea what was going on. As it turned out, he wasn't even a doctor—*he was practicing to be a doctor!* He quickly called in another doctor who was a knowledgeable plastic surgeon. Together they found some pain killer and deadened the pain.

I was still in tremendous pain so I demanded they let me up. "I don't want this operation! Unstrap me! Let me off this table!" But I had signed a paper giving them permission to perform the operation.

"Well, we've already started the operation and we've got to finish it now," the second doctor announced.

"Let me off this table! Let me off this table!" I screamed. "Those guys just want to kill me!"

Two of the convicts were sitting off to one side, smiling. They told the doctor I was a little unbalanced and not to worry about me. The doctor didn't know what to think so he insisted they finish what they had started.

He had the cons hold my head and they started in with the chisel again. Even with the drugs, the pain was absolutely incredible. They finally put me out.

I opened my eyes when they were wheeling me out. A familiar face was looking down at me. It was Jack Griffith. "How ya doing, Bob?"

"Hey, Jack! Those suckers tried to get me."

"Yeah, I found out about it and straightened it out." Although he hadn't been at the Rock long, he was head nurse in charge of all the other cons. "Don't worry, I put the word out you're my friend. You won't have any more trouble.

They placed me in a little room to recover. I was supposed to get shots for pain every hour, but never received anything. Outside my door, four inmates began to play dominoes. Each man would slap his down on the table. The racket hurt my throbbing head. I got out of bed and staggered to the door.

"Hey, man, give me a break on those dominoes."

One of the men got smart, so I tipped over the table sending their game to the floor. One of them slammed his fist into my face knocking off the metal cup taped over my nose. We began to fight, but Griffith came running and everyone fled. He helped me back into bed.

"Bob, you broke your nose again. It's swelling like a tomato."

They called the specialist and told him what had happened. But they couldn't come back until the next day. All night I was up with the pain.

The next morning the doctors returned and gave me some shots. One grabbed my nose between his two fingers and squeezed it. I could hear cracking sounds as he straightened it, but he did it so fast I didn't have time to react. They covered it with another metal cup and applied ice packs to help the swelling go down. By now, both my eyes were almost completely closed.

Jack came up to see me again. He had heard rumors they were transferring him to the East Unit where I lived. He was concerned for my safety and told me if he came over he would train me in karate. After seven days in the hospital I was returned to the prison.

I went to my first movie, which was shown in the gymnasium. They called one wing at a time, lined us up and searched for weapons, then marched us into the gym. Only one officer was in the room and he sat toward the front.

I made the mistake of sitting in the seats below the bleachers. Several guys threw things down at me; some tried to spit on me. I finally left my seat and watched the movie with my back to the wall.

Not too long into the movie, a fight broke out in the bleachers. In the light from the projector I could see someone running across the floor. The officers immediately turned on the lights.

One con had a long knife and was chasing another inmate. The fellow being pursued sprinted to the stage but missed the step and fell. The aggressor reached him and slammed the knife into his body. After he was stabbed, the victim pulled the knife out and knocked it aside. Then he jumped up and stumbled back toward the bleachers. The attacker picked up the knife, caught his prey from behind and began to thrust the blade in over and over.

I couldn't believe what I was seeing. It was so brutal and senseless. But no one raised a hand to stop it—not even the guards. The man was stabbed twelve times before he collapsed and died.

The emergency squad burst in and everyone lined up against the walls. They started to shake us down, but then the lieutenant said, "Ahh, the hell with it. If they want to kill each other. Let 'em go. Run the movie!"

The slain prisoner was carried away and they made another inmate mop up the blood—then they turned the lights out and finished the movie! I couldn't believe it. It was as if nothing had happened. The other cons were totally indifferent to that guy's death. In fact, they laughed and joked through the rest of the film.

I couldn't sleep that night. I realized how completely worthless my life was in prison. Death could strike so quickly. Nobody really cared about anybody. We were just a number and whether we lived or died was of little concern to anyone.

The majority of guys still wouldn't talk to me; most couldn't forget I had been a pig. As I listened to some of the guys tell how they had been arrested and physically abused, I found myself starting to resent police and authority. Many of the arresting officers had lied in order to secure convictions of my friends. I knew about how the police could lie because of my trial. I began to see things more and more from their point of view.

After I had been in Railford for a month, heavy-set Lieutenant Cook called me into the radio room. "Tyler, I want to tell you something and I want you to keep it between you and me."

"Yes, sir."

"You're one of the first cops that's ever been able to make it in population, and I respect that. But I expect you to have some serious problems soon."

"Why?" I asked.

"I'm gonna show you a picture of a guy. I want you to look closely." He pulled out the medical records of another inmate. I had seen the man. He was a six foot six prisoner with red hair. "This guy is crazy," the lieutenant continued. "He's been in and out of prison all his life. He's been in eleven years on his most recent sentence. When he was arrested, the police in Jacksonville handcuffed and beat him to a pulp. He hates cops and he's been telling everyone, the first chance he gets, he's gonna kill you."

The lieutenant's words sent an electric shock through my body. The guy was a monster and he lived in the wing opposite mine. On several occasions I had noticed him glaring at me, but so many inmates did that, it hadn't seemed too unusual.

"Listen," the lieutenant continued, "I know you've got a lot of time. But I want to tell you something if you can keep it between you and me. You promise?"

"Yes. Of course."

"If you have to kill this man, I'll make sure you don't get any more time for it."

Fear tightened my stomach muscles. "What do you mean, *kill him*!? What am I gonna kill him for?"

"I think you've realized, in prison the best defense is a good offense. He's a dangerous man; he's a mental patient. Just remember, you've been warned!"

My heart was pumping madly. I took a last look at the man's records and thanked the lieutenant. Back on the wing, I asked another prisoner about the redheaded inmate.

"That guy's dangerous. He's a cop hater and is stirring up trouble for you. He's tried to talk other inmates into bushwhacking you." My friend's words only added to my fear.

On several occasions I found notes in my cell warning me not to go to a movie or out in the yard because prisoners were laying for me. The first time I went out in the yard, several cons threw rocks at me while my back was turned. None hit me, but when I turned around everyone looked the other way.

I strode over to the group which I was sure had thrown the stones. The tall redheaded con was part of it. "I don't know which one of you guys is throwing the rocks, but you're pretty brave to my back. If you got any guts why don't you let me see who you are."

Nobody said anything; they just stared. After I turned and walked away a short distance, someone tossed another stone. I went to where several cons were lifting weights and grabbed a small iron bar. I held it in my hand and walked around the yard. The other cons looked at me uneasily; no one was sure what I was going to do next.

Prison life is a jungle. Whenever a fight broke out in the mess hall, the officers would slam the doors, allowing the inmates to have it out while they sent for the "goon squad." It seemed everyone had knives and if there was any trouble, the cons would break out their weapons for protection.

There is a definite social status in prison—a pecking order. The most feared and respected inmates are murderers. Armed robbers rank second, followed by burglars and other violent criminals. On the very bottom of the list are those in for sex crimes and child molesting. Those cons are treated roughly, they're hounded and beaten up—and if they are weak, they're turned into homosexuals.

A Korean named Kim Wha lived on J Wing. Everybody was afraid of Kim because he had wiped out a couple of guys in a fight. He had a black belt in karate and I asked him to teach it to me. He refused, but I kept after him, asking him several times a week. Kim took a liking to me because I knew some Korean. I described what the country had looked like when I was there in the service and it turned out we knew some of the same people.

Finally one day, he took me to his cell, and explained that karate was ninety percent mental and only ten percent physical. I didn't understand because the karate training I had had in Korea was so limited. All I knew were the basic exercises.

"Watch," he said. He walked to the wall of his cell and fired directly into the solid concrete with his fist—with maximum power. He pulled it away and struck again and again—a total of ten times. The force of his blows would have broken any normal man's fist and arm.

When he turned to face me, I saw his eyes were spaced out—he was gone. Slowly he came back and began to shake his hand loose, because it was frozen in place.

Kim pointed to his temple. "That's weapon. You still want be student?" Before I could answer he punched me hard in the chest and my first reaction was to hit him back. He shook his head. "You have bad attitude. I cannot teach you."

I tried to keep to myself as much as possible. There was a lot of drug traffic, homosexuality, and fights on the wing. Some of the guys would steal yeast from the kitchen and with pieces of fruit they would make their own liquor. They sold the booze to other cons and everyone got drunk.

All known homosexuals in the state prison system had been shipped into the East Unit and were housed in K Wing opposite us. These gays and transvestites were assigned to one-man cells in Sissy Wing (as it was called). On most nights, the "girls" put on a "spook show." They dressed up like women with clothes they had smuggled in from the clothes factory. They would put towels around their heads, paint their lips red, and dance sensually in front of the windows.

Even our wing was full of "marriages." Guys would walk around holding hands. When they went to the movies they would sit together. They also had homosexual sex. The guards knew about it but never tried to stop it. What a bizarre world to be thrown into.

The environment was so artificial and weird I began to wonder if it was real or if I was just dreaming about its existence. I kept telling myself it couldn't be real.

There were just over 1100 men at the prison. Of these, over 700 were locked up in maximum security or on death row. Many of these guys got so bored and lonely they would mutilate themselves by slashing their wrists and cutting their bodies just so they could get out of their cells and walk down the hallway to the clinic. On the average, about 70 to 90 men came to the clinic each month to get sewed up.

The doctor had become calloused to these men who came in again and again and he began to sew them up without any pain killer. It almost seemed that inmates were subhuman. They acted and were treated like animals.

I lived in a world of fear. There weren't many places I could go without asking for trouble. I couldn't allow myself to be isolated in the gym or in the yard because it would have been too easy to get attacked.

One day I heard Jack Griffith had been transferred to the East Unit. I walked to the control room and discovered he was in the holding tank.

"Hey, Jack! Are you ready to start working out?"

"Yes, I am. Just get yourself ready. Make sure you're in good shape."

Jack was assigned to my wing. His first day in his cell, he introduced me to Lester Woods, who had been a student of his both at the Rock and on the street.

"I'm gonna have Les work with you when I'm not around. He's a brown belt and can teach you a lot." Les was a young guy serving a twenty-five-year sentence for armed robbery. I spent several hours with him every day doing body stretches and the other exercises he showed me.

They opened our cells at 5:30 every morning, but we were not called to go to work until 8:00. I would use this time to work out everyday. On the job, I had a lot of extra time, so I did exercises there too. I was learning how to punch and kick and stretch out my body.

Because Jack was a Master, he outranked Kim, who was only a black belt. Jack ordered Kim to start working out with me and give me sparring experience called *kumite*. As I worked with Kim in the corner of the bottom floor where the guards couldn't see us, most of the guys on the wing would crowd around. Jack would pay a pack of cigarettes to have them "spook" for us. When a guard came to make his rounds, someone would yell "fire in the hole!" We would stop sparring and do push-ups so the guard couldn't tell what we were doing.

At first the other inmates laughed at my awkward looking attempts to become proficient in karate, but soon I began to develop powerful techniques. Because I worked out at every available moment, I developed rapidly.

Jack was an extremely high-ranking karate Master—a red belt. He had learned the art in Japan. Like me, he had been a boxer, but soon discovered the superiority of karate. He was one of the first white men ever allowed to learn the martial arts. He became a black belt in the 1940's. While he was in Japan he won the all-northern Japanese championship and held three black belts in different karate disciplines, another in judo, one in jujitsu, and one with samurai swords.

He began to explain to me the oriental philosophy of being a warrior. Once the vow is taken to be a warrior, one lives by the code of *Bushido* (a code of chivalry, which values honor above life). Each day is lived as an individual, and if anything happens, one is supposed to rely on himself.

Griffith had lived with a Master in a dojo (a hall of meditation). His stories about the death matches and the warrior philosophy captured my imagination. I could easily apply his stories to my own life. People had tried to kill me and I lived with the daily threat of hand-to-hand combat.

I totally gave myself to being a warrior. Jack kept referring to me as a *kamikaze* (a suicide fighter). He respected the way I would fight back even when severely hurt. He told me I could be a champion black belt, which became my goal. I dedicated my life, my whole existence, to learning the martial arts.

Jack was into Zen Buddhism. Although I didn't have any religious belief, he would discipline me by having me sit in a half lotus position each night for a half hour. I was to empty my mind in order to build my mental fighting power called *ki*. I grabbed onto karate like a dying man would grab onto a life raft. I saw it as the only means that could possibly save me and give me a chance to live in prison peaceably.

Jack took a burlap bag and a two by four and made a striking board for my hands and feet. I began to punch and kick the board to harden my hands and feet. I worked on it daily. For a while my knuckles looked like hamburger.

Our schedule was six to seven hours of physical workouts every day. Jack had me jog outside until I was so exhausted I had to depend on my mind, not my strength. He took me to the gymnasium and instructed the boxers to punch on me so I would get used to being attacked. He instilled in me the idea that regardless of whom I fought, if a man could not hit me, he could not hurt me.

I was taught all the ceremonial aspects of karate and respect. Before a match, I would bow to the east in honor of the master, then I would bow to Griffith for our workouts. The first time we went to the gym, Jack reminded me of the past.

"Bob, remember in county jail when you gave me a break?"

"Yeah."

We bowed and when Jack came out of the bow he spun all the way around me with arms and legs flying everywhere. He kicked the back of my head and punched my face lightly with numerous blows just to show me what he could do. His performance was so extraordinary I simply couldn't believe it.

"Boy," I said, "am I glad I gave you a break!" We both laughed.

Jack also started to teach me judo. Because we could not work out if any guards were around, we put our mat up on the stage behind the movie screen so we couldn't be seen.

One afternoon Jack flipped me wrong and hurt his leg. He checked into the hospital and found he needed an operation. He was going to be in for several weeks, and there was no way I could get to him. I was now a brown belt and Les could no longer teach me.

The next day I walked to the prison control room and faked a fall on the wet floor. The guards came running and I claimed to have hurt my back. They immediately took me to the hospital. The doctor told me I would have to stay in bed until they knew how bad my injury was.

Immediately, Jack and I began to use the whole medical dormitory for karate. He had me work out from 9:00 at night until 3:00 in the morning. He showed me how to walk and punch and kick; it was constant repetition and hard work. In the daytime I slept and faked my injury so I could stay in the hospital.

Within six months, everyone knew I was improving greatly in karate. I found most of my troubles had ended. Nobody wanted to tangle with me because they were afraid they would get hurt. And because I didn't stick my nose in anyone's business and didn't inform, I found the other cons beginning to accept me more and more.

About this time, a good job came open in the radio room which broadcast music to all the cells. The position was normally given to an inmate who had been in for ten to fifteen years. It was an easy job that segregated one from the other inmates.

I walked into Captain Combs' office and asked if I could have it. He thought for a few moments then replied it would be a good way to keep me from the other inmates and said I could.

There was enough area in the radio room to work out—and with the light demands of the job, I was able to put in almost eight full hours a day. Jack drew some diagrams of the human body that showed where to strike for maximum effect. I hung these drawings up and practiced striking at them.

Because I had taken such a bad beating in Korea, I had a mental block about working out with Kim. Every time we sparred, he beat me. Kim had been a black belt for over twenty years but Jack told me my mental outlook was the only thing stopping me from whipping him.

One day we were out in the yard sparring with about thirty guys watching. Kim ran in and grabbed my throat and twisted it. I couldn't find the right counter move. Then he did it a second time, and I got extremely mad. When it was time to bow in for the third sparring session, I bowed and turned on mentally—one hundred percent. I was determined to tear him up; he had hurt me enough. When he looked into my eyes and saw my mental state he realized I had the confidence to beat him. He bowed out and refused to fight.

I went to Jack and said, "*Sensei* (teacher), I can beat Kim!"

"I knew you could beat him a long time ago; I just wanted you to find it out."

Whenever a new inmate came into the prison who had any knowledge of karate, Jack would make me work out with him. A new prisoner came in who was a black belt. There was a lot of publicity about his case because he had beaten a guy to death. I asked him to meet me in the gym and in front of a large crowd. I won the match. I was only a brown belt at the time and Jack immediately promoted me to *1k kyu* (first degree brown belt). After that match, more of the guys started being friendly—even the old timers.

Sensei Griffith insisted I start teaching at least two students. You can't learn karate fully unless you teach it to others. I could no longer be promoted unless I was qualified to teach. I took Les, whom I had surpassed, Norman Tripp, a 34-year-old college grad, and Phil Wineshanker, a short muscular man. Every student is different and my sensei explained how to teach each one on an individual basis.

Sensei Griffith told me, "Don't trust anybody. Are you sure you understand that? But you can trust me." But when I wasn't looking he would creep up and punch me. A couple of times, when I was in the shower and had soaped up, Griffith ran in and attacked me, knocking me down with punches and kicks. He instilled in me that I was never to be unaware. I was always to be alert. This was *karatedo*—the way of the warrior.

The officers knew I was into karate, but the majority turned their heads when they caught me working out. They all knew what I had been through and that I needed some way to defend myself.

EIGHT
"THEY KILLED NORMAN!"

The longer I stayed in prison, the dimmer the light from society became. We were completely shut off from the outside world. It was like living in a foreign society. We never knew who we were around or what we were in for. We never knew when someone was going to flip out and attack us. Often we would be sitting in the day room watching television when someone would go crazy for absolutely no reason. We lived in a world of fear, violence, and bloodshed.

My attorney kept telling me my appeal had been rejected in one court after another. I knew cons who had been in eight to ten years and the courts had still not made a final ruling on their cases. Everyone had a lingering hope that their convictions would some day be overturned. One day I was certain they would exonerate and free me.

Every four or five months a member of my family would come to visit. They would stay for a few days, then return to Phoenix. The outside world became more and more distant. I lived on memories.

Greg Nelson, a friend in the cell next to mine had one of the few prison jobs that paid money. He was the officers' barber and made over a hundred dollars a month. Greg had been accepted for parole, and because I wanted to earn some money, he suggested I try for the job. I checked out books from the library on the subject and went to Captain Combs.

"Sir, I'd like to be the staff barber."

"I didn't know you knew how to cut hair, Robert."

"I've never cut a head of hair in my life."

He laughed, "Well, how do you expect me to make you the staff barber, then? The only men who have ever held that position were master barbers with licenses on the outside."

"Captain, if you'll give me permission to go down to the inmate shop, by the time Greg goes home, I'll be good enough to cut the officers' hair."

Combs raised his eyebrows and studied me. He put his hands behind his head, leaned back in his chair and said, "You're serious, aren't you, Erler?"

"Yes, sir, I am."

"Don't you think you'll have trouble with the inmates while you're trying to learn?"

"No, sir. They might have trouble, but I won't have any." We both laughed.

"Robert, I'm gonna give you permission to go down there and cut hair—if you really want to."

"Yes, sir. I'll do it all on my own time. Thank you."

I started cutting everyday. I would do it after hours and on weekends. Sometimes I would take over for another barber who wanted time off. Because of my karate, many of the guys tried to win my friendship, and let me practice on them. I soon became quite proficient at cutting hair because I worked so hard at it.

Some of the guys wouldn't let me touch them. One was the big redheaded con who was out to get me. One day, when I was the only barber in the shop, he refused to let me touch him. The guards insisted he get his hair cut and sent him back.

"I ain't lettin' no punk cop cut my hair!" he said coming back into the shop.

I stood up. "Mister, you've caused me a lot of trouble. You really think you're tough, don't you? If you're so tough, let's get it on right now!" He wouldn't fight and walked back out, but he was starting to respect me. Later we became friends.

After a couple of months, Greg began to teach me up in the officer's shop. One night Lieutenant Davis came in and sat in the chair.

"All right, Erler, I've seen you cut hair. Cut my hair."

I threw the wrap around him as two other officers walked in.

Davis began to tell them how he had been moose hunting in Alaska. As soon as I turned on the clippers I started shaking. Greg told me if I ever had any trouble, to engage the man in a conversation and my fear would go away.

"Did you get any moose?" I squeaked. My voice sounded so strained the officers stopped talking and stared at me.

"Yeah, I got one," Davis answered and turned back towards the other officers. I almost threw the clippers down and walked out. Greg was watching and making encouraging nods for me to continue. I decided to ask another question to calm myself.

"How did it taste?" I said, in a voice so squeaky it would shame any self-respecting mouse. Everyone looked at me and busted up laughing.

"Look," I confessed, "I'm scared to death."

The lieutenant smiled and said, "That's okay, just go ahead and cut it."

I gave Davis a pretty good haircut until I had to use the straight razor. I clipped him up around the ear and he had to use his hankerchief to wipe away the blood. I couldn't apologize enough. Several officers allowed me to cut their hair after that.

A few days before Greg was to leave, the prison erupted in an inmate riot. Everybody on the wing refused to go to work. Word came around that anybody who went to work would be severely beaten or stabbed. The whole prison had to be locked up tight.

The strike was started at the Rock because of bad food and lack of canteen privileges. I didn't believe in striking because somebody told me to, so I told the leaders I wasn't going to strike. They agreed to let me go to work. They wanted to listen to the radio anyway and hear what the newscasters were saying about the strike.

Greg was so close to release he didn't want to jeopardize his parole. We asked the two mafia guys in charge of the strike if he could work to avoid blowing his parole. They agreed.

The strike became a major incident. The authorities called in the governor's task force and the Marine guards, who stormed the prison. Looking out my window, I saw the task force march through the front gate. Having had riot control, I knew what they were capable of doing.

They charged on our wing with shotguns and night sticks. Everyone had to come out of their cells and go down to the bottom floor; anyone who resisted was dragged out.

They told us they were taking over the prison and asked if anyone had any questions. One guy said, "Yeah, I've got a question." They pulled him out of line, and without any warning, smashed the guy violently with their night sticks.

"Does anyone else have any questions?" the warden asked.

A chorus of voices cried out, "*No, sir!*"

The officers up on top jacked shells into the chambers of their shotguns. We could hear all the weapons clicking. The warden continued, "We're taking this prison back over. Do you people understand that!"

"*Yes, sir!*" everyone again chorused together.

Some of the guys had been beaten up pretty badly, and they shoved them to one side while the rest of us were thrown back into our cells. They went through the entire prison, a wing at a time, tear gassing or beating up anyone who gave the slightest provocation.

In the maximum security section, the guys booed when they saw the cops. So the riot police gassed the whole section—every cell—whether or not they had done anything.

Afterwards, the officials came around and asked everyone individually if they were going to go to work. Greg and I had already been cleared to work, but several others went too. That night, all the guys who had gone to work, except Greg and I, were beaten up. One con's jaw was broken; another was stabbed.

The next morning, a con came to my door and said, "Bob, stay in your cell. We're gonna cut Greg Nelson."

I jumped up. "Why are you gonna cut him?"

"Cause all the blacks who went to work got busted up. We don't have no whites to beat up to show we're still supportin' the strike."

"You mean you're making a racial issue of it just because Greg's white?"

"Listen, be cool. He's going home in a couple of weeks anyway. It won't make no difference to you. We're not gonna kill him; we just want to smear some blood around so everything will be cool with the blacks."

I immediately went to Greg's cell and told him what was coming down. All the inmates were milling around the front deck. The strike leaders came out and asked me what was going on.

"Greg and I went to work. I went 'cause I felt the strike was wrong, but none of you guys are jumping on me. Now you want to cut Greg when you gave him permission to work. I'm stickin' with Greg. If you guys want to fight, jump on us right now." We both pulled off our watches and everybody just stood looking at us.

"Hey, man, cool down," the strike leader said to me. "You're lettin' your temper get the best of you."

"You guys wanna make a show. I'm going down with my buddy if I have to."

Nobody tried to do anything, but the situation was explosive. Everyone was mumbling. Greg and I decided to get off the wing and go to the barber shop. Greg just didn't know what to do.

Finally, I got an idea. Greg had false teeth. He took them out and with a razor blade I made several small cuts on the inside of his lip and on his eyebrow. I smeared the blood over his face and mouth and on his shirt—which I ripped. He got on the ground and I put a few foot marks on his back and stomach. We messed up his hair and then he walked back to his cell alone.

When he got on the wing, he was a mess. It looked like he had been viciously attacked. He went into his cell and slammed the door. When everyone gathered to look in at him, he cursed and told them to leave him alone.

Our act appeased everyone. Rumors spread that his "attackers" were trying to keep it quiet so no one asked questions.

The warden came down to the wing, saw Greg and asked who beat him up. Of course, Greg said nobody had beaten him up. So the warden had the strike leaders locked in max thinking they were responsible. I went to the warden on the sly and explained what we had done so they would release the leaders. He and the captain had a good laugh about it.

The riot left a bad taste in most of the guys' mouths; so many cons had been busted up over almost nothing. At the Rock, the inmates were lined up on the athletic field and ordered to work. When they refused, without warning, the troops opened fire. Over 200 inmates were hit with buckshot. Fortunately nobody died but many were badly injured. One of my friends lost an eye.

Finally the time came for Greg to go home. I had been practicing for so long I was getting pretty good, but was still not as good as a master barber. The captain called me in.

"Robert, do you think you can hold the job in the officers' shop?"

"Yes, sir, I do."

"Well, I've decided to give you a chance at it."

I transferred from the radio room to the shop, which was *the* elite job in the prison, and there was a great deal of hostility towards me in general population because of the move. Everyone felt the administration was giving me special treatment because I was an ex-cop.

The officer's barber shop was located next to the area where all the squads lined up before going or coming to work. One squad was the chain gang that worked outside. Those men had been responsible for putting snakes and rats in my cell to harass me.

They would kick on the door or knock on the window of the shop just to aggravate me. Because there was a curtain on the door, I usually could not see who was doing it. Often I would open the door and ask what they wanted, but no one would say anything. This went on for a month and it was getting to me.

I decided to stop the problem. I went to the maintenance shop, where a buddy of mine worked, and got some wire. I took a wet mop and soaked the hall outside the shop. Mr. Newman, the officer in charge of the metal detector, asked what I was doing. I told him, "I'm gonna electrocute some cons."

He laughed. "Are you serious?"

"I've got some wires in here," and I showed him what I had rigged up. He busted up when he saw what I was going to do.

"Just don't tell anybody you told me," he said.

"I won't. If you come up here, I'll be looking out the window so if you touch the door, it'll be okay. But if anyone else touches it, I'm gonna jolt 'em."

Newman walked back to the metal detector and soon the chain gang walked into the area for their line-up. I was standing on a wooden chair inside the shop and had a cord stuck into the electric socket. The other end, with its exposed wires, was ready to be touched to the metal door handle.

Three guys cleared the metal detector and walked to the barber shop. They looked back to see if Newman was looking, then began to beat on my door. One grabbed the handle and started to rattle it so I hit it with the wires. A three foot arc shot out on the other side of the door and my victim cut loose a bloodcurdling scream. They all ran to Newman like a bunch of scared rabbits.

Everyone complained they had almost been electrocuted. I was laughing so hard I fell off the chair and almost shocked myself. Newman walked down to the shop with several of the cons. He yelled out, "Is there anyone in the barber shop?" He was warning me he was there. Then he touched the door handle. Of course, nothing happened and he began to chew the guys out for lying to him.

"Hey, man, I swear it! I saw fire come out that door. Honest, man!" But Newman refused to believe them and walked away.

The first guy showed everyone his hand and the burn he had received. "Man, don't touch that handle, it will burn fire right through you!" But some of the others kept messing with it. When one grabbed the handle, I juiced it again. It shot electricity out four or five feet. The guy screamed in sheer terror and pain and everybody again fled back to Newman.

I unplugged the wires and hid them in the bathroom. After the squad had gone to work, I locked up the shop and left. The guys went to the captain and complained, but Newman called the captain aside and told him what I had done and why and they let the matter drop.

Two days later, while I was cutting the warden's hair someone started to open the door to the shop then let it close again. "Warden, I'm having a lot of trouble with these guys playing with that door and I'm not gonna take much more guff from them."

The door started to open again, then closed. I figured with the warden sitting in the shop, no one would give me any trouble. So I strode to the door and quickly swung it wide open. There stood a startled Captain Combs. He had been talking to someone as he was about to enter the shop.

"Oh, sorry captain. I thought it was some of those punks giving me a hard time with this door."

He grinned. "That's right, Robert, I forgot I could get electrocuted fooling with your door." We all laughed.

Working in the shop I got to meet and make friends with all the officers. They had a television in the shop and many of the guards came in to watch TV during the lunch hour. One of the officers noticed a big spider in the back of the shop. He was going to kill it until I explained it was my pet. Out of monotony I kept this tiger spider and fought him against other inmates' pets. He told me, "I know where there are some giant spiders. I'll bring 'em in to you."

The next day he brought two giant female gold orb weaver spiders. I put them in the rest room and the next morning I discovered one had fallen off the window sill and had killed itself, while the other had made a king-sized web that practically blocked the door. It became a big joke to feed that mammoth spider different insects to get it as big as possible.

About this time, I had several run-ins with the Black Muslims. They were an extremely militant group. Everywhere they went they went as a group. They posted guards and wouldn't let any white come near them. They wanted to learn karate, but Jack and I refused to teach them. They practiced what they called "karate," but it was self-taught techniques out of books and was very weak.

When I sparred with my students it was difficult to find a place where we were out of view of both the officers and the other inmates. The Muslims met in one of the rest rooms off the gym for their training while I worked with my students, Phil and Norman, behind the movie screen.

In prison, many guys claim to be karate experts. I beat several blacks who challenged me during our workouts. They provided no contest at all. Most were quite militant and the idea that a white guy could whip them really upset them.

One of the top Muslims on the street, a black belt who had been training their people to fight, got busted and came to the East Unit. He was well-known by all the Muslims. Because he was a black belt, I approached him in the mess hall and offered to work out. He wouldn't talk to me and was extremely hostile.

"As long as you approached the guy and made yourself available to work out," Griffith told me, "you have complied with the normal protocol of a karate man."

Later, when the work squads came through, a sealed letter was pushed under the shop door. It was an official challenge for me to meet the Muslims in the bathroom during gym call. The letter finished with, "Come alone—*if you're not afraid.*"

I took the letter and showed it to my sensei and students. Of course, they all wanted to come with me, but I told them no. Griffith was sure I could handle whatever they threw at me. By this time I was a high-ranking black belt and had been working out with karate for several years.

I went down to the gym that night. It was filled with blacks. The majority of the inmates in the prison were black and they ran the sports programs. I walked to the bathroom where two guards were posted. After making me wait for a few minutes, they opened the door.

The room was lined with shaved-headed Muslims. They were all standing at semi-attention with arms folded defiantly. I approached their minister and asked, "Are you the one who issued the challenge?"

"No," he answered, "it was Brother Three X." He pointed to their karate instructor who had just come into the prison.

I walked to him and held out my hand. "I appreciate the offer to work out with you. I'd like very much to spar with you in kumite."

He didn't say anything and wouldn't shake hands. He just glared back with the eyes of a killer.

I looked around. There was a ring of fifteen Muslims, all staring at me. They had closed off the windows with cardboard and tape so nobody could see in. "Are you ready to begin?" I asked.

"Any time," Three X answered toughly.

I had already warmed up on the wing, but I went through a few quick exercises and some body tensions, then turned to my opponent. "Is this contact, or semi-contact? Or do you just want to work out and pull all the punches?"

Brother Three X answered. "Full contact karate. The best man wins." I acknowledged with a nod.

Walking to my corner, I said, "I don't mind the sparring session, but don't let anyone get behind me. I get paranoid when there's someone behind me." The head minister made the guys get out of my corner.

We bowed and Three X came at me with a kick to the groin and a punch to the face. I blocked them both and hit him with a side snap kick and a back punch. It knocked him to one side. He managed to kick me once in my side, but the blow glanced off my hip. He also managed to scratch my cheek with his fingernails. Other than that, it was completely my fight. He was not a very advanced black belt.

I swept him to the floor. I kicked him in the ribs, then broke his arm. When I back-fisted him in the face he had had it. He kept trying to kick me, but he had lost, so I backed up and bowed.

Three X jumped up, wanting to continue. This time I gave him no mercy and with a flurry of kicks and punches dropped him back to the floor. He was finished. The fight had lasted only one and a half minutes. I bowed and said, "Is there anyone else who wants to spar?"

Nobody said anything. A couple guys ran to help Brother Three

X on the floor. Everyone was glaring at me. I smiled, bowed, and walked out.

In fifteen minutes the word had spread throughout the entire prison that I had demolished the number one Black Muslim. A heavy tension quickly developed between the blacks and whites, especially with all of our karate people.

Within a week, rumors spread to the officials as well as the inmates that the blacks were going to start a riot and run over to our wing. At 5:30 in the morning, just after the cells were opened and we were still sleepy and groggy, they were going to kill me, Jack, Norman, Phil, Les, and Kim. Sergeant Allen came down and opened my door each morning, to make certain I was awake so no one could creep up on me.

The officers also advised me to carry a weapon. I talked it over with Jack, and we decided if there was going to be a fight, we were going to be ready. We started working out with weapons—I practiced with a straight razor.

The tension continued to build for three or four days. Finally, word came down that the riot was going to take place on Wednesday morning. All the white guys on the wing came out to the quarter deck and stood around. Everyone knew we were armed and ready. When the blacks in our wing saw all the whites sticking together, they slid their doors back and locked them. The blacks in W Wing started gathering together, but as they looked across and realized we were ready, they decided not to come over to our section. Nothing came of it and things quieted down after that.

The monotony of prison began to get to me. Daily the bells clanged, the PA blared—the noise pollution was tremendous. There were self-mutilations, stabbings, every now and then a suicide, weekly rapes, occasional murders, robberies—all the vices on the street.

I spent many nights thinking about my son Bobby. Not hearing from him or knowing where he was, I began to wonder if he was alive. I didn't know what he looked like or if he even knew I was his father.

I had to cut hair only during certain hours and the rest of the time I could practice karate. When I went off duty, I trained my students for two hours each day. Norman and Phil progressed fast and both made brown belt.

About this time, Florida abolished the death penalty. This

meant several men who had been on death row came back into the general population. One of these men, Willy Jacks, was a militant black who was the leader of a black group on the street. He had massacred several whites with a machine gun in Fort Lauderdale and openly advocated killing all whites. He was extremely racist.

Jacks was assigned to work in the kitchen where Norm worked. The first day he was in the kitchen he got into an argument with Norman, who was not a very aggressive guy.

I was in the barber shop cutting hair when a friend ran in and said, "Bob, the blacks just stabbed and killed Norman in the mess hall!"

I dropped the clippers and ran to the kitchen. Norm was lying motionless on the floor in a large pool of blood. One of the guards had the eight-inch blade which had been used to stab Norman four times in the back. Six officers from the emergency squad had Jacks and were marching him toward the door. I went crazy. I jumped right in the middle, knocking a couple of officers to the side and started thrashing the black. The officers subdued me before I could do too much damage. Four of them held me while the other two ran the black out into the hallway.

The officers kept telling me to be cool. They didn't want to hurt me. I calmed down and they told me to go back into the barber shop and lock the door. I went back to the shop, waited a few moments, then put my straight razor in my pocket and walked into the corridor.

Jacks was in the bull pen outside the control room. I walked up to the electric gate and the officers opened it for me. Several blacks were standing in front of the pen talking to Willy. I ran to the cage, stuck my arm through the bars and took three or four swipes at him. He backed away and managed to escape the razor, but he was scared. The other blacks fled down the hall.

I couldn't reach him, but I told Jacks I was going to kill him. He knew I meant it. He countered by saying he would get me first. "Yeah!" I said in a rage, "we'll see who gets who!"

The officers in the control room could see what was happening and the razor in my hand. Sergeant Mobley got on the PA and ordered me back into the barber shop. After a minute or two of coaxing, I folded up the razor and stuck it in my pocket and walked back to the shop. I felt terrible. My good friend was dead.

After about fifteen minutes there was a knock on the door, but nobody came in. Finally I heard a voice calling to me. It was Captain Hicks.

"Bob, can I talk to you?"

"The door's open."

"But will you let me come in?"

"It's your prison. Of course I'll let you come in," I answered.

He cracked the door and stuck his head around the corner and said, "Are you all right?"

I was really upset and frustrated. "Yeah, I'm all right. But that nigger killed my buddy."

"No," Hicks answered, "Norman's not dead. He's up in the hospital. They're operating on him right now trying to save him. Can I come in and talk to you?"

Behind Hicks was the whole emergency squad. "Hey," I said, "if you come in here and try to jump me, we're gonna tear this barber shop to pieces."

"We don't want to fight. I just want to sit down. Why don't you make yourself some coffee; I've got to talk to you." Hicks and several others came in and sat down. After I made some coffee, the captain said, "Bob, you realize I have to lock you up, don't you?"

"Yes, sir, I do."

"Are you gonna give us any trouble walking down the hall?"

"Who's going to escort me down the hall?"

"The emergency squad."

"Then I'm gonna give you trouble. You're not going to belittle me."

Lieutenant Harris, whom I had known ever since I came into the prison, said, "Bob, if I walk you down the hall to your cell, will you pack up your things and then let me take you down to max?"

"Yes, sir, if you walk me without trying to handcuff or bully me."

So I went to my cell, packed up, and from there was taken to N Wing in max. About twenty of the officers came down to see me and find out exactly what had happened. I told each of them I could not live in population with Jacks. One of us would end up killing the other guy. Hicks also came to see me. I had been in prison, at this point, for about five years and my record had been good up until this incident.

Hicks said, "Bob, I really don't know what to do with you. I know you've had a rough time in prison. I also know if I leave you here, you're either gonna kill that guy or they're gonna kill you. So we've decided to send you down to Belle Glade—a medium security prison—for your own good."

After four days in max, they transported me out of the prison and down to Belle Glade.

NINE
THE ESCAPE

I was placed on a bus and driven down to southern Florida. Belle Glade Correctional Institution is a medium security prison located at the south end of Lake Okeechobee. I was to be housed in an area with close security.

Belle Glade has about 700 inmates. When I stepped off the bus a large group of guys I knew met me and began to slap me on the back and shake my hand. In prison, everyone knows who is coming before they get there. These old friends seemed to look at me almost as a folk hero. Everyone pulled marijuana and other drugs out of their pockets to show off their new freedom. It was incredible. I couldn't believe a prison could be this lax.

I looked at the surroundings. The prison was really beautiful with green grass and trees. I hadn't seen a tree in five years; we don't miss things like that until they are taken away. Shrubs and bushes and the beauty of singing birds had been absent for so long, this place seemed like heaven.

We walked to the prison laundry and I was issued new clothing and bedding. As we strolled over to the dormitory several guys ran ahead to get me a good bunk. The place looked like a college campus.

Before we stepped in, a big fat inmate ran out one of the dormitory doors. Right behind him came a gimpy-legged sergeant. Everybody turned to watch the show.

"What's going on?" I asked.

"Ozzie's running again!" someone grinned. "That's Sergeant Columbo and he's caught Ozzie with dope."

Ozzie was running around the yard pulling marijuana out of his pockets and throwing it on the lawn. He ran around the library three times until he had emptied all of the contraband. Finally, he pulled his pockets inside-out and stuck his hands up in mock surrender.

Because Ozzie no longer had drugs in his possession, the sergeant could only write him up for insubordination. If he had been caught with drugs, that would have been enough justification to transfer him to a tighter security prison.

After everyone had a good laugh, I asked where all the officers were. "You've just seen him! There's one officer for each dorm. That's it!"

I couldn't believe this was prison. There was no "goon squad"—no close supervision. There were tower guards, but the most awesome part of the security was a moat filled with alligators and poisonous snakes surrounding the compound. We could even approach the high chain-link fence on the edge of the moat and watch the water animals swim around.

After living for five years in a one-man cell, and being able to lock it up at night, I had difficulty adjusting to a 128-man dormitory. I didn't sleep at all the first two nights. I knew stabbings and murders often took place at night and I wasn't about to go sleep with so many guys around. But by the third evening, I realized if someone was going to kill me in my sleep, there wasn't much I could do about it. I finally passed out and slept so solidly the guard had to shake me the next morning to get me awake.

I was assigned to work in the school. Because I liked to work out, I requested and was accepted to work on the athletic field. I was given the job as college coordinator, working on the athletic field. I took over the college program from Miami-Dade Junior College and signed up everyone for courses they wanted to take. I signed myself up for twenty-four units.

Before long, I picked up a couple more karate students. They let me make a striking board and hang it up near the little athletic shed. We started getting in top notch shape.

There were numerous wild cats at the prison. Rocky, one old

gray cat with a white chest, was everyone's special pet. Many of the inmates fed it meat laced with LSD. The cat was mentally gone because he had received so much acid. He would suddenly jump in the air, claw, spit and do all kinds of crazy things, then get up and calmly walk away. Everybody enjoyed watching that cat.

There was another cat, who was dubbed "the phantom." He wisely refused to eat anything the inmates gave him. He was a large Siamese and he killed mice and snakes and lived outside the fence. This cat would actually swim the moat, come into the compound and mate with all the other cats. Phantom was everyone's hero because he came and went as he pleased.

Before long my other karate students were also transferred down from Railford. Then Jack Griffith was shipped in. We had our old karate club together again.

When Jack got off the bus, he and I immediately went behind a building, stripped down, and began to spar. It had been so long. But after a few moments, we were surrounded by club-holding guards who commanded us to stop working out. The captain called me in and told me if I was caught working out again they would send me back to a maximum security institution.

I told the captain I was a black belt and karate was my "religion." After complaining for several weeks, the administration decided to let me work out by myself and do *kata* (form fighting) as long as I didn't spar with any other inmates.

Right after he arrived, Jack told me he had something heavy he wanted to lay on me. "Listen, I'm gonna escape. What are you gonna do?"

"No. I'm gonna stay, Jack. I don't want any part of that. I'll get my college degree this semester. I've had a near perfect record and I'm gonna go for it. I'm gonna let them overturn my conviction and give me a new trial. At the very least, they'll let me out on parole in a couple of years."

"I understand, Bob. But, if you change your mind, let me know, because I'm definitely going over the wall. Don't tell any other cons what I'm gonna do."

"You know you don't have to worry about that."

Over the next few weeks, Jack kept trying to convince me to escape, but I refused. Another prisoner, who was in for killing a police officer, also told me he was going to escape and invited me along. Again, I refused, and he escaped the next day. He was captured after a few weeks and returned to a maximum security prison.

About this time, my brother Paul came to see me. He was driving a brand new gold Datsun with mag wheels. We sat under a big awning out on the grass in the visiting area.

"I've got a surprise for you and I don't know how you're gonna take it," he began.

I figured he must be getting married or something like that. Paul was twenty-one and had just returned from Viet Nam. He had been a paratrooper in the 173rd Reconnaissance and had been highly decorated. We had mutual respect for each other.

"What is it? Lay it on me."

He looked at me cautiously then said, "I accepted Jesus Christ into my life and became a Christian. I was baptized two weeks ago."

I really didn't understand what he was talking about but he seemed quite happy about it. "Well, that's cool," I said.

"What do you think about it?"

"I don't think anything about it. You do what you want to. Do you like it?"

"Yeah," he said, "it's the best thing that's ever happened to me." He paused for a few moments. "I've got to lay something else on you. You know I've never told you any stories or tried to lie to you."

"Yeah. What is it?"

"I had a dream," Paul began, "after I accepted Christ. In that dream, I walked into a lounge—and it was as clear as day—it just seemed so real. As I walked into the lounge, a bartender pulled a gun and shot me and I was severely wounded. I was laying on the floor and Danny was with me. Mom and De De came running in and there were police officers everywhere and they all thought I was going to die. I didn't hear any voices but I had this feeling God was saying to me if I would live for him I wouldn't die. In the dream I made a commitment to live for him."

"Go ahead, tell me more," I replied with a sarcastic grin. As far as I was concerned, it was just a dream.

"You're taking it as a joke, but I'm really serious." He told me exactly what was supposed to happen—with all kinds of details.

Paul had always been pretty wild, but he didn't seem as I had remembered him. He was much more mellow than in the past. He told me he was going to stay in Florida for a while and would see me again before returning to Arizona.

When I went back to the dorm, Jack called me aside and told me he had set a date for his escape. He was giving me a chance to go with him again. "Don't tell me anymore 'cause I want no part of it."

But Griffith continued to talk of his plans and what he was going to do when he got out. As the day drew near, I tried to stay as far from him as possible. I was really wasting my time because everyone knew we were close friends.

Jack had been reclassified and was working on the outside on a paint detail. He was painting the assistant warden's house. The morning of his escape, I shook hands with him. When he walked out the gate with the other men, I was certain I would never see him again. We had talked about the *kamikaze* code and how the warrior would never be taken alive.

He was gone for several hours before anyone knew it. He had set up a ride and was probably out of state before the authorities discovered he was missing. Immediately they brought in helicopters and busloads of people to search the surrounding swamps.

The compound was closed and all of us were in the dormitories when the escape alarm went off. Over the loudspeaker, the assistant warden called out, "Attention dorm two. Robert Erler, 023619, report to the captain's office." I was the only inmate being called in for questioning.

Everybody in the dormitory started laughing. "We know where you're going. We know what they want from you." The way it was done, there was no secret what they wanted. I hesitated, and in a few moments the PA system boomed out again. "023619! Erler, Robert! Report to the captain's office *on the double!*"

As soon as I had walked into the administration building, I was met by the new assistant superintendent. His name was Dowling, and he seemed anxious to impress everyone.

"All right, Erler," he began toughly, "I know you know where Griffith is. Now where is he!"

"Mr. Dowling, sir, you're really putting me on the spot. I'm an ex-police officer and I'm the only inmate you called over the loudspeaker."

"I don't care what you were or what you are. I called you here to answer some questions. Now tell me, where is Jack Griffith?"

"You don't care if I've got to live here and do the rest of my ninety-nine years, do you?"

"You've got a choice. If you want to be a tough guy, I'll be twice as tough as you are."

"Mr. Dowling, I'm not trying to be a tough guy, sir. I just don't want any trouble. I don't know where Jack Griffith is. And if I did know, with the kind of attitude you've got, I wouldn't tell you anyway."

Dowling leaped up from behind the desk. His face went very red and he began to swear at me. "I'm gonna get you for this. I'm gonna take care of you. Get yourself back over to the dormitory, Mr. Tough-guy, 'cause you've got something coming!"

As I walked out I really felt sick. I had blown it with the assistant warden. He was in a position to keep me in prison for a long time. When I returned to the dorm, the other cons said, "Hey, you weren't in there long." At least they knew I wasn't squealing on anyone.

I told everyone what had happened with Dowling. They were concerned for me because he had a reputation of laying for guys and then when he had the opportunity he would really sock it to them.

I had met a woman named Mrs. Lucy Bachelor who taught a class out in the visiting park. She came that day and I told her what had happened with the assistant warden. She suggested I let things cool off and the following morning meet him as he came to work.

The next morning, I stood by the gate and waited. When he walked in I stepped out and said, "Mr. Dowling, I'd like to apologize for my conversation yesterday. I'm sorry you took it the way you did, because I don't want to have any problems with you, sir."

He stuck his hand up in my face. "You and I understand one another perfectly, Erler. We have nothing further to say to each other." He stomped off.

Now I was really scared. I told Mrs. Bachelor what had happened and she suggested I wait a few more days, then she would try to talk to him for me.

About three days later, the assistant was walking through a hallway and I stepped up to him. "Mr. Dowling, can I talk to you sir?"

He glared at me, then said, "No, you can't!" and stomped away. Now I knew I had a problem.

I talked to Danny on the phone. He said, "Listen, you've got a visitor who just showed up here today." I realized he must be talking about Jack and I couldn't understand that.

"What's he doing out there?" I asked.

"He said all of his friends refused to help him. He said he saved you in prison and you owe him a favor. He wants us to help him."

Now my head was really spinning. Jack had talked about being a *kamikaze*, and he wanted my family to take care of him! I just didn't know what to say.

My family was caught in an ambiguous situation. If they turned him in, he would probably kill me or have someone else do it. On the other hand, if they harbored him, there was no telling what would happen if the police discovered his whereabouts.

"Danny, I don't know what to say. You'll have to give me time to think about this. This is too heavy. Tell him I said to get away from the family."

I called Danny back the next day. "Hey, I don't know what to tell you. He says he isn't leaving, because this is the only place where he'll be safe."

I didn't know what to do. All the karate students were upset that Griffith would go to my family and put me under such pressure. At the same time, of course, I had tremendous anxiety worrying what Dowling was going to do. My mind was being torn.

Over the next two weeks, I kept calling home. Danny told me Griffith was getting drunk and using a lot of dope. But worse, he was in love with my sister and had talked about killing her husband so he could take her away. My family was terrified. They kept asking me what to do.

I really didn't have an answer. Should I talk to the administration and tell them where he was? I had just about made up my mind to break my loyalty with Griffith for my family's sake, when I was called into the assistant warden's office. I hoped he would be in a friendly mood.

"Hello, Mr. Dowling."

"Sit down," he said gruffly.

"Mr. Dowling, I'd like to talk to you."

"There's no need to, tough guy. You're going back to Florida State Prison, with your friends up there." He was referring to my problems with the Black Muslims.

"Why?" I panicked.

"Because I just called the bus! You'll be leaving in a few hours. It's coming special just to pick you up." Then his mouth widened into a smile from ear to ear. "Now I hope you won't think this is anything personal between you and me, Robert." He laughed sadistically. He was telling me he had finally succeeded in giving me the shaft.

"Mr. Dowling, sir, I've got twenty-four college credits coming and I'll graduate in a couple of weeks. If you could just let me stay here until then."

He told me what I could do with my college degree. "You can get a college degree in your cell up north. That's all, Erler. Go pack your stuff and stand by for the bus."

"I guess there isn't any use for you and me to talk this all over, is there?"

"Like I told you before, Erler, we don't have anything to talk about. Of course, it isn't personal, like I said." He started laughing again.

I burned with a rage. I wanted to smash him right in his arrogant face, but I knew I couldn't do that. Slowly I returned to the dormitory.

"What's happening, Bob?" someone asked. The other guys could tell by the expression on my face something was terribly wrong.

"They're sending me back to maximum security. I know I'll have all kinds of trouble back there."

"Well, why don't you hit the fence and take off?"

For the first time, escape looked like a serious alternative. I began to reason out the possibilities. If I escaped, all kinds of attention and pressure would come down on my family and Griffith would have to leave. I wouldn't have to be a rat. It seemed the perfect way out of both problems.

There were several tough dudes who had just come down from Railford who had respect for me and how I had never put anybody's business in the street. One of these cons, named Bill, said, "Look, Bob, if you can get to an area away from this prison, I can have a vehicle pick you up."

"I don't know, Bill, let me think."

"Make up your mind, but be quick. I'll go out and make a telephone call and they'll be there. These people are very big in organized crime and they know about you."

"Go drop that dime," I replied. "I'm gonna go."

A 1968—
Officer Robert
Erler
Hollywood (Fl.)
Police
Department.

B April, 1968—
Graduation from
Broward
County Police
Academy. Erler
is seated on
the front row,
far left.

C August 12,
1968—Officer
Erler (left) on
the road where
victim was
found. (Photo
credit:
*Gainesville
Sun.*)

A August 12, 1968—Hollywood, Florida, front page news.

B August 12, 1968—*Fort Lauderdale News* front page.

C December 15, 1968, *Sunday News.*

D September 15, 1968, headlines.

E Police artist's sketch of murderer circulated in local newspapers.

F Erler in police lineup in which Mrs. Clark was unable to identify him. Erler is second from right (no band across eyes).

1. Hollywood Sun-Tattler

Suspect Arrested At Scene

Teenage Girl Murdered, Woman Shot, Police Search For Possible 3rd Victim

'CATCH ME!' SLAYER CRIES

Murderer Hunted In Bizarre Case

Detective Links Police Officer With

The Miami Herald

Ex-Policeman Is Hunted In Murder

A

B

Erler Trial Starts
With 'Gag' Orders

C

Hollywood Sun-Tattler

Led To Arrest, They Testify

7 Policemen Identify 'Catch Me' Voice

D

E

F

Hollywood Sun-Tattler

Jury To Begin Deliberating

Erler Case Arguments Closed

G

A September 17, 1968—*The Arizona Republic* news clipping.

B January 30, 1969—Newspaper photo of Erler with defense attorney Joseph Varon (right).

C News coverage of the trial.

D January 29, 1969—Still front page news.

E Erler's family at the trial (left to right: sister Lynne, mother, and sister Betty).

F Erler talks to attorney Varon during trial.

G January 31, 1969, headlines.

A Erler family with attorney Joseph Varon (left to right: brother Danny; sister Lynne; Varon; mother, Mrs. Winifred Erler; and sister Betty).

B & C February 1, 1969, headlines.

'Don't Forget Marilyn Clark'

Erler Case Goes To Jury
After Dramatic State Plea

FORT LAUDERDALE NEWS

Catch Me Killer' Gets 99 Years

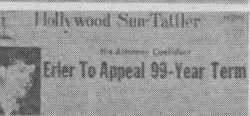

Hollywood Sun-Tattler

His Attorney Confident

Erler To Appeal 99-Year Term

A Webster County (MS) Sheriff's Department photo of Erler, taken shortly after the high-speed chase and arrest

B Webster County Sheriff W.E. (Bill) Middleton, who arrested Erler in 1973.

C Erler sparring with brown belt karate student in Florida State Prison

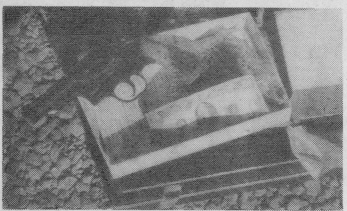

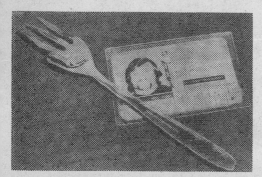

Top: Bob's escape car with tires and windows blown out.
Middle: The package containing a gun, drugs, and money Bob picked up at Mathiston post office.
Left: A key made from a fork to open the cell door and Bob's fake I.D. he used while on escape.

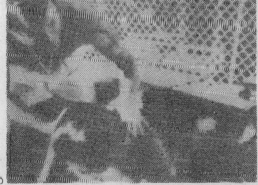

A Jack "Murph the Surf" Murphy, Colonel Hiaas and Erler at prison Christmas party.

B Erler preaching in baptismal service in Arizona State Prison yard.

C Erler leading prayer before baptismal service.

D Erler baptizing fellow inmate. Note Special Forces tattoo.

E Moments after Erler baptized "Bulldog," former high priest of black occult group. Note devil tattoo on Bulldog's forehead.

A Florida prison chaplain Max Jones with Erler.

B Erler and Gainesville, Florida, television personalities at Jaycee Banquet sponsored by the prisoners (Photo credit: *Gainesville Sun*).

C Erler shares his testimony with Pat Robertson of the 700 club during filming of TV program, "Maximum Security."

He went out and made the telephone call. I immediately walked out in the compound to analyze what would be the best possible escape route. I left Dowling's office at 4:00 o'clock and was not sure how much time I had before the bus arrived. Two of my karate students, Jimmy and Scott, told me they would make the distractions necessary for me to make it over the fence.

At 5:30, when the college call came, I went to classes as usual. I had told Bill I would be at the pick up point at 9:00, but wasn't sure how long it would take to get through the swamp or if they would manage to shoot me during the escape.

As soon as it got dark, I excused myself, telling the teacher I had to go to the rest room. There was an officer stationed in the hallway and he allowed me to go down the hall by myself.

As soon as the door was closed, I took off my shirt and pants and put them in the sink. I turned the water on, and they immediately darkened and lost their shine. Quickly, I put them back on.

The officer was walking toward the head, so I stepped into a stall, sat down and flushed the toilet. The guard entered the room, walked around a bit, then left. As soon as he left, I pushed out the small window as far as it would go, then squirmed through and down into the main yard. After dropping to the ground, I realized there was no way to climb back up. It was either escape or be captured.

Roving officers walked the yard checking it at night. Cautiously, I searched for one. I had to travel over fifty feet of open space from the school to the shelter of a trailer. If the guard in the tower had been looking in my direction, he would easily have seen me. I began to belly crawl across the open area and made it safely.

Once past the shelter of the trailer, I was faced with another open area of approximately 150 feet—again in full sight of a guard tower. I decided to belly crawl within a few feet of the tower, figuring they wouldn't look for an inmate to crawl that close. If I made it, I would have to climb the fence, the top of which was almost eye-level with the tower.

As I crawled across the yard, two officers came out of the control room and walked across the compound. I stopped crawling and pushed up against a wooden well covering about six inches high. The officers came to a stop about three or four feet from my head! I thought sure they had caught me. Slowly I looked up and saw they were facing in the opposite direction. It was a dark area and I lay perfectly still. One of them struck a match on the well cover, and after three or four minutes—which seemed like an eternity—they walked off.

I continued crawling towards the gun tower, finally reaching the fence. This was the tricky part. I had to take off my shoes and throw them over the tall fence; periodically the searchlight ran up and down this 18-foot barrier. One at a time, I threw my shoes over this obstacle. One landed in the water with a splash. The guard heard it and shined his searchlight up and down the moat. After a few moments, he aimed it back on the fence. I sat motionless for another five minutes until I felt it was safe to go.

Carefully I began to climb upwards. Because I was at a corner, I could grab two sections and it was much easier to scale. When I reached the top, my hand got caught in the tangled barbed wire and my efforts to free it shook the whole fence. I was bleeding badly.

The guard in the far tower, approximately seventy-five yards away, began to make another long pass with his searchlight on the fence. I hung at the top, motionless, waiting for him to finish.

Once he had completed his sweep, I freed my hand and carefully lifted my legs over the top of the fence. Again, I gouged myself badly on the barbs, but managed to quickly descend down the other side. As I stepped on the ground at the edge of the ditch, the far tower began another sweep. There was no place to hide except in the moat. I slipped into the ditch, up to my neck. There were all kinds of noises in the water from gators, snakes, and frogs.

By now my heart was pounding like a sledge hammer. As the light passed over, I ducked my head underwater. If they spotted me after coming out of the moat on the other side I would be a sitting duck; they'd shoot me for sure.

There were some big alligators in the ditch, some eight or nine feet long. I was concerned about them, but because of my size, I didn't think they would bother me. My biggest fear were all the poisonous snakes that swam out in the middle. As quietly as possible I started to swim across the moat.

Arriving at the far side, I discovered a jeep was coming down the road surrounding the prison. It was making a security check. Although I desperately wanted to get out of the moat, I submerged myself again in the water while the jeep drove by. After it was a good distance away, I crossed the road and lay down in the ditch on the opposite side.

Breathing heavily, I waited for a few more minutes, then slipped under another fence and began belly crawling through the field on the far side of the moat. By now there were thirty yards between me and the nearest tower.

This was the middle of nowhere and everything was very black. When I had gone about 200 yards, I stood and looked back. The prison, with its high fence and four searchlights, looked like a picture right out of a Gothic novel. A heavy mist was rising up around it off the swamp. The night was filled with the noises of alligators and frogs; unseen creatures scurried in the bushes. It was an eerie scene.

I turned and ran, full-out. I couldn't see anything in front of me, but I just felt like running. Suddenly, I smashed into something big and black, knocking both it and myself into the marshlike grass. The force of the blow knocked the wind out of me, and I was stunned for a moment.

I had collided with a large black cow. She had heard me coming and was just starting to stand when I toppled her over. We both stood and fled in opposite directions.

Soon I reached the end of the pasture. The area was unfamiliar to me and I was depending solely on the descriptions of the prisoners who worked outside. There was supposed to be a mile and a half of swamp before coming to a road.

A canal lay across my path. As I slipped down the bank, my feet were caught in quicksand. I struggled to pull my legs out but the mud sucked off one of my shoes. When I entered the canal, I could hear several creatures slip in off the bank to join me in the water.

After swimming across, I entered the swamp. It was difficult slogging with one shoe, so I threw the other one away too. I had to move through a marshy area covered with moss and some other slimy stuff. The biggest problem was not knowing what my bare feet would step on next. Without shoes, they were getting all cut up.

After covering a mile and a half through the swamp, I came to a bank supporting a road. I had reached an intersection which had one street light and a small dark supply building. I was certain my ride would meet me somewhere in the area—in a new burgundy-red Cadillac.

I lay on the side of the bank and waited. In a few moments headlights appeared down the road. As the car came into view I realized it was a police car. Immediately panic filled my brain, thinking they knew I was waiting to be picked up. But I hadn't heard the escape sirens go off at the prison. The deputy couldn't know about me.

The sheriff stopped at the intersection, turned off his engine and lights, and sat in his vehicle with the inside light shining. After about ten minutes, I began to wonder what would happen if my ride appeared and saw him.

Sure enough, another set of headlights came down the road and turned through the intersection in front of the police car. It was the Cadillac. They drove down the side road. The sheriff looked up and watched for a moment, then went back to whatever he was doing.

In about five minutes, the Cad returned, made a turn at the intersection and drove off in the direction in which it had come. I figured the police car had scared them off and they probably wouldn't return. After a few more minutes, I determined the only way out of the area was to sneak up on the deputy, overpower him, and drive off in his car. Just then, he started his engine and drove away.

I was in the middle of nowhere. There was no traffic whatsoever. I didn't know what to do now that I had lost my ride. I started walking down the highway in the direction the Cad had gone. After a few minutes, I spotted another set of headlights coming. Fearful it might be the sheriff, I jumped off the road. It was the burgundy-red Cadillac, but by the time I got back up on the pavement they had passed at about 30 miles an hour.

They drove back the other way for about a half mile, turned around and stopped with just their parking lights on. I started jogging towards the car and in a moment they turned on their lights and met me on the road.

There were two women in the front seat. Angie, the driver, was a strikingly beautiful dark-haired woman, heavily into organized crime. I had met her in the visitor's park and she had shown a strong attraction towards me. With her was the wife of the guy who had made the call for me.

I was covered, from head to foot, with mud and weeds and grass and the interior of the Cadillac was white; but I crawled into the back seat and we drove off.

Immediately they gave me my choice of two pistols, a .38 and a .45. I took the .45 and stuck it into my belt. They had also purchased some clothes for me approximately my size.

Angie asked what my plans were. I really didn't have any plans beyond my escape. I knew, in many ways, I had blown it by escaping. But it had seemed the only decision I could make.

She asked me if I wanted to stay with her for a few days until things blew over. That seemed to make sense, so I agreed. We rented a room at a Holiday Inn, where I washed up and got into the clothes they had purchased for me.

TEN
THE UNDERWORLD

Angie was a cold, sadistic woman. I had heard stories about how she had been involved in many armed robberies and killings. She was known as "the black widow" because she had had several husbands who had been killed in gang warfare or from drug overdoses. She was well-known in the underworld and had profited greatly from her life of crime.

Angie was also beautiful. She had jet-black hair, green eyes, stood five feet seven inches tall and was quite well-built. Having been in prison for five years, it was not hard to fall for her. I decided to stay with this unusual woman.

We moved closer to Miami. Angie owned several apartments and property in Miami and wanted to get back into her territory. We checked into a Howard Johnson's motel.

The next day we sat in front of the television and watched the newscasts on my escape. They interviewed the prosecuting attorney, Dan Futch, who was now a judge. He was scared. He was afraid I would try to get even because he had sent me to prison. He talked about how he had a pistol and would use it in self-defense if he had to. We laughed as we ate our steak.

Les Cochrane, the guy who helped set up my escape, was classified as a minimum security prisoner and allowed to leave the prison on weekends. He found me at the motel through Angie and filled me in on how the guys had covered my escape.

When the teacher in the college class asked where I was, they told him I had gotten sick and returned to the dorm. After class one of my friends was bouncing a handball and hit the guard, who was taking the count, in the groin. The officer lost count and everyone continued into the dorm without being counted. They didn't discover I was missing until bed check at eleven o'clock.

Once my disappearance was discovered, Assistant Warden Dowling appeared and headed the search. Dowling kept saying, "He's got to be here. He's just got to be here! He just *can't* escape!"

Les told me his friends in organized crime were impressed with how I handled myself in prison. "Bob, you won't have any problems working yourself into crime. They want you to get involved in murder for hire and armed robbery right away."

"I don't know, Les, I'm still not sure what I wanna do. They'll have to give me a few days to make up my mind."

"That's cool. Just lay low for a month. They'll take care of you. Then you can get involved."

The news bulletins about my case were frequent; the heat was really on. Angie thought we should get out of the state as quickly as possible. She was from Tennessee and had family and friends there, so we decided to drive there.

Angie purchased some dye and I colored my hair dark brown. I also began to let my mustache and beard grow. She bought a complete wardrobe for me, spending over $4000.

When we arrived in Tennessee, I met all her friends and family. Angie and I were quite involved and she seemed pretty crazy about me. But I knew she had a history of overwhelming young guys with sex and drugs and then she would have them commit armed robberies to earn money. It was a big joke among all her friends that she was quick to put a gun in a guy's hand and make him go to work. I knew it, but I was still drawn to her.

One morning Angie told me her father was wondering if we were married. "What do you think about that?"

"Do you want to get married?"

"Yes, I do," she answered.

"Okay, let's do it."

She obtained a birth certificate of a guy named Bruce Strickland, who had died years before. I got myself a hunting license, then a driver's license, social security card, and finally a marriage license.

We were married in a nice wedding ceremony fifteen days after my escape.

We stayed in Tennessee for about two weeks. For a while we lived on a houseboat and went up and down the rivers. But Angie was afraid to stay out of Florida too long because of all her commitments.

We started back towards Florida but decided to stop in Atlanta so I could make contact with my family. After all this time, I was concerned to find out what had happened with Jack Griffith. Angie called some friends of my brother Danny in Phoenix and asked them to call him to a telephone booth in the middle of nowhere.

Once Danny was on the phone, I told him we wanted him to come see us if he could evade the FBI agents that were constantly shadowing the family. He agreed and flew to Dallas, then Chicago, Memphis, and when he was convinced he had lost everyone, he flew into Atlanta. Angie picked him up at the airport.

"Did anyone look suspicious?"

"Yeah," Danny replied, "everyone on the plane, including an old lady in a wheelchair!"

Actually, we learned later Danny was still under direct FBI surveillance at that very moment. They even spotted me, but my hair coloring and mustache fooled them and they didn't move in on us.

Danny spent several days with us and told how Griffith had to leave because of the pressure my escape had put on the family. But he was still with my brother Paul, who had been captivated by Griffith's many karate tales.

The three of us drove to Florida and by now it seemed much of the pressure was off. While we were driving, I saw a sign with directions to Disney World. The amusement attraction had been built after I entered prison. We decided to go to the park and enjoy ourselves. There were hundreds of people walking around, and although nobody stared at me, I still felt uncomfortable around people.

Many things were hard to get used to after five years in the pen. I felt uncomfortable driving. On a couple of occasions, I asked people for permission to have simple things, like straws in a restaurant. I was used to asking for permission for everything, and Angie got quite upset with me over it.

When we arrived in Miami, Danny flew home. Angie felt I

should take the first six months and do nothing but unwind and have a good time. No one knew there was any connection between her and me. She decided it would be best if I stayed in her apartment. I couldn't go out during the daytime, but I would climb over the eight-foot fence at night so we could go out on the town. No one in the other apartments even knew I existed.

Angie was a witch. Every week she went to a meeting of witches. At night she would turn on some electric candles and leave the windows open so the breeze would move the curtains. She did some pretty strange things. But I was playing the tough guy role and shrugged off her antics.

In the evenings we went out and had a good time. People who have a lot of money don't stand out in Miami; they blend into the crowd—and Angie was quite wealthy. We went to the best restaurants and really spent the money.

About this time, Angie and I had our first of many arguments. I was beginning to have difficulty putting up with this domineering woman. She insisted on running everything and telling me what to do like I was a child.

One night we went to the Executive Club, an exclusive membership restaurant. Right after we had ordered some cocktails, one of Angie's former boyfriends came up to our table. His name was Stanley Harris and he had been in prison when I was at Railford. He was a professional killer and it was rumored he had put away more than twenty people.

"Who is this guy?" he asked Angie. She introduced me under my alias. He had been drinking heavily.

"I don't like you! I think you're a punk!"

I didn't say anything. I figured maybe it was time for us to leave. But Harris turned his drink over on our table. "And I think you're chicken, too!"

By this time, people at nearby tables were beginning to notice his loud talking. Angie excused herself and went to the ladies room. Stanley didn't have any idea who I was so I suggested we go outside. He quickly agreed.

Once outside, we walked between Stanley's new Lincoln Continental and our Cadillac. He turned and said, "I want to ask you something, punk. Are you sleeping with Angie?"

"That isn't any of your business."

He tried to hit me and I dropped him. It wasn't much of a fight because he was so drunk. I took his pistol away, emptied it, and handed it to Angie who had just come outside. Then we drove away.

The next day Angie received a call from Stanley and some other underworld people. They wanted to know who I was; they wanted to meet me at a restaurant. Stanley had murdered a guy in our apartment and it wasn't difficult to figure out he was after me, too. Angie said she would come by and explain.

I owned a new Cadillac, a speed boat, an apartment complex—everything a person could want—but I wasn't happy. My relationship with Angie had deteriorated to the point where I really didn't care about her anymore. She wanted to dominate me. I told her I would probably be the first man in history to break back into prison to get away from his wife.

My old karate student, Les Woods, was out of prison and in Miami. One night he came to the apartment and Angie told me he was in our living room. I decided to let him know I was there.

I jumped in front of Les; he just couldn't believe it was me. We hugged and laughed. It was good to see this old friend. He had jumped parole and was involved in organized crime. I told him about the problems I was having with Angie and that I didn't think we'd be together much longer.

Angie went to a meeting in Miami with several underworld people to discuss how they could use me in some armed robberies. I had played "tough guy" and they figured with my background I would make a great killer.

When she returned, she told me Stanley Harris and the others didn't know much about me, but I was one guy they didn't want to mess with. It blew my mind to think those vicious killers were afraid of me.

They had staked out a lady who had a large diamond they wanted. The lady had an oriental houseboy who was supposed to be a karate man. Angie's friends figured if there was trouble, I could take care of him. With my luck, he would be a master like Bruce Lee and I'd get wiped. I told Angie it was no deal.

I was also receiving pressure to rob a jewelry store with Harris and some of his partners. Angie kept telling me I had to prove myself and commit a crime. Others warned me not to do it; they said Stanley would blow my brains out after the job.

We had a twenty-two-foot inboard-outboard cabin cruiser which we took into the canals at night to race around. I had worked for the North American Boat Corporation, water-testing racing boats in this same area.

One night we were going to meet a shipload of marijuana coming in from Jamaica. We had some prearranged signals and I cruised the entrance of the harbor for several hours looking for the boat. It never showed. I found out later Harris and his friends met the boat and stole the marijuana. They killed three of my friends, then sank the ship.

When Les Cochrane came out of prison on weekends he was notorious for sleeping with the wives of different guys. One night he called to tell us he was having problems with one particular guy, who happened to be a friend of Stanley's. A few hours after his call, Harris phoned and asked where he could get Les when he got out on furlough. They wanted to kill him.

I told Les later that Stanley was really after him. But Les claimed they were punks and he would take care of them. A few days later, Cochrane was found on a Miami golf course with his hands tied behind his back and five bullets in his brain.

Angie had picked up several thousand dollars' worth of counterfeit money that had come down from Atlanta. She went to sell it, but when she drove back to our apartment, I suddenly heard tires squeal and sirens blare. I looked out the window to see the building surrounded by cops. Angie was arrested outside.

I was sure somebody had finked on me to the police. Because of the notoriety of my case, I knew they would kill me when they ran me down. There was a closet full of machine guns, rifles, sawed-off shotguns, and burglary tools in the apartment. I threw a blanket over the weapons, then ducked into another closet just as the detectives broke in.

I could hear the men searching the apartment. One checked out the bedroom and another examined the area about eighteen inches from where I was hiding. I could hear the officer's breathing; I was sure he would open the door. I had a loaded .45 in my hand.

"I hope he doesn't open that door," I thought. One side of my mind said, "Bob, this man is a brother. He's a police officer—you can't hurt him!" The other side of my mind said, "You're on escape; you're a convict; they'll put you in prison!" A war was going on in my head and I was afraid. I didn't know what would happen.

I realized that I was not a tough guy. I was not a gangster. All my frustration and hate were my problems. These people were good, and law and order was good. I was wrong.

I laid my pistol on the refrigerator and said a prayer. "Please, God, don't let this officer open that door, please." I really didn't know what would come out, the good guy or the bad guy.

The other detective yelled from the bedroom. "Hey, Mike, look at this! Look at all these weapons!"

The officer went into the bedroom, so I stuck the .45 in my trouser band and walked out through the kitchen and down the steps leading to the pool. An officer in civilian clothes stood outside the door. I looked like one of the officers, so I told him, "Mike wants you inside." He looked at me, nodded, then entered the apartment. I quickly jumped the fence and got away.

As it turned out, the cops were local police, FBI, and Treasury agents who had come to arrest Angie after she had sold them the bogus bills. They didn't even know I was in the house.

Angie and I had made arrangements if we ever got separated to go to a certain motel and check in. That evening, she was released on bond and came to my room. They had confiscated the Cadilliac because she had transported counterfeit money in it. She went back to the apartment after a few days.

Les Woods came to see me at the motel. He was excited about a big shipment of cocaine coming in from Central America. I reminded him they had killed all the others.

"Well, we'll just have to be cool."

"Not me, man. I quit. I'm not a tough guy anymore. If I keep this up, I'm gonna kill someone or get killed for sure. I almost killed a cop back there in Angie's apartment. I'm tired of playing gangster."

He looked in my eyes. "You're for real, aren't you?"

"Yeah, I'm for real. Les is dead and all those guys on the boat. Harris will kill me the first chance he gets. I'm just sick of it all. I don't want any part of it anymore. I'm even thinking of turning myself in."

"Oh, man, don't do that. What would everyone think in the joint? They'd think you lost your guts."

"Well, I don't know what's gonna happen, but I know I'm sick of having this woman tell me what to do. I'm leaving."

My marriage to Angie wasn't legal anyway because I had married under an assumed name; I determined to leave her. I took a taxi back to the apartment but could tell by the cars out front that Stanley and another professional killer were inside. I put my pistol in a shoe box and entered the apartment.

When I walked in, Harris looked at me face-to-face for the first time since our fight. He knew instantly who I was. I made no secret about the weapon in the shoe box so they wouldn't try anything. I was certain Angie had put them up to giving me a hard time; I would have nothing but trouble until I was out of the area.

I packed my things and went to the Trailways Bus Station. I bought a ticket to Tallahassee, but before going too far, stepped off the bus and caught a Greyhound to Orlando. I kept switching buses until I arrived in Alabama. There I called Mississippi and reached Greg Nelson, from Railford days.

He met me at a bus station in Mississippi. I stayed with Greg for a couple of days and he introduced me to a number of friends. One guy, whose name was Jimmy, immediately wanted me to help him steal cars. He picked them up in other states, changed the serial numbers, then got new papers for them. I didn't want to steal cars. The risk was too great considering I had a ninety-nine year sentence hanging over my head. I was determined to get a job and go straight.

Jimmy asked what kind of work I wanted. He said he knew everybody and could get me a job. He got both Greg and me employment at a construction company in West Point, Mississippi.

I decided it wasn't a good idea to ride around with Jimmy in all his hot souped-up cars. We began to look for a vehicle with local tags that wouldn't attract so much attention. After a little searching, we bought a local 1964 Ford two-door.

My job consisted of doing manual labor on a construction site. It was the heart of winter and the temperature sometimes dipped to 26°—but I loved the job. At night I went jogging and worked out in karate.

Jimmy came to me and said he had some stolen jewelry and wanted to know if we could get it fenced for him. I told him I knew of several fences, but would rather not get involved. He knew I was draining my family to pay for all of my expenses so I wouldn't have to commit any crimes. He offered me 10 percent of anything I could get for the stuff.

Greg took the jewelry and put it in a bag and placed it under the front seat of my car. I called a fence in Miami and set up an elaborate system for him to call me back. A few days later he returned my call.

"Bruce, you've got a problem. There's a contract out on your life."

"Who put it out?"

"Stanley Harris and his gang."

"Why are they after me?"

"They think, 'once a cop, always a cop.'"

I knew there were other reasons. I had beaten Stanley up. I had married Angie. Sooner or later he would try to fulfill that contract and there was a chance he might know the area where I was staying. I immediately moved and started carrying my .45 everywhere.

A month earlier my brother Paul had been arrested with Jack Griffith. I felt morally responsible for leading Paul down the road to being a hardened criminal. He had been impressed both by my life and Griffith's. When he got out on bond, he came to visit me. We decided to get a motel in Boonesville, Mississippi, and talk. We watched the Super Bowl on TV and after a couple of days of talking sense to Paul, I took him to the airport. Greg and I were going to check out of the motel the next day. We drove into town to get something to eat. As we pulled down the main drag, four police cars pulled in around us. Two were city cop cars, one was a highway patrolman, and the other was the sheriff.

They jerked us out of the vehicle and handcuffed us. We found out quickly there had been a burglary at a local laundromat and because we were the only strangers in town, they naturally suspected us. I knew as soon as they checked my fingerprints, they would find out who I was and send me back to prison. When they searched my car, they found my .45 caliber pistol with several boxes of shells and the jewelry under the front seat.

They put both Greg and me in the same cell. I motioned for him not to talk while I shook it down for a bug. Sure enough, down behind the vent I could see a small silver microphone tip. I pointed it out to Greg and we started carrying on a phony conversation. We knew the sheriff would be listening to our conversation.

I talked about just coming back from Viet Nam and wondered how my family would take this arrest. I made up an elaborate story about my father being a captain on the police force back home and how I hoped this wouldn't kill my chances of becoming a cop.

They called me out first for questioning. "What's your name, son?"

"Bruce Strickland, sir."

"Where you from?"

"I'm from Tennessee, sir."

"What you doing 'round here if you're from Tennessee?"

"I came down to see Greg. I just got out of the service, from Nam, and I wanted to see Greg."

"How many times you been arrested?"

"I've never been arrested," I lied.

The sheriff looked at my Special Forces tattoos and asked what I was going to do. I told him my father was a captain on the police department back home and I was gonna apply for a job as an officer.

He asked why I was carrying the .45-caliber pistol. I told him it had saved my life in Viet Nam and I had kept it. He asked about the jewelry and I claimed my grandmother had passed away and left it to me—it was my stake for a better life.

The sheriff asked my age and I gave him the wrong answer.

"How come your age is different on this birth certificate and your driver's license?" My phony license had the real Bruce Strickland's birth date on it.

"Sheriff, this is the first time I've ever been arrested. You've got me so upset I can't even remember my age. I don't know if I should get an attorney, or what. This is a felony you're arresting me for. If I get a felony on my record, I can't ever be a police officer."

Sheriff Elder and the chief of police questioned me quite closely for over an hour. They believed my story, and because they didn't take my fingerprints, they didn't learn my true identity.

"I'm not going to charge you with a felony," the sheriff said at last, "but I'm gonna keep your weapon." He brought in the town judge and they fined me $100 dollars for carrying a concealed weapon and confiscated the pistol. They let us go after eighteen hours. The sheriff even gave me an application to become a police officer for the city!

Greg and I got in our car and started to pull away when the sheriff and the chief of police came out of the station and began to yell. "Hey you! Strickland!"

My first impulse was to stomp the accelerator to the floor, but I knew we couldn't outrun them in the Ford so I waited as they approached.

"You want this jewelry or are you just gonna leave it here?" He was holding up the bag containing the stolen merchandise.

"Oh, I'm so upset I forgot all about it." They gave us the jewelry and waved as we pulled out of the parking lot. After we had driven away, Greg and I started laughing. "That sheriff doesn't know it, but I would have bought him a gold-plated submachine gun to get him to let us go."

I telephoned a friend and informed him I had been arrested and lost my weapon. I asked him to send me another pistol. He told me he would get it to me in two or three days. I instructed him to send it "General Delivery" to a small post office about thirty miles away.

I was teaching karate several nights a week in Columbus at the Golden Triangle Club where I had been offered the job of head instructor. On two alternate nights I taught karate at Mississippi State University. I was so involved with karate it was all I was really interested in.

I called the post office in Mathiston, Mississippi, where my friend was sending the gun, and asked if there was a package for Bruce Strickland. The woman on the other end said, "I wouldn't come here if I were you."

Her warning didn't sink in. "Is the package there for me?"

"Well, yes, it is," she replied, then hung up. I decided to drive to the post office between karate workouts and pick up the package.

ELEVEN
A HUNDRED MILES AN HOUR

It was March 31, 1973, a cold but sunny Saturday afternoon. I drove to the town of Mathiston and cruised around the post office several times to see if anything looked suspicious.

There was no way anyone would know the package was for me; it was addressed to Bruce Strickland. I parked my car and walked into the small rural post office. Stepping through the swinging doors, I approached the clerk, who was an older lady.

"Do you have a package for Bruce Strickland?"

She looked at me strangely. There was fear in her eyes and panic started welling up in my head.

"Yes, I do," she said nervously. She placed a package on the counter, then ducked down. Her actions definitely confirmed something was wrong. I grabbed the package and fled. Jumping into my car, I burned rubber taking off.

After driving fast for a few blocks with nobody chasing me, I decided to slow down as I approached the main part of the city so I wouldn't call undue attention to myself. I stopped at a red light.

In an instant, four or five unmarked police cars converged on me from several directions. A bright red Chevrolet pulled up beside me; the car was driven by the local sheriff and his deputy was hanging out the passenger's window with a sawed-off shotgun.

"Pull it over, son," the deputy called.

I looked over at him and down the muzzles of his shotgun. Suddenly I became angry. I was angry at myself for not being more careful. I was angry at these officers for coming down on me. A million thoughts raced through my mind in a matter of seconds. Looking down the two barrels of the deputy's shotgun told me I preferred death to going back to prison. I nodded towards him, then punched the accelerator to the floor.

I expected buckshot to blast my head off, but he didn't fire. I quickly swerved through a gas station and squealed through the other side—right through someone's yard and fence. In a second I was back out on the main road but there was a line of cars in front of me. Swerving onto the shoulder, I raced past them, then cut back into the lane. I flew over some railroad tracks and in a matter of seconds was up to 100 miles an hour.

My evasive driving in and out of traffic had left all the unmarked police cars in the dust. But the sheriff was driving a high-performance Chevy and a few moments after I hit a long straightaway, he pulled up behind me. By now we were both speeding at 125 mph. The deputy began to shoot at my car with his shotgun.

One of the first blasts knocked out my back window and the glass sprayed through the interior of the car, showering me from behind. My head and neck burned and started trickling blood from many small cuts. I was sure I had also caught some shotgun pellets. I kept the accelerator punched to the floor but the sheriff stayed right with me as they pumped shotgun shells into my tail end.

My mind flashed back to the 100-mph chase I had had in the black section of town. It's funny what one thinks of in a crisis situation. I saw myself in that sheriff's car giving pursuit—it was like I was chasing myself.

My mind was racing faster than the car. All the talk of being a kamikaze flashed into my brain. I was that kind of warrior. Either I would escape or die trying.

I flew down a hill toward another small town. The deputy was really blasting me. Pieces of the car were falling off—I could see them in my mirror. I expected some lead to come flying through the back window hole and end it all. If the pellets didn't kill me the car crash would—we were going so fast. My back tires had been hit and were getting spongy.

The sheriff started to pull alongside on another straightaway.

When he was almost even with me, I slammed my battered Ford into him and knocked him off the road.

In a moment I was in the small town. Coming out the other side, I could see they were trying to block the road ahead with a police car and a logging truck. My first impulse was to slam head-on into the truck at 100 mph and end it all. But in a fraction of a second I thought it wouldn't be fair to the innocent truck driver and those standing around. At the last possible moment, I swerved and aimed for the small space between the truck and the cop car, hoping there was enough room to make it. My car touched the vehicles *on both sides* as I blasted through the small opening and on down the road.

The small town disappeared behind me and I was coming to a flat area. In a moment, the sheriff caught up again and began blasting on me. My car was becoming hard to handle. The back tires were just about flat and I was beginning to weave from side to side.

The sheriff tried to pass me so I jerked the steering wheel in another attempt to knock him off the road; but the swerve sent my car completely out of control and I slid sideways off the road, down an embankment, and into somebody's yard. By now my tires were completely flat. I tried to accelerate once I had regained some control, but all the other officers were converging on me. My car was caught in a crossfire and began taking blasts from several directions.

I grabbed the package, jumped out of the car, and ran into a big field. Frantically I tried to rip open the package, but they had wrapped it tightly with nylon tape.

Bullets were flying everywhere. The grass around me looked as if it was being strafed by a machine gun. I kept expecting the lights to go out—one of them had to find my number. I was trying to make it to a grove of trees for protection. After running about fifty yards into the clearing, a bullet seared into my back. I was running so fast, the lead was enough to throw me off balance and knock me down. I spun around and jumped up. When I reached down to feel my back and leg, my hand was immediately covered with blood; it was pouring out. I knew I was going to die—there was just too much lead in the air.

I screamed profanities at the approaching officers. One reached me and aimed his weapon at my head. I was screaming and spitting at them with rage. They quickly handcuffed me.

An officer yelled from my car, which contained my black belt and several karate magazines. "Watch out! He's a black belt! He's a karate expert!"

One of the officers, who was some kind of inspector, started shaking me and said, "I ought to blow your head off, you punk! I ought to kill you right now!"

"Do it, do it! You're nothing! Kill me! Kill me!" I screamed and swore and spit on him like a maniac.

I was surrounded by officers. They took one of the handcuffs off and locked my hands behind my back. They were roughing me up and telling me what they were going to do to me. I didn't want to go to prison and was trying to bait them into killing me.

The sheriff came running into the field. Because he was a large muscular man, and had a real mean look on his face, I figured it was "head knocking" time.

"Kill me! Kill me! I hate you! I hate you!" I screamed at him.

"Leave him alone!" he yelled to the others. "He's my prisoner!" Turning to me he said, "Nobody's gonna hurt you, son."

I spit right in his face, and swore at him.

He looked at me and said, "I love you and Jesus Christ loves you." His words totally blew my mind. I hadn't expected that. I didn't know whether to laugh or cry. He had short-circuited my mind and I stood there numbed and quiet.

In a moment, a pickup truck pulled up with an old-timer in it. He ran out to us with his shotgun and yelled, "Get away from him, Bill. He ran me and my wife off the road. I'm gonna blow his head off!" But the deputies quickly overpowered the man and took his shotgun away.

The sheriff immediately took control. He made everyone leave me alone and he and his two deputies took me to the hospital. He kept asking if I was hurt. At the hospital they x-rayed me. The bullet went in my back and came out the other side, through my hip. They patched me up, then took me to the county jail.

When we arrived, it was crowded with deputies and curiosity seekers. Everyone kept asking who I was. I wouldn't talk to anyone. After I was in a cell, one of the other prisoners said, "Hey man, what's happening?"

"That sheriff out there shot me," I announced.

"Oh, yeah?" he said.

"Yeah. He shot me, and then he told me Jesus loved me and that he did too!" Everybody in the jail roared.

The sheriff came back into the cellblock and started to talk to me. "Who are you?"

"You've got my identification," I replied toughly.

"No, that's not you. Nobody ever ran like that for nothing. What have you done?"

"That's for you to find out."

"Well, you know we're gonna do that."

"I want to get out on bond."

He started laughing. "Come on, give us a break. You know I'm not gonna let you go until I find out who you are and what you've done."

I refused to talk to the sheriff further and he left me alone. After he was out of sight, I reached up to the light socket and unscrewed the bulb. I broke it off and made two deep gashes with it next to my wound. Then I started yelling for the sheriff. In a moment he came back with several deputies.

"Hey, man, I'm bleeding real bad. Get me to a doctor."

"I'm not gonna let you out of that cell. With the karate you know, you'd try to go through all of us and we'd have to shoot you."

"Look, I'm bleeding bad. You're not gonna let me bleed to death are you?"

"I can't let you out. I'll call the doctor at the hospital and have him come out here and look at you. Take that towel over there and put it on the wound."

The sheriff, whose name was Bill Middleton, had read me well. If they had opened that door, I would have gone absolutely berserk; I would have fought all six of them and tried to get one of their pistols to shoot my way out. I grabbed the towel and stopped some of the bleeding.

When the doctor came they made him work on my wound through the bars. He gave me some heavy medication because I told him I was in pain. A few moments after I took the medication, Sheriff Middleton wanted to take my fingerprints through the bars. I refused.

"Listen, even if we have to bring the army in here—and we can do that—we're gonna get your fingerprints. So why not cooperate?" But I still refused.

Several local bigwigs came in and stared at me. My arrest was one of the biggest things to happen in that town. Before long, the doctor's medication knocked me out until the next morning.

On Sunday, they told me they were going to bring me out of my cell for questioning. They had called the University and found out I was a ranking black belt and could be quite dangerous if I wanted. There were so many officers lined up around my cell, I knew it would be impossible to fight my way out. I had to stick my hands out through the bars so they could handcuff me. Then I was brought out for questioning.

I was spaced out. I knew they would eventually send me back to prison, so I wouldn't give a straight answer to any of their questions. Middleton was friendly to me, but all the others were playing the "good-guy-bad-guy" game. I finally refused to cooperate at all. I did let them fingerprint me, though, because I knew they would get my fingerprints anyway.

After I was back in my cell, the sheriff came back to see me. He brought his wife in and she had cooked me some special food. He sent a deputy downtown to buy me some clothes; they took all my bloody things away. I appreciated that.

Middleton rapped with me and tried to be friendly. But I was hostile. "There's just no meaning in my life."

"God has a reason for everybody's life," he responded.

I laughed. It was absurd to think God had a purpose for my life after all I had been through. The sheriff's wife said she was praying for me and I thought that was cool. They were both so nice I couldn't help but like them.

When the FBI report came back on my fingerprints, many of the officers came running back into the cellblock. "Hey, we know who you are, Robert Erler. You're an escaped convict from Florida." My destination was inevitable now.

Middleton came back a few hours later, and said, "How you feeling, Robert?"

"Oh, okay, I guess," I replied in a daze. "I don't know what it's all about. I just don't know what's going on. Hey, sheriff, I know there's gonna be a lot of reporters wanting to get to me. I'm so tired of being put in the newspapers and being looked at as a complete animal. Can you keep 'em out?"

"There's going to have to be some, but I'll keep it at a minimum for you. Listen," he continued, "we've got to bring you out for questioning again. I want to treat you like a man if you'll act like one. I don't think you're as bad as you like people to think. I know you can be a tough guy if you want to be, but I don't think you are inside."

"I won't give you any problems," I promised. The sheriff moved me out to a room filled with people. I began to tell them who I was, about my life as a police officer, and about prison and the problems I had had as an ex-cop.

One inspector, the one who had threatened to kill me when I was captured, was extremely cool towards me. He said, "I just want you to know, when we get into court, I'm going to make you out to be a bad guy."

I smiled. He thought he was really scaring me.

"Listen, Erler, we've got a lot of felonies we're going to charge you with: possession of a weapon by a convicted felon, fleeing an officer, sending firearms through the mail, and possession of narcotics. You could get fifteen years tacked onto your prison time."

(They had discovered the contents of the package when the clerk in the post office had dropped it and the pistol barrel had popped out. There had also been some narcotics in the package.)

I laughed in his face. "You know, I could care less what you do. I'm already doing ninety-nine years! Don't you understand? I hope you do charge me with all that!" The man made me mad and the sheriff had to calm me down.

"If this jerk has me tried for all that stuff," I addressed the sheriff, "it would give me an excuse to get out of my cell. I'll need a vacation. I hope he tries me for everything."

They just looked at me. I'm sure most of the investigators felt sorry for the situation I was in. The next day I was told, "If you'll waive extradition, we'll drop all the charges and send you back to Florida." I agreed to waive extradition, and they sent to Florida for officers to take me back.

While I was sitting in my cell, I began thinking about the sheriff. He had been true to his word about all the publicity. He had really kept it to a minimum. I realized capturing me was probably the biggest arrest of his career and yet he wasn't capitalizing on it in the least. He was more concerned with me than he was with all the publicity.

Sheriff Middleton even offered to buy my bullet-riddled car because he knew I needed money in prison! He told me he was a

Christian, but he never forced it on me. I couldn't believe this man. He was so polite and courteous I began to feel guilty for the way I had acted.

The next day Florida police came. They restrained me with handcuffs and leg chains. There were two deputies in my car, two in the car ahead of us, and one in the car behind. They took elaborate precautions because they thought I was connected with organized crime and someone would try to free me. I felt like Al Capone.

When I arrived at the East Unit, my classification officer told me, "I hope you know you're gonna be buried in max. And you're gonna get more time for escaping."

I was put in an isolation cell. Lying back on my bunk, I wondered about my life and how all the pieces fit together. I didn't see any purpose in it at all. Life didn't really make sense for me. Being back in prison seemed the end of the world all over again. I began to think seriously about suicide.

I was back in the zoo. Max was full of the criminally insane who screamed out at all hours of the night. The guy in the cell next to me was always going berserk and beating his head against the bars.

In a few days I received a receipt for a hundred dollars. Sheriff Middleton had purchased that battered old Ford of mine and had the money deposited into my account. I couldn't believe he did that; the car was going to be confiscated anyway.

Because I didn't have anything else to do, I began to read. Under my bunk was an old, half-destroyed copy of a Gideon Bible. I started thinking about religion. My oldest sister had wanted to be a missionary—but she had died in a car crash. How could there be a God, if he would let somebody die who wanted to serve him?

I remembered all the times in my life when I had faced big trouble and had called out to God. There was a time in the army when my parachute had opened only moments before I hit the ground, there was the 100-mph car crash when I was with the police force, then there was that time I was in the closet when the Treasury men came in—I wondered if God had really helped me or if I had just been lucky.

Sheriff Bill Middleton's words came back to me, "Jesus Christ loves you." That frightened me. I wanted to laugh it off, and yet, I was afraid of the whole "God thing." I picked up that old Gideon Bible and started reading.

Before long the prison chaplain came into the cellblock. His name was Max Jones, a big jovial man with silver-gray hair. He walked up to my cell and said, "How ya doing?"

I just shrugged my shoulders.

"Jesus loves you," he offered.

I threw the Bible on the floor. "Hey, man, I've had enough of that." He smiled and asked what was wrong. I asked if he would take a message back to Murf the Surf and the rest of my buddies and he agreed.

"Murphy's been coming to chapel quite a bit lately," he informed me. "Is there anything I can get you?"

"No, not really."

"Can I pray for you?" he asked.

"You really think that would do any good?"

"Prayer is always heard—if you're sincere."

"Sure, you can pray for me," I said, surprising myself. After he prayed, he went to all the other cells and seemed not to notice the abuse he was receiving from the inmates. Every few days he would come back. Although I didn't buy his message, it was easy to tell he was sincere.

I decided to take a correspondence course from the University of Florida in religion. I started reading the Bible to answer the questions in the course. In some ways the Bible was pretty interesting, but there was a lot of it I simply didn't understand.

After I had been in max about a week, Captain Hicks came to my cell. "Hello, Captain Hicks."

"It's Major Hicks, now," he replied.

"Man, it wasn't very long ago you were a sergeant and you were my coffee boy, bringing me coffee." He frowned. "How in the heck did you make major?"

"Bob," he said, ignoring my sarcastic remarks, "I just came back here to see how you're doing."

As we talked, I realized I was jealous of Hicks. I was feeling sorry for myself because if I had been able to stay on the police department I probably would have made captain by now. It was easy for me to resent Hicks because he had advanced so fast. I found myself giving him smart answers and calling him "field marshal."

My bullet wound got infected and ruptured. They took me to the hospital and I saw Hicks again—only now he was a colonel. I couldn't believe how fast he had advanced. Hicks wanted to know if I would have any trouble with Willy Jacks, the black guy who had stabbed Norman. I told him I didn't know how to answer that question.

Dope was easy to get, even in max. Friends would bring it in balloons when they came to visit, and the guys would smuggle it in by swallowing the balloons. I was using a lot of acid and grass.

After a month, I looked up to see Mr. Dowling, the man with whom I had had so much trouble at Belle Glade. "Well, well," he said, "look what I've got here."

I didn't bother to get off my bed. "Hello, Mr. Dowling."

"Hello, Erler. I hope you know you're going to be moldy by the time you get out of max." He smiled, turned, and walked away.

A few days later, the wing officer let me out to clean up the cellblock as the "run-around." I was allowed to take food trays down to the other men, clean up the mess and sweep the floor. While I was cleaning up the cat walk, Dowling came by on a tour of the cellblock. He immediately screamed at the wing officer.

"Put Erler back in his cell! Don't ever let him out!" The officer, who had been a deputy sheriff in Broward County and liked me, had to put me back in my cell.

"I'm sorry Bob, I've received a direct order to keep you in your cell."

A few days later I had to go to the hospital for my bullet wound again. I saw Hicks in the corridor. "Hey, field marshal. When you gonna let me out of max?"

"Listen Bob, it's not me. I'd let you out. But there's somebody here who's holding you in and I think you know who that is."

One day when I awoke, there was a little green frog sitting on my toilet. I stuck my hand out to the frog and he jumped on it. We immediately became good friends. I fed him and he slept in the water that leaked from my toilet. He stayed in the cell with me for eleven months.

An officer slipped me a newspaper from some of my friends in population. The headline read, "MIAMI GANGSTER SLAIN." It was an old newspaper, dated February 14, 1974. While I was still out on escape, Stanley Harris had been machine-gunned; he had been shot twenty-two times. I really can't say I was unhappy about it, as Stanley got what he deserved.

One of the guys had a visit and passed me some Columbian

grass. Right after I smoked it and got high, the loudspeaker blared out, "Inmate Erler, prepare to go to the colonel's office."

I panicked because I was high. The wing officer came down and asked if I was ready. "No, I don't want to go."

"You can't refuse to see the colonel. He wants you in his office right now." An escort officer came down and after they had strip-searched me, they marched me up the hall.

Once I was in the colonel's office, I saw his expression change as he looked into my dilated pupils. "Look, sir, I'm high. I just got through doing some dynamite grass. If you want to send me back and lock me up and put a write-up on me (which would take all my food away), just go ahead and do it."

He squinted at me for a second, then said, "Bob, sit down. Why don't you and I have a talk." I sat down. "Bob, how are you? I've been worried about you."

"How do you expect me to be doing? I'm doing ninety-nine years in isolation."

"Well," he said. "You feel like talking about anything?"

I told him I didn't see any purpose to my life. I didn't know what was going on and I didn't care about anything. I was so high, I broke down and started crying like a baby. I had to get some Kleenex off the colonel's desk.

"Colonel, I'm sorry," I said between sobs. "I don't know why I'm crying like this."

"That's okay, go ahead and cry."

"Colonel, what have I done with my life?"

He was at a loss for words. "Bob, I don't know."

"Colonel, how can I ever repay the damage I've done?" By now I was sobbing out of control.

"Bob, I really don't know what to tell you."

"What about my family? I've hurt them so bad. I've cost my family thousands of dollars. I've led my brothers astray so they hate authority. Colonel, what about my son? How am I ever gonna tell him I'm in prison for murder?"

Hicks looked helpless. "Bob, I don't know." The colonel talked to me for two and a half hours. Everytime he got a telephone call he would tell them he was too busy to take it.

Finally he said, "Bob, I'm so happy you broke down and talked to me like this. I finally got to see the real you. I always knew you were like this."

"Colonel, I really appreciate your spending all this time with me. But, please don't tell anyone I broke down like this."

For the next few days, I felt pretty good, like a load had been taken off. Word soon came down there was going to be a "revival" in the prison. They were bringing a group of Christian athletes in, including Roger Staubach of the Dallas Cowboys, whom I greatly admired. They were also bringing in Mike Crane, a karate black belt.

Crane was supposed to put on a demonstration. My first thought was I would like to meet the guy—I was sure he was a phony. When the chaplain came back, I started asking about the program.

"Chaplain, what are the chances of me getting out to talk to this karate guy and getting to go to the meeting?"

"I don't know, Bob, but I'll try to work it out."

Max Jones went all the way to the warden to get permission for me to attend one of the meetings. I was taken into the chapel during the third day of the revival and had an opportunity to meet Roger Staubach and all the other men. They were really super people.

They allowed me to go into a small room with Mike Crane. He was wearing his karate *gi*. I looked carefully into his eyes. If you are into karate heavily, you can usually tell what another guy's *ki* is. I told Crane, "I'd like to work out with you."

"What rank are you?"

"I'm just a black belt, but I think you're a phony."

He laughed. "That doesn't make any difference. But for the sake of the argument, you can beat me."

"No, that's not good enough. I'd like to get down with you in front of everybody." What I really wanted was to work out with him in front of all the other inmates and wipe him out.

Crane told me he couldn't do that. We had a real good talk and covered a lot of different subjects. Whenever he talked about God, I just turned him off. He asked me what I wanted to talk about. I told him the only real interest I had, besides karate, was my son. We talked for quite a while.

Finally, he said, "You know, Bob, you'd make a good Christian if you'd just accept Christ and give your life to him."

I didn't want to hurt the guy's feeling and before long, I agreed to bow and he coached me in a prayer asking Jesus to come into my life. As soon as we were done praying, I leveled with him.

"Listen, I don't want to hurt your feelings, but I wasn't very truthful. I still don't believe in Christ."

"Well," he offered, "why don't you test God? The Bible says you're not supposed to test God, but I believe God would honor some kind of challenge."

"How do I do that?"

"What's the most important thing in your life?"

"My son, of course."

"Why don't you go back to your cell and pray for him, Bob."

"Well . . . okay. I guess I will."

We shook hands and he gave me his address and told me to write to him. I went back to max. I started thinking about what I had done and what Mike had said. Just in case there might be something to this Christianity thing, I decided to pray. I looked outside my cell to make sure no one was looking, then got on my knees.

"God . . . Lord . . . Jesus . . . whoever you are, if you really care about me, I want to know my son someday." I got up off my knees and immediately forgot about the whole thing.

Two weeks later, I was called out for a special visit. I walked into the visiting park and my little son Bobby was standing there all dressed up in a little suit. He had a smile from ear to ear. Patty, my ex-wife, was with him.

I kneeled down and Bobby ran to me. I wrapped my arms around my little son. I hadn't seen him in seven years! Tears welled up in my eyes. He gave me a beautiful hug and kiss.

"Bobby," I said, "do you like your daddy?"

"No, Dad. I don't like you. I *love* you!"

I started crying. The first thing that came to mind was God had answered my prayer. I kept saying "Thank you, Jesus, thank you, Jesus!" over and over.

My ex-wife gave me a cold stare and said, "What, are you one of those bead-rattlers now?"

I laughed. "I accepted Christ."

"Oh, yeah?" she said turning in the other direction. She didn't want to hear anything about it.

"Tell me. Why did you come and see me after all these years?"

"I don't know. I really don't know how to answer that. I just had a strange feeling it was time to bring your son down here to see you.

That's what we're doing here. I'm not staying long, so if you want to spend a few minutes with him, go ahead, 'cause I'm going back to Kansas."

My ex-wife and I didn't get along at all, but Bobby and I had a great time talking. After a while he asked me if I had done the crime for which I was in prison.

"No, Bobby, I didn't do it. I didn't do it, son."

"I want to know if you done it, Dad."

"No, Bobby, I didn't do it. I'm a good guy. I'm innocent."

He gave me a big hug. After forty-five short minutes, Pat told me she had to leave. I went back to my cell and immediately got on my knees.

"Father, if you can take my life, and all the pieces that I've shattered it into and put it back together, whatever you want me to do, I'll do it." I finished my prayer in the name of Jesus like I had been told. I felt super good. I felt fresh and clean on the inside. God had answered my prayer!

TWELVE
MAXIMUM SECURITY

I sat back on my bunk in maximum security. There wasn't much to do but read, so I started getting deeply into the Bible. I read it constantly.

"Hey, man, you a Christian now?" another con asked one day.

"Yeah, I'm a Christian."

He looked at the cigar in my hand. "Christians don't smoke."

"Where does it say that in the Bible?"

"Doesn't it say you got God in your life now and your body's God's temple?"

"I don't know if it says that or not."

"Well, Christians aren't supposed to smoke," he said, just like he knew what he was talking about.

I had just purchased four boxes of cigars. I smoked them because I thought they added to my "tough guy" image. After looking at them for a moment, I got down on my knees and started to pray. The chaplain had told me if I couldn't do something on my own, I should pray and ask the Lord for help.

"God, if you'll take the cigars away from me so that I don't have any desire for them, I'll quit smoking. And I'll do something for your glory."

Right after I said that, I began to wonder what I could possibly do for the glory of God. About the only thing I could do was sit and read my Bible. Finally, I decided I would take all the junk in my cell and build something to the glory of God.

Sure enough, my desire to smoke went away, so I built a house out of matches and cigar boxes. The house was extremely detailed, with rooms and furniture and lamps and window shades. I used everything. Old flashlight batteries wrapped in aluminum foil became propane tanks outside the house. The small thin containers of medicine I had been given for my wound became electric lights throughout the house. The house took me 1400 hours to complete, and I did it to bring glory to God. (Later, Ripley's Believe-It-Or-Not Museum offered me $500 for it.)

I didn't fully understand what it meant to be a Christian, but I was concerned how the other inmates would accept my decision once I was allowed back into population. After twelve months in maximum security, I began to press hard to get out.

They began to let me out one day a week to attend Mrs. Bachelor's human relations class. She had moved from Belle Glade to the Railford area. When I told some of the guys in the class I had accepted Christ, they began to snicker and laugh, thinking I was joking.

Whenever anyone went to chapel or read the Bible, everyone figured they were trying to fool the parole board and make everyone think they were rehabilitated. I kept telling the guys I believed the Bible was true and I wanted to live as a Christian. But everyone was skeptical, including the prison officials.

Chaplain Max Jones called me out to his office on several occasions and I had Bible studies with him and his assistant, Austin Brown. They encouraged me not to worry about what the other prisoners thought or said. They told me if I was going to be true to myself and to God, I should do his will, study the Bible, and stay out of trouble.

The guy in the isolation cell next to me often screamed that demons were trying to get him. One morning I woke to hear officers in his cubicle. He had hanged himself during the night. I really felt sorry for him.

It is amazing I didn't go off the deep end myself. So many strange things happened in max. One con committed suicide by eating the chemicals from inside several flashlight batteries. Guys were constantly having arguments and would try to settle them violently whenever they got the chance. One day, while we were being allowed to shower, one inmate shot another right between the eyes with a zip gun, killing him instantly. Max was a bizarre place to live.

I found out that shortly after I was shipped to Belle Glade, a major race riot had exploded in the prison. Of the ninety-six guys on the wing where I had been housed, eighty were black. They attacked the sixteen whites and cut everyone they could reach. One young prisoner was stabbed to death.

Two guards came back and told me that Willy Jacks, the man who had almost killed Norman, was leading a large group of black militants which had been responsible for many stabbings. They told me he would probably try to kill me when I came out of max.

One of the officers passed me another newspaper clipping from the guys in population. The article told how two highway state troopers had pulled Les Woods and his new wife over on the turnpike. His car was loaded with drugs and weapons, and when the officers started to search it, the newspaper said, Les killed both of them and fled.

The article brought a sick feeling to my stomach. Les and I had been so close; he was my brother in karate. But one of the men Les had killed was Phil Black, a friend from police academy days. I had just finished reading Genesis and my mind flashed back to the story of Cain and Abel. I saw Cain rise up against his brother Abel and kill him. It really shook me. I said a prayer for Les.

Max Jones came back almost every day to help and encourage me to get into the Bible. He kept telling me I could do anything in Christ; I could be a shining light for Jesus.

"Tell me, Chaplain, how I could ever be a shining light sitting in an isolation cell with nothing but an old Gideon Bible? How can I change anything? How can I be of any value to God?"

The chaplain told me to pray. He said many people were praying for me. The Christians out in population were concerned about me and were happy I had accepted Christ.

After I had been in max for fourteen months I received a letter telling me they had dropped all escape charges. They had investigated the situation which caused me to go over the fence and decided the institution was partly to blame for my escape. I was excited about that piece of news.

Colonel Hicks came to see me and said they were seriously considering letting me back into population, but were concerned about my problem with Willy Jacks. They were afraid one of us would murder the other.

I was taken before the classification committee and spent two hours convincing them I would not try to kill Jacks if I was let out of max. Finally, the paperwork was sent through and I was allowed into population.

When I saw all my buddies, their first question was, "Did you get the newspaper articles we sent back?" Everyone offered me different drugs: grass, cocaine, speed, acid, all of which I turned down. Everybody thought I was joking when I told them I had accepted Christ.

Jack Griffith and I had a quick conversation about the past. He had been sure I would want to kill him because he had stayed with my family against my wishes. We settled the problem and renewed our friendship.

Willy Jacks was on my wing. I found out he was on a work detail and would be back at 4 p.m. I went to the control room, and when his work squad came in, walked up to him. Before I could say anything, he saw me coming and held out his hand.

"Erler, I'd like to be friends, if you'll let the past be gone. We've both got too much time to be fightin' each other."

I looked deeply into his eyes. He was a dangerous individual and I was afraid he might be trying to get me off guard to throw a sucker-punch. But he seemed truthful so I stuck out my hand and we shook. We met later in his cell and he convinced me he didn't want any trouble. Still, I knew my guard would have to stay up against him.

Every morning at 5:30, the wing officer opened the locks on all the cell doors. If I didn't get up, I became extremely vulnerable to attack. I made myself a burglar alarm so no one could come into my cell without my knowing about it.

Early in the morning, the next week, Jacks and two other blacks attacked Joe Anderson, the guy in the cell next to mine. I heard screaming and came out to investigate.

Joe, a black brother and good friend of mine, had been stabbed at least a dozen times. He stumbled out of his cell and slipped in his own blood. The attackers caught and finished him right in front of me.

It happened fast and my body quickly flooded with adrenaline. Jacks looked up at me, his long butcher knife still dripping blood.

Immediately I went into a fighting stance, but before Willy could try anything, the doors started slamming and the emergency squad came running down the hall. Jacks and the others fled to their cells. Within fifteen minutes all three were in max on murder charges.

In population, I was spending less and less time reading the Bible. Everyone gave me a hard time about being a Christian because they thought I was playing a game. There were only a few solid Christians in the whole prison at the time.

Everyone kept telling me I wouldn't be let out of prison no matter what. The prophecies of doom discouraged me and I began to smoke grass again. Griffith wanted me to work toward a higher degree in my black belt. I started working out more and more and reading my Bible less and less

The chaplain allowed me to call my lawyer. "Hey, kid! I've just gotten news they're gonna overthrow your conviction!"

"Are you serious?" I asked.

Varon told me the Appeals Court had already discussed my case and was going to overturn my conviction. That meant I would soon be a free man! The news ended my Bible reading. I began to take drugs heavily and went back to my kamikaze frame of mind. Many of my karate students saw me as the ultimate warrior because of the way I had resisted arrest. I began to get back into that macho role.

A very well-known black belt named Frazier had been arrested and convicted of assault in south Florida. He was due to come to Railford and while he was in the county jail, he heard about me and that I was a Christian. He told everyone, "If Erler is a Christian, he can't be anything but a turkey."

Word came back to me through the prison grapevine of his remarks and everybody began to make fun of me because I was a Christian. Everyone told me he was much better than me. Men in prison love to see a good fight—as long as it doesn't involve them. They continued to tell me all the things he had said. I intensified my training, knowing when he came to the prison we would have a serious match.

One day, word came down that Frazier was in the holding tank. I walked to the control room and introduced myself. He was very standoffish. I noticed his knuckles were heavily calloused, indicating he worked out a lot.

"Would you like to spar with me?" I asked.

"Yeah, I would." He told me he didn't want to play around; he wanted to do some serious sparring. He was implying he could beat me. I immediately accepted his challenge.

Frazier was in isolation for about six weeks. When he came out, they moved him onto a different wing. He had made a lot of caustic remarks about me and everyone was convinced he could beat me. He avoided me on several occasions in the yard. Still, he told one of my students I was nothing but a turkey.

I became determined we would have a showdown and found him in the yard teaching some students. I approached him and asked if he was interested in working out. He said he was busy.

"Look, Frazier. You've called me a turkey and claimed I'm nothing but a phony to all my friends. I think it's about time we sparred. One way or the other we're gonna do it right now!"

A huge crowd was gathering. He realized he was on the spot. If he didn't fight, everyone would think he was a chicken. Finally, he said he would spar and told me to warm up. I immediately donned my karate *gi* and began to prepare.

My sensei told me not to play any games with this guy because he was a high-ranking black belt. He felt I could take him if I was careful. I already knew what his weapons were, but he didn't know what type of fighter I was.

As soon as we bowed, I came up into my ki. We were pretty even for a while. He was a good kicker and managed to drop down low and sweep me to the ground. I jumped to the side and counter-attacked but it is an embarrassment to be taken down. I kicked hard at his stomach and he blocked it with his leg, breaking my toes. I was so deeply into ki, I blocked out the pain and continued fighting.

Finally, I won the match by a series of punches and a wheelkick to the side of his head which caught him in the jaw. I was going to pull the kick but he moved into it and I knocked him out, breaking his jaw.

I stood over him and told his karate students, "When he wakes up, tell him *super turkey* was here!" All the cons howled with laughter. I then hobbled off to get medical attention for my three broken toes.

Three days later, when I came back to my cell, I discovered my karate students had painted a giant turkey on my wall, complete with an oversized stomach (like mine) and a black belt.

Later I went up to see Frazier in the hospital. We talked, but never did get friendly. My victory spread throughout the prison. Everyone knew I had beat him and why.

My attorney had convinced me my release could come down any day. Griffith kept telling me about a national champion he wanted me to fight if I got out. We began to train for it. I worked on building my mental control or ki. Jack told me very few people could get heavily into ki and control it completely, but that I had the ability. The ultimate was to induce a state so deep in which one could smash like the Japanese charged in World War II. Many had to be shot to pieces before they could be stopped.

One of my brown belt students told me he had really gotten deeply into ki with the help of LSD. I took two tabs of Orange Sunshine acid and began to meditate. I wanted to prepare myself for the day I walked out of prison to be a champion. My sensei felt it was possible for me to become the greatest champion in the world.

As the LSD came on, I was overcome by pure energy. I had always been afraid of Kim because he had such a deep ki. He could smash his hands into stone walls and totally block out any pain or injury. When I looked at him, I looked right through him, I was so deeply into ki. I was the cat and he was the mouse.

I took up a fighting stance. *"Hajami!"* (which means "begin" in karate). Kim looked at me and could see how deeply I was into ki. He waved me off with his hands and bowed. He wouldn't fight. He backed up, but I started to follow him.

I wanted to enter into a death match. My mind flashed back to that time in Korea when I had been wiped out. I was filled with hatred and aggression which was driving me to attack. "Yami!" Griffith yelled, stopping me in my tracks.

Fear knifed through me. I had submitted to the force of ki; it was like I was overcome by it. I felt so guilty. I apologized to Kim and everyone else and returned to my cell.

The next day I went to the chaplain and confessed. "Chaplain, I'm a phony; I'm a hypocrite. Since I've become a Christian I've been smoking grass and taking all kinds of drugs. Ever since I found out I was getting out of prison, I decided I didn't need God anymore. I've just turned my back on him."

Max pulled out his Bible and turned to 1 John 1:9 and read: "If we confess our sins, he [Jesus Christ] is faithful and just to forgive us our sins and to cleanse us from all unrighteousness."

"Chaplain, I believe God came into my life, but I just don't think I'm good enough. I don't have the strength to live for him and I don't know what to do about it."

Max and I got down on our knees in the chapel and began to pray. He prayed first, then I asked Jesus to come into my life and take control. I told him I was really sorry for the way I had been living. Max was a beautiful Christian brother; he helped me so much.

Walking back on the wing, I spotted Murphy. "Jack, I asked the Lord in my life again; I want to live my life right but I just can't seem to get it together. I'm gonna be going out on the streets and I just can't get it together."

"Well, don't worry about it. Just be cool. Hey, they've got a black Pentecostal group coming in here on Sunday." We considered most black groups to be "holy rollers" because of the way they carried on. I went to chapel services every week, but was really only living for myself.

Because I had been labeled the "Catch Me Killer" my conversion placed me at the center of attention. Many outside Christians wanted to come in and talk to me and find out why I had become a believer. I couldn't understand all the attention I was receiving.

That Sunday the black group came in as planned. Most of the men and women were quite old. The service began and we started to sing. Jack and I were there primarily because it was expected of us. We were both somewhat skeptical of this type of Christian.

An eighty-year-old black lady stood up and searched the inmates with her eyes. She walked up and down the aisles until she came to Billy Jacks, Willy's brother. Billy had been on death row for murder, but the state of Florida had eliminated capital punishment and he and a lot of other convicted first-degree murderers were allowed to come back into population.

The old lady pointed a finger at Jacks and said, "You've got a devil!" He just stared at her but didn't react in any way. "You've got a devil and you're gonna hurt somebody!"

I looked at Murphy. We had never had any incidents with outside people and we were both afraid of what could happen. An incident would probably blow the whole program.

In a moment, the lady called some of the others off the platform.

Several of the older men and women came down and stood in front of Jacks. "This man has a devil in him, and he's gonna hurt someone if he doesn't accept Jesus Christ."

She put her hands on Jacks' forehead, but he didn't move. She told him, "You've got to accept Jesus Christ or you're gonna do it and you're gonna regret it."

I couldn't understand what was going on. All the visitors started praying and jumping up and down and started what we called "the hallelujahs." I was sure we were headed for a major incident.

Jacks just stared straight ahead. When the women began to plead with him to accept Christ, he stood up, smiled and walked out of the meeting. The visitors returned to the altar, had prayer, and then the service continued.

When the program was over, I went up to the chapel advisor. "What was that all about?"

"That woman is a prophetess," she said. "The Lord told her that man had a demon and he was going to kill somebody." When I told Murphy what the advisor had said, we both had a good laugh. More of "the hallelujahs," we thought.

The next day I was in the gym. After going through a pretty heavy karate workout, I came off the stage to get a drink of water and stepped into the weight room. Murphy and a guy named Harold Johnson were both lifting weights.

Harold was a 250-pound man with a tremendous muscular build. He was a leader of the blacks and was the prison weightlifting champion. He was a product of the system. He had been raped when he first came into the prison fifteen years earlier, and as he grew, he became a homosexual rapist himself and had made many enemies. We had tried to lead him to Christ, and just a few days earlier, Max Jones had brought him to the verge of becoming a Christian.

This particular day, he was bench-pressing 350 pounds. When he lifted the weight into the air and locked his elbows, Billy Jacks suddenly raced out from behind the curtain with a twelve-inch blade. With a powerful thrust, he buried the long blade in Harold's chest. Again and again he slammed it into Johnson's stomach and chest.

Harold was still holding up all that weight, but his arms were shaking. He was in shock and didn't know what to do—he couldn't drop it. I stood there dazed; murder always happens so fast. Jacks kept plunging the blade in and out. Finally the weight fell on Harold's chest, crushing it.

Jacks had been laughing satanically as he committed this murder right in front of our eyes. Almost as quickly as the attack began, he dropped the knife and calmly walked away.

There was blood everywhere. Murphy and I ran to Harold and started to carry him to the clinic. He was bleeding badly. We kept falling because he was so heavy. We got him to the clinic, but his heart had been pierced and he died moments later.

His death really shook me. I had known him for years. We had both been "tough guys" and I had really gotten to like him. Murphy and I returned to the wing, but we were both shaken. Jack turned to me and said, "You want to hear something really weird?"

"What's that?"

"What did that woman, that prophetess, say yesterday about this?!"

I looked at Jack and suddenly it "clicked" in my mind. I got goose bumps all up and down my back. *"Oh, man, that just freaks me out!"* Jack and I were both shocked when we realized that woman had seen it all.

"Murph, I've lived my entire life at a 100 miles an hour. Right at this very moment, I dedicate my life to serving Jesus Christ. I'm gonna go 100 miles an hour for him." The impact of the spiritual warfare around us had overwhelmed me. Murphy and I got on our knees and said a sincere prayer of dedication to God.

From that moment, my life changed radically. I stopped taking drugs completely. I started studying the Word every day and began to go to chapel services faithfully. I began to seriously ask Max for help in my personal Bible study. I became consumed with Jesus; he became my life.

THIRTEEN
FLASH BACK

I received an emergency call from Phoenix. When I picked up the telephone my mother's voice came through.

"Butch, I've got bad news," she said, then started to cry. "Paul has just been shot and they don't expect him to live." Mom really started to weep.

She told me how Paul had walked into a bar and got into an argument and the guy pulled out a pistol and shot him. The doctors cut out his kidney, spleen, part of the upper and lower intestines, and part of his liver. They had given up hope he would live. He was in extremely critical condition in the hospital.

After I hung up, I told the chaplain, "Max, my brother's dying."

"Let's pray for him," Max said. "Let's get all the Christian brothers and pray for him."

When the Christians had come into the chapel, I shared with them how my brother had been shot and we all began to pray. While we were praying, I suddenly remembered Paul's visit at Belle Glade and the dream he had. I jumped up.

"Chaplain! When I was down at Belle Glade, my brother came to visit me. He told me he had accepted Christ and how he had seen a vision he would be shot. He was told in that vision if he would serve Christ, he wouldn't die." I was overwhelmed by the memory of his words and immediately went back to prayer.

"God, if you'll save my brother as you said, I'll give you my life and I'll do anything you want me to." I'm sure the other guys must have thought I had really gone off the deep end. But I loved my brother deeply and wanted him to pull through in the worst way.

I had never been superstitious or believed in the supernatural before I became a Christian. Now I knew there was a supernatural world and that God was in control. I was absolutely convinced God would not let Paul die, even though my family kept calling to tell me he had not improved. Finally, they telephoned to say he was pulling out of it—he was beginning to regain consciousness. God had answered my prayers!

Later, I had a dream of my own. "Chaplain, I had a dream the other night in my cell. I really don't know if it was a dream, or if I was thinking it, or what. I had a dream God was going to use me to be great."

Max opened his Bible and read a verse which said if you wanted to be great, you had to become the servant of all. "If you're gonna be great, you're gonna have to be a servant. Even Jesus said he came not to be served but to minister to others."

I started to think about that. "You know, Chaplain, I've got something I want to lay on you."

"What's that?"

"It's really been bothering me ever since that day when I prayed with you about guilt." I told him about the incident with Harold Johnson and how that woman had predicted it would happen. I told him I didn't know what to do.

Max said if I really wanted the Lord to reveal himself to me I should pray. We prayed together right then. Max was like my spiritual father. He helped me through so many difficult problems.

I went back to my cell and asked God what he wanted to do with my life. The Scripture passage, 1 John 1:9, kept coming to mind. "If we confess our sins, he is faithful and just to forgive us our sins, and to cleanse us from all unrighteousness."

I began to think about my family and all the trouble I had caused them and everyone else. Now they were going to turn me loose; I would no longer be a convicted felon. I was really confused.

For the first time, I honestly faced the past. In my mind, I drifted back to August 12, 1968—the night of the crime. I had been working seven days a week and six nights. I had been suffering from non-stop headaches, personal problems, and overwork.

That particular night, I remember going to deserted Dania beach after work to have my nightly run. After jogging a couple miles, I jumped in the ocean to cool off, then walked back up to the showers to wash off the salt.

While I was showering, a female voice called out to me. I couldn't make out her question so I turned off the shower and walked to an older Ford Falcon, where the woman was sitting.

"Do you know if it's okay to sleep on the beach?" she asked.

"No, ma'am. I'm a police officer and I know you can definitely not sleep on this beach."

The light was bad; I couldn't make out what the woman looked like. She told me she had no place to stay. I mentioned I was separated from my wife and was staying alone. She invited herself to stay in my trailer. The thought crossed my mind that maybe we could get something going. I drove back to my trailer and she followed in her Falcon.

Once we arrived at my place, I saw the woman closely for the first time. She was short and squatty, smelled strongly of body odor, and her clothes were wrinkled. She was unattractive to me. Her daughter had been sleeping in the back seat of the car. She was a young girl, overweight, and with no front teeth.

We entered my trailer and I apologized for the condition of the place. I explained my wife and I were getting a divorce. The woman told me she understood; she had been married and divorced several times and told me she "really knew how to take care of a man." She offered herself to me.

"Lady, I think you've got the wrong idea. I think you better leave."

"I need seventy-five dollars."

"For what?!" Her request took me by surprise.

The woman told me she hadn't been working and needed some money. I told her I didn't have any money. "Even if I did, why would I give it to you?"

She looked up at the picture of me in my policeman's uniform on the wall. "What would the chief of police say if I called and told him one of his married officers was entertaining a woman and her daughter alone at this hour of the morning?"

Her threat made me flush with anger. "That sounds like blackmail to me."

"Call it what you like. I'll just call it a loan." She turned and walked to the telephone, letting me know she was going to make good her threat.

Something snapped in my head. At that moment, my sanity disappeared. I became completely detached from what was happening. "Lady, you just blew it!" I said in a rage. I twisted the phone from her hand and slammed it down. (Ironically, the phone had been disconnected after I was unable to pay my wife's bill, but I was so mentally exhausted I wasn't thinking rationally.)

Horrible diabolical laughter rang in my brain. It was like an evil person was in my head with me. The laughter scared me. My mind went black. The evil voice began screaming in my head, "Kill her! Kill her!" There was a loaded .22 caliber pistol on top of the TV. I picked it up, turned towards the woman, and pulled the trigger.

I watched myself do this horrible deed—my mind was detached and uninvolved. Apparently the girl screamed. Everything is so hazy and confusing. I must have reloaded and shot her, too.

The next thing I remember, I was outside on the railroad tracks near my trailer. Down the track I could see the circling white light of a moving engine coming toward me. I was laughing, that same horrible evil laughter, and I began to run full speed towards that oncoming train. I tripped on a railroad tie and fell to one side. In an instant, the train swooshed by. I rolled on the ground, laughing satanically. Later, I had many nightmares about that train.

I remember thinking, "I have to get these women to the hospital." I don't know how I transported them to where they were found, but at some point I realized the girl was dead and there was no sense taking her to the hospital. Everything is such a blur. There was no real reason for what happened.

For years I had been running from the responsibility for the crime. I convinced myself I was innocent. But I was not innocent. I was guilty. I did it. The woman pushed me over my limit, and I snapped, but nothing can justify what I did. There was no one to blame but myself. I was overwhelmed with guilt and truly understood the word "sin" for the first time. I was a sinner of the worst kind. I broke down into uncontrollable sobbing.

Max Jones had told me God forgives all sin. All sin is the same in his eyes. I wanted someone to forgive me and I realized no one could but God.

My mind flashed back to that terrible morning. I saw myself, in uniform, get out of my car and enter a phone booth. I dialed the sheriff's department to turn myself in. There was a mad throbbing in both my temples. My mind was confused. When the officer answered, fear swept through me, and the evil voice told me to hang up. Yet, another voice pleaded with me to turn myself in. Hallucinations filled my head. For some reason I claimed to have killed three people and cried, "Please catch me!" I hung up, but before arriving at the police station, I made a second call. Again I had a strong urge to confess and seek help, but the evil force within me impelled me to hang up.

Now, years later, with a tear-stained face, I sunk to my knees. "Father, in the name of Jesus Christ . . . and through his blood . . . I'm sorry for this horrible thing I've done. Please forgive me . . . and take over this life I've shattered." A warm peace flooded over me. A 200-pound weight lifted off my back. I knew God had forgiven me. I got up and lay on my bed and drifted off to sleep.

Later, a friend came up to my cell. "Rick," I said looking up, "I'm confessing to this crime, because I'm guilty."

"Hey, man, be cool. Don't blow it. You know you're doing ninety-nine years."

I went to see Max. "Chaplain, there's something I've got to tell you. I've lied to you. All the years I've been in prison I've lied to my mother. I've lied to my brothers, to the judge, to myself. I've lied to everybody. I even lied to God."

"About what?"

"Chaplain, I'm guilty. I committed that crime." He looked at me and put his arm around my shoulder.

"Bob, I just want you to confess it to God. Jesus' blood cleanses you of anything, because Jesus Christ came for sinners. And you're a sinner, Bob." Max pulled out his Bible and showed me where Jesus died between two thieves and one of them was the first person to go into paradise.

"I want to call my attorney," I said. Max didn't ask why. He just picked up the phone and dialed.

"Varon? I want to tell you something, Joe."

"What's that, kid? How you doing?"

"I've never been doing better in my life. Varon, I want you to know I've become a Christian. I've accepted Jesus Christ into my life."

"That's good, kid, if it helps you, that's real good."

"Varon, the Bible says the guilty must own up-to it. My whole life I've refused to accept responsibility for myself. I just want to tell you I appreciate everything you've done on my case, but I want you to take my appeal out of court because I did it, Joe. I'm guilty."

"What?"

"I said I'm guilty of the charge and I don't want to fight my case anymore. I'm confessing that I'm guilty."

"Hey!" he said. "*Shut up!* You're on the telephone; they've got this thing bugged. Kid, they're gonna turn you loose. You're doing ninety-nine years, don't you understand that?"

"Yes, I understand that, but there's got to be a deeper meaning in my life, Joe. God says I've gotta confess."

"Kid, you're flipping out. Shut up, I'll fly up there tomorrow morning—first thing. But don't say anything to anybody."

"No, Joe, I've made up my mind. I've prayed about it. God has told me to confess to this crime, 'cause I'm guilty. Just pull my appeal out of court."

Varon thought I had totally flipped out, but I knew what I had to do. After we hung up, I asked the chaplain to dial my family. My mother answered.

"Mom," I began, "God healed Paul."

"Oh?" she said. "At least he's alive."

"Mom, God healed me, too."

"What do you mean?"

"Mom, I'm a Christian. And I'm gonna live like one. I've lied to you all these years, Mom, because I'm really guilty of committing that crime." She started crying. I kept telling her how badly I felt for what I had done and how it had been eating me up like cancer. Telling the truth was like taking a thousand pounds off my soul.

I told Mom I had taken my appeal out of court. She didn't know what to make out of it all. My sister Bette quickly flew to Florida. My whole family thought I had become a mental case. My sister wanted to know what had happened.

"You know," I told her, "I'm really sorry for the way I've lived my life. I've caused all of you so many problems. But Jesus Christ has come in and changed everything."

I told my sister about a dream I had. In it, a person appeared wearing a karate outfit with a black belt around his waist. But the man was wearing a police badge on his chest, a night stick and pistol were strapped on his hip, a parachute was on his back and a green beret was on his head. I was afraid of the man, but I looked up and saw my own face on the image. God was showing me what I projected to other people and it scared me. As I walked through the jungle, the beast I feared most was really myself. I was afraid because I never knew who I was or what I'd do next.

"As I understand faith in the Bible," I told my sister, "God has called me to trust in his promises. I finally realized I am standing on nothing but his promises, and that Jesus Christ is God, and that he is in my life."

Before accepting Christ, I had been half a police officer and half a convict and didn't know if I was a good guy or a bad guy. When Jesus Christ came into my life, he divorced me from being "half" a police officer and "half" a convict and made me a "whole" Christian born again in the Spirit. All of a sudden I had direction in life.

My sister had a difficult time accepting what had happened. She thought I was going overboard on religion. She couldn't understand why I confessed to the crime, even if I was guilty. I told her God didn't want me out of prison yet, but there was a mission for me inside even though I didn't understand it. Before she left, I gave my match house to my sister to take back to Arizona.

I wasn't sure what my calling was, but I knew God had something for me. Max kept telling me God was calling me into a deeper relationship with him for a very special mission in life. I believed it. I started sensing God was going to do things through me and for me.

All the guys began to say I had overdosed on God. But I didn't care. I read my Bible and prayed and prayed. A Bible seminar came into the prison and I had an opportunity to hear a lot of teaching. The teacher taught us to learn spiritual truth from the men in the Bible and apply it to our lives.

I became particularly impressed with the life of Jonah. I could really identify with what he went through. He had been swallowed by a great fish and I too had been swallowed by an iron and steel monster. Many men in the Bible had been heavily persecuted, but God had used them in tremendous ways. I wanted to be used like that.

After the seminar, a group of students from a local high school were brought into the chapel service on a tour of the prison. The chaplain introduced himself from the pulpit and asked the inmates if anyone wanted to stand and give a testimony. I didn't know what a testimony was, so I asked the chaplain what he meant. He repeated his question, only this time he said, "Does anyone want to stand and tell our visitors about how they found the Lord?"

I stood up and introduced myself. "My name is Bob Erler, and I'm the 'Catch Me Killer.'" There was a little stir from the students. I had always loathed the title before I became a Christian. Now I realized it offered me the kind of notoriety that would help people listen. As I told my story, everybody seemed to listen intently. I became so wrapped up in telling it some of the kids began to cry. My personal experiences seemed to reach out to these kids and touch them. At the end of my testimony, I praised God for what he had done in my life and sat down.

Afterward the chaplain asked, "Bob, why didn't you give the audience a chance to receive Christ?"

"How do you do that?" I was such a new believer I had no idea how to lead anyone to Christ.

"Bob, the Spirit of God was flowing through you so powerfully that if you had given an altar call, many people would have been saved. They would have had eternal life in this prison today."

Reflecting on his words, I felt I had really let God down. I determined if an opportunity like that ever came up again, I would give some kind of invitation.

The prison psychologist was with the students. After everyone had gone, he came to me and asked, "Are you for real, Bob?"

"What do you mean, am I for real?"

"Well, do you really believe in Christ?"

"Yes, I believe in Christ." I really didn't know how to explain what it all meant but shared the depth of my trust in the Lord.

"I've got to talk to you when we get a chance," he said.

About a week later, they brought another group of students in, this time from a reform school. Again, the chaplain asked if anyone wanted to give a testimony, and again I stood up.

I shared my background as a green beret, as a police officer, as a karate black belt, and with my crime. I told about my escape and capture and how I had met Jesus. All the kids seemed mesmerized by my experiences; they were locked into what I was saying. I asked how many of the guys were Christians and a few hands went up.

"Don't be ashamed to say you're a Christian. I'm a Christian and it's the greatest thing in the world. How many of you would like to have eternal life?" Almost everyone raised their hands. "If you want to accept Christ," I continued, "just come forward and I'll pray with you."

To my amazement, almost everyone came forward, including the teacher. There was barely enough room in the front of the chapel to hold them all. The chaplain had told me when someone received Christ, he had to repent and admit he was a sinner. I had everyone bow in prayer and led them through a sinner's prayer. When we had finished praying, everyone had smiles on their faces. All the Christian inmates came up and began to shake the hands of their new brothers and sisters in Christ and we all began singing. I was overwhelmed with a dynamic good feeling. I was excited that God had used me to change these young people's lives.

Word got back to the warden about how the reformatory kids had responded to the chapel program and he gave permission for groups of students to come into the prison every week. They made a special request that I be allowed to stand up and talk to each group coming in. This began to happen every week and many each week trusted Jesus as their Savior.

Before long, the reform school superintendent came to see me. He said, "I've never seen such a tremendous effect on these kids like what you're doing in this prison. I'd like you to keep it up, only . . . I'd appreciate it if you wouldn't talk about religion. Some of the kids came back to the school crying. They were afraid they were going to hell because they had not become Christians."

He didn't understand what we were doing. "You know, sir, I really love being able to help these kids. But I made an agreement with God that I would tell everyone about Christ and what he did in my life, and if you ask me not to talk about Christ then I really don't have anything to say." I don't think the superintendent was pleased with that, but he continued to let his kids come into the prison.

When speaking, I often told how I had almost killed a police officer. There had been two voices in my head, one telling me to do it and the other telling me not to. I explained how God had kept me from doing it. A lot of the prisoners and reform school kids seemed to be able to identify with the war that went on in my head as they had had similar experiences.

The prison psychologist kept calling me into his office and I kept telling him about Jesus Christ. I didn't understand it at the time, but he was under conviction from the Holy Spirit. God was working in his heart. After talking to me, he and his girlfriend went to church. Both became Christians. He came back to the prison and invited me into his office again to tell me he had decided to quit his job as prison psychologist and enroll in Bible school. It was exciting to know my life was touching people.

There was a big meeting of prison brass at the Railford facilities. They brought in superintendents and assistant wardens from all the prisons within the state. These administrative people wanted to talk to some of the people who were involved in the human relations classes to determine if they should expand the program.

Eight of us prisoners were invited into the meeting. Mr. Dowling was there as well as Mr. Wainright, the superintendent of the entire Florida prison system. Each of us was asked to say something.

When it came my turn, I was praying, asking the Lord to help me say the right things. I looked up to the director of prisons and said, "Mr. Wainright, I want to apologize to you and to you, Mr. Dowling. If any of you have been holding anything against me, I would like to ask you to forgive me for all the things I've done to hurt you, the division of corrections, and the state of Florida by my escape."

Everyone just stared at me. I'm certain none of them expected me to say that. "I want you to know that I have accepted Jesus Christ as my Lord and my Savior. I've given my life to him and I'm going to serve Christ for the rest of my life. If it has to be in this prison, then that's where it will be. I am confessing to my crime. I'm guilty. I did it. I've pulled my appeal out of court and will serve my ninety-nine-year sentence without appeal."

I thanked the men and sat down. No one seemed to know what to say. Afterwards we had a small party for the human relations class and Mr. Wainright shook my hand and kept staring at me. It was as if he couldn't figure me out.

FOURTEEN
MOVING OUT

Right after I had been in several sparring matches, the chaplain and his assistant began challenging me about my involvement in karate. They told me I had set a terrible example. God was calling me to a spiritual ministry.

Max pulled out his Bible and showed me verses which said I had to die to self. It was difficult to explain how I had depended totally on myself for survival. When people came against me, I couldn't just stand there and let them cut me up.

Almost every day Max talked to me about dying to self. As Christians, he said, we have to flee from our egos. It was not right to hurt people physically, and he explained that Christ would never hurt someone. I had a hard time with what he said.

He talked about idolatry and helped me see I had devoted much more time to karate than to serving Christ. I was a contradiction. Could I be a karate champion and serve Christ fully? He asked me to pray about my karate.

I started studying about demons. In Ephesians I read that we wage war not against physical powers, but against wicked spiritual powers in high places. That caused me to analyze all the people in prison who had severe problems, character disorders, and the guys who claimed they were being attacked by demons. I became convinced their problems were indeed caused by demonic forces.

In prison, there is no doubt evil exists. I began to realize how much power the enemy has. The more I studied, the more I believed I needed deliverance from my violent nature.

Frank Costantino, a Christian minister who had a deliverance ministry, came to the prison. Frank had become a Christian as an inmate and returned to preach every year. I was greatly impressed with his Christian faith.

I stepped forward in one of his meetings and told him about my situation. He wasn't sure if a Christian could be demon-possessed, but he had all the Christian brothers in the chapel step forward and lay hands on me and pray for my deliverance. I felt a sense of relief after that; I felt cleansed.

The Bible verse on the chapel wall began to speak to me. It said, "Not by might, nor by power, but by my Spirit, saith the Lord " (Zech. 4:6). I was still living an ego trip and that was not what the Lord wanted.

I discussed my involvement in the martial arts with all the Christian brothers. They came up with several Scriptures to convince me I should not be involved with karate. Almost all of them were against me even working out. To lose karate was a hard thing for me.

After a lot of prayer I made my decision. The more I became a warrior the farther I got from the Lord. My God was Jesus Christ, not karate. I decided to quit karate; I even decided to quit working out. I made a covenant with God that he would be first in my life.

Jack Griffith had given me his own personal black belt dating back to the 1940s. I returned his belt and said, "Sensei, I've decided to quit karate."

"You can't quit karate. You're a warrior and warriors never quit." He couldn't understand how I could stop working out.

When I told Jack why I was quitting, he said I was becoming fanatical and cursed God. We had a big split and I turned my students over to him and stayed away from the karate people after that.

The prison officials decided to open up more programs for inmates. We started the Florida State Prison Jaycees. The program seemed to draw all the hard core cons who had shown open hatred for me when I had first arrived. Surprisingly, they asked me to become head of the program. After praying about it I accepted and was elected as first president.

Two weeks later, I became involved in Alcoholics Anonymous even though I had never had any real drinking problem. Some of the guys asked if I would consider heading the group. "I'm president of the Jaycees; I can't run. The administration won't let anyone run more than one group.

But they put my name in on a write-in and the 100-man organization elected me. I was also coordinating the college program, and before long, was placed as manager of the officers' canteen. I was one of the first inmate human relations counselors and was heading the Christian Men's Fellowship. As it ended up, I was in charge of every inmate program in the prison.

No attempt was made to stop me from leading the different groups. Mr. Wainright, director of the Florida prison system, said I was the only inmate they had ever let run more than one program—let alone all of them.

I had been reading about Joseph in the book of Genesis, and couldn't help identifying with him. My days on the police force were like those he experienced with his brothers. They sent him away as a slave and prisoner, but God raised him up. It seemed God was raising me up, too. I felt the Lord was calling me to be a leader.

We had been praying God would give us a Christian warden and sure enough, a new warden came in who was a believer. His name was Bobby Leverette. He called me into his office on several occasions because I represented so many groups. I invited him to our meetings. He came and showed more personal attention than any administrator had ever shown. And he openly encouraged the Christian Men's Fellowship.

The warden gave me permission to go to every area of the prison and talk to guys in the different programs. I was the only inmate in the entire prison who could do that.

We got the Jaycees involved in many self-improvement programs. The nucleus of our group was composed of Christians who helped me with everything. The inmates began to clean up in the offices, the kitchen, and do other odd jobs to raise money for our programs. We painted the visiting park and started a camera concession in the visiting area to take pictures of prisoners and their families.

One day while reading the paper, we noticed a little black girl in Tampa needed a kidney. The Jaycees adopted her, donating several hundred dollars towards her respirator and kidney machine. A family's house burned down and we raised money for them. Our programs were beginning to change the prison. The Christian Men's Fellowship was expanding like never before.

The warden called me in about a plan I submitted to have a banquet for the Jaycees. They had never had such a program inside a maximum security prison. I told him we wanted to invite in women, the local sheriffs, the professor of criminology from the university, judges, and people of that caliber. He looked at me closely.

"Bob, if you'll give me your word we won't have any problems, I'll risk my career on what you tell me." I told Mr. Leverette there would be no trouble, so he let us have the banquet.

We set it up in the gymnasium inside the maximum security section. Over 400 people attended, including the chief justice of the state supreme court, several judges, and three county sheriffs. Numerous prison officers came with their wives; the director of prisons, the news media, and the parole board also showed up. My family flew in from Phoenix.

We had a great program. At the end of the meeting I stood to give the president's message and gave a testimony explaining that the change in my life had come not in rehabilitation but by regeneration in Christ. The banquet came off perfectly with no incidents.

I was receiving a lot of attention from different Christian organizations. Because the International Prison Ministry wrote short versions of my testimony to distribute nationally, I began to receive stacks of mail.

Jack Murphy was one of the closest friends I had ever had. We lived cell by cell for several years and shared much together. When we made the decision to dedicate our lives to serve the Lord, we knew God could use our publicity for his Kingdom, if we would lift up the name of Jesus.

The Christian Broadcasting Network came down and said they wanted to film a television program inside the prison which they would call *Maximum Security*. Both Murphy and I agreed to have them film our testimonies for the show. We assured the warden there would be no problems. The program came off beautifully and we began to receive mail from thousands all over the country who had seen the program. But the publicity scared the authorities.

My parole hearing came up. I had been recommended for parole by the colonel and the classification team and there were several hundred letters in my file recommending release. The parole officer took my folder home and read all the letters. The next day he told me I had a phenomenal record. He doubted they would parole me because of past publicity but highly recommended parole or at least work release. I was thrilled by his recommendation and shared my testimony with him before he left.

Right after that, an article appeared in the newspaper about a parole commissioner (a superior of the officer who had talked to me) who stated, "People think just because they tell someone they accepted Christ, they're going to walk out of prison." The article was very negative, and obviously directed at me. I was disappointed, of course, knowing I had been turned down and would spend at least another year in prison.

A member of the board came to see me and said they wanted me to transfer out of state. He felt there was too much attention and publicity focused on me because of my Christian faith. He said if I went out of state, it would enhance my opportunities for parole. I put in a request to be transferred to Arizona because my family lived there. Normally, such a request took anywhere from eight months to two years to be approved. Mine came back in just a few days; they wanted to transfer me immediately.

The swiftness with which the paperwork came back scared me. I wondered why they wanted to transfer me so fast. It just didn't seem right. I also knew I would have to start over in a new prison and the memories of being assaulted and losing my teeth came to mind. No matter where I went, the cons would never forget I had been a cop. I decided to turn the transfer down.

The parole officer returned, along with the head classification officer. "Listen Bob, I think it's best you go out of state. It's your decision, but we want you out of state. We want your case to cool off. You shouldn't be in the news media like you have been."

I told the chaplain about the situation and he encouraged me to pray for God's will. "God knows best. We should open all avenues in our lives to let God work the way he wants."

I ran so many programs and had so much freedom it was difficult to think about leaving. I had become a sort of Christian celebrity and didn't want to walk away from it. But there was so much pressure to go out of state, I put in for the transfer again. When it came back quickly a second time, I denied it again.

The assistant warden and colonel called me in. "I think you better go out of state, Bob. We think this would be the best thing for everyone. You could get visits every day in Arizona." That idea appealed to me because I loved my family very much and they were not able to visit much because of the tremendous expense in coming to Florida. "If you turn it down again, you'll stay in Florida and have to do many more years than you would do in an out of state prison."

I prayed harder about accepting the transfer. I told the chaplain I didn't really want to go to Arizona because of what might happen; I was certain to be stabbed or have other problems. We prayed together and I told the Lord, "If you want me in Arizona, I'll go. But you know I don't want to."

"Bob," Max said, "sometimes, even as Christians, we get so powerful and influencial we believe we're eagles. But God doesn't want eagles; he wants sparrows. It has to be God's will and not man's in our lives. We don't understand it but we have to do it his way because he knows what's best."

I decided to put in for the transfer again. I assured the authorities if it came through, I would take it, believing it was God's will for my life. Soon I received word from the front office that they had received the paperwork and would ship me to Arizona, Sunday night at 1:00 a.m.

I stayed in my cell for two days prior to leaving. I still feared the transfer because I didn't know what to expect. I hoped my initiation wouldn't be as bad as it had been in Florida.

The warden called me into his office, on the weekend, just to say good-bye. "Bob, you are a very powerful inmate in this institution. You're the most powerful inmate we have here. And when you go to Arizona, you're not going to have the relationship you've established over the years here with the officers.

"The prison you're going to is run differently than this. I had the opportunity to take that prison, but denied it and took this prison instead. I'm familiar with the situation out there and it's possible you'll have problems. I'm not trying to scare you. I just want you to be prepared for a totally different environment."

Mr. Leverette and I had a good talk. He was a warm, kind person. He admired my stand for Christ and I really felt affection for this man who had taken some of his off-duty time to say good-bye to a convict. I let him know I appreciated everything he had done for me and considered him my friend as well as the warden. We shook hands and embraced.

He then told me there were some guests coming to see me before

I left. Professor O. J. Keller, the professor of criminology at the University of Florida, had come with his mother, a very dear Christian woman. He and his college students with whom I had worked would miss me. Mr. Keller was President of the American Correctional Association, and had allowed me to join this group from inside prison. It was good to know he recognized I had been able to make contributions to the prison system as an inmate.

The warden gave me permission to walk all over the prison to say good-bye. It was really difficult for me because even the hardened cons, whose friendship had taken so long to win, embraced me. Saying good-bye was so emotional I again began to have second thoughts about leaving. Was I really being led of God to leave or was I convincing myself it was God's will?

Back in my own cell, I started praying. "Lord, I hope I'm doing the right thing in leaving this prison. Lord, I want to ask you to protect me in Arizona." With my publicity, I knew everyone would know who I was within days after my arrival. I was fearful I would have incidents like those at Lake Butler.

I lay back on my bed and prayed and prayed. Picking up my Bible, I read about Gideon. I was inspired by this man. I identified easily with him, noticing how he asked God for a sign.

"God, I pray in the name of Jesus Christ, that you'll give me a sign so I'll know I'm doing the right thing." I didn't know if I had the right to ask God for a sign, and after praying for some time, I forgot about the request.

That evening, at 1:00 a.m., they came to get me. While they were getting the vehicle ready to move me, all of the officers inside the control room came out and shook my hand and wished me the best. They marched me out the back and put me in a squad car. I received two sets of handcuffs and was shackled to the floor.

As we drove out, I looked back at the outline of the prison against the black sky. I had spent years in that place and it was almost like leaving home. Even though it was dark, I stared at the trees and the beauty of the outside world. There were no trees for a mile around the prison.

It was also the first time I had been around a citizen's band radio. They had one in the squad car and when we got on the highway, I could hear trucker's say, "A smokey is coming up behind you with big blue eyes." I asked the officers about the radio and they used it to show me how it worked.

After we were on the road for eight or nine hours, my guards started asking questions about my religious experience and if I thought it was going to get me out of prison. I told them how I had become a Christian and they listened attentively.

The lieutenant turned and said, "Didn't you confess to your crime?"

"Yes, I did."

They quizzed me as to why I would confess. Nobody confessed anymore, even if they really did it. The driver asked, "Why did you make those telephone calls to the police department asking them to catch you?"

I had to think about that. "I really don't know. But as a Christian, and looking back, I believe I wasn't really calling out to the authorities to catch me . . . but I feel it was my lost soul crying out to God to help and save me." Both the officers turned and looked at me.

I leaned back in my seat and started praying silently. I talked to the Lord about that sign I had asked for. So far, there was nothing to reassure me.

Before long the officers started to tell me how rough it was in this Arizona prison. They had picked up prisoners out there and it was tough. They told me how many killings there had been and encouraged me to be careful. Their warnings began to bring on a state of paranoia in me.

They had orders to drive me straight through. They were not to let me out of the car except to go to the bathroom. It was dark out when we reached Arizona. It was my first time in the state in nine years. As we drove across the desert, they kept telling me how many more miles it would be. The closer we got, the greater my anxiety became.

Finally, at about 3:00 in the morning, the lieutenant pointed off across the desert and said, "About twenty miles over there is the prison."

I looked out the window of the squad car and searched the dark horizon, half dreading my first glimpse of it. Suddenly, a giant lightning bolt flashed into the sky in the form of a cross. It stood there for almost two full seconds right over the top of where they had said the prison was.

"Did you see *that!* Did you see *that!*" I called out.

Both of the officers looked at me, then out the window. "You mean the lightning?"

"Yes! Did you see what it did?"

"That's just heat lightning."

They were looking at me strangely. I figured I had better keep quiet or they would think I was crazy. But as far as I was concerned, God had given me a sign. As I sat back in my seat, a Bible verse came to mind, 2 Timothy 1:7. It said: "God hath not given us the spirit of fear, but of power, and of love, and of a sound mind."

A warm, comforting feeling came over me. I started to feel good again. I knew even though there would be some rough times ahead, everything was going to be okay.

FIFTEEN
BREAKING IN

The prison was located in the desert near a small town called Florence. The buildings were old forbidding structures with a high wall surrounding them. The place seemed much more oppressive than Railford had been.

I was taken to a small room where they unshackled me. One of the officers took my three baskets of clothes, including my karate *gis*, and piled them onto the dirty floor. I walked over and picked up my *gis*.

When one of the officers saw what I was doing, he picked up my master's text on karate, and my black belt.

"Are you a karate-ka? I'm a *San-kyu*," which meant he was a third degree brown belt.

"I'm a *Sandan*," I replied. My rank was third degree black belt which was five ranks higher than his.

"What's the problem, sensei?"

"I don't appreciate this man kicking my gi and the rest of my gear all over the floor."

The young officer said he'd take care of it. We shook hands and quickly became friends. He had been a police officer in Phoenix for eleven years and knew my family. He was happy to see me at the prison.

Immediately he warned me about all the gangs. As an ex-cop he thought I would have trouble with the Mexican Mafia, the Aryan Brotherhood, and possibly some blacks. He explained the prison was divided into these three groups, plus the Indians, who were fewer and stayed to themselves.

They let me pick up my karate gear to ship it to my family. I was taken into another office and a lieutenant told me, "If you're really a karate expert, you won't be allowed to work out, introduce any material of a martial arts nature, or to do any karate exercises."

I was placed in a one-man cell and the next day they started processing me into the prison by giving me a battery of tests. They also cut off all my hair.

At the beginning of my second week in Arizona, I was called in front of the diagnostic center with about thirty other new inmates. The counselor walked down the line and asked the men about answers on their forms. He called out to me, "What was your occupation before coming to prison?"

I had purposely left that space blank because of all my trouble in Florida. I wasn't certain if inmates handled the prison's paper work and didn't want "police officer" on my record jacket. I didn't answer his question.

"36516, what was your occupation?"

"Just put anything you want on it, it doesn't make any difference."

"I asked you a question. What was your occupation before you came to prison?"

"I've been in prison nine years; I've done a lot of things."

"Well, what was your last position?" He was getting insistent. By now everyone in the line was looking at us. I didn't have any choice.

"I was a police officer."

I could feel the eyes of all the other cons burning holes in me. When we returned to our cells, they immediately spread the word. Several yelled threats down at me.

Two days later, as we were marching toward the mess hall, four guys crowded in front of me, pulled a knife and stabbed the black in front of me; then the four attackers ran. A seven-inch blade was sticking out of the black's side. He fell and I stepped forward to help him.

"Don't get near him!" some inmates yelled. "The tower officers will shoot you!"

Looking up at the tower I saw several rifles aimed at me. They told me to back away.

"I need to help this man and pray for him!" I yelled back.

One yelled, "Make any move toward him and we'll shoot!"

With that, I backed against the wall. The guards came out and took the guy away on a stretcher. After he was removed, our wing was allowed to line up again to return to the mess hall. This time I was first in line. When I walked past the entrance to the cellblock, two big white guys jumped in front of me. Their knives gleamed in the sun.

"*Kiai!*" I screamed. A quick kick sent the first attacker to the ground. Turning fast, I backhanded the second, then decked him with a hard blow with my foot. I kicked both of them a few times on the ground to make sure they didn't get up, then whirled to see if anyone was behind them. The line of cons that had been following me had turned to flee like a covey of scared quail.

I picked up the knives my attackers had dropped, threw them off to one side, then turned and walked back to my cell. A few minutes later, the sergeant came up. "Erler?"

"Yes, sir."

"What happened down there?"

"You probably know more than I do about that."

"The only thing I saw," he said, "was you fighting with those two guys. What was it about?"

"I don't know what it was about. As far as I'm concerned, they fell down the stairs."

"There's an investigator comin' to talk to you. He'll be here in a minute."

I picked up my Bible and started reading. By now, almost everyone knew I was a Christian. Chaplain Ray's books, which contained my testimony, were all over the prison. In thirty minutes a lieutenant came to my cell. "What happened down there, son?"

We were standing next to the bars, right where all the other inmates could hear. "I don't know lieutenant. I think those guys fell down the stairs."

"I understand they tried to stab you."

"I don't know anything about that, sir."

"Both those guys are at the prison hospital, banged up pretty bad.

Did you know they're *bikers* (motorcycle gang members) and members of the Aryan Brotherhood?"

"I don't know who they are."

"You know I'm gonna have to write this up don't you? I'm gonna have to take you to court over this."

"Yes, sir, whatever you have to do."

He hesitated for a moment. "I thought you were that Christian from Florida."

"Yes, sir, I am a Christian."

"Well, how come you got yourself in this?"

"I didn't get myself into anything."

"Well, doesn't the Bible say you're supposed to 'turn the other cheek'?" A big smile formed on his face.

"Yeah, the Bible says a lot of things. But it also says Jesus wants us to have life and have it more abundantly. He doesn't want us to get cut to pieces or have somebody kill us."

His smile got bigger. "I thought you were supposed to pray for people instead of beating them up."

"Lieutenant, I don't mean to be a wise guy, but sometimes I find in my position as an ex-cop in prison, I've got to lay hands on people, and feet too, and pray for them later." We both laughed.

"Erler, you're my kind of Christian. As far as I'm concerned, it's like you said; those guys fell down the stairs." He took the write-up he'd made and ripped it up and instructed me to flush it down the toilet.

"I suspect you'll have more trouble with these guys. There are many gang members and they've done a lot of killing in here recently. If you want to go to protective custody, I can put you over there.

"Lieutenant, I appreciate the offer, but I've never been in protective custody and I've got ninety-nine years to do."

He looked deeply into my eyes. "Erler, you're either crazy, or you're a heck of a man."

"Well, maybe I'm a little bit of both," I laughed.

Finally, they let us go back to chow. After I had my food and sat down, the sergeant called me away from the table. "That was karate, huh?"

"Yes, sir."

"I've never seen anyone change so many gears so fast. You scared the daylights out of me. When I saw what happened to those guys, I had to run." He paused and motioned toward some convicts around my place at the table. "See those Mexicans sitting over there?"

"Yes, sir, I do."

"Those guys are all members of the Mexican Mafia. They trade off contracts with the Aryan Brotherhood. If one group can't reach somebody, the other group will do it for them."

"I appreciate your telling me. I don't want any trouble, I just want to do my time."

"Well, sometimes you can't do your time. People are gonna mess with you."

"If I have to," I said with a wink, "I'm not above doing the Mexican hat dance on their hats with their heads still in it." We both laughed.

Word quickly spread through the prison that there was a tough Christian around. The other prisoners looked on me as a Christian warrior. In the next few days, a lot of guys came to my cell and told me they were Christians, too. I realized many looked up to me because I was willing to stand against the gangs.

I asked to see the chaplain but was told he didn't visit the cellblock. So I wrote a note to him, asking to get in to the Sunday service. But they wouldn't let me go to chapel for two months, until I was out of the diagnostic center.

I was soon classified as a barber; my job was to cut the hair of all the incoming men. The position presented great witnessing opportunities for me. Word spread through the county jail about the incident with the bikers and Chaplain Ray had flooded the state jail system with books containing my testimony. By the time an inmate reached the prison, he knew all about me and was usually friendly and respectful.

Every guy who sat in my chair heard the Gospel. I would witness to them as I cut their hair. Several accepted the Lord right away. Soon we had twenty or thirty new Christian brothers.

One day, as I was witnessing to an inmate, the chaplain walked in. It was the first time I had seen the chaplain and because the man in the chair had just asked to receive Christ, I turned to him.

"Chaplain, this is Jim, he wants to accept Christ. Would you pray with him to accept Christ?"

The chaplain looked around nervously. Several cons and officers were watching us. "Listen, let's not pray here and embarrass anybody. We can do that later."

"What?" I couldn't believe my ears.

"I'm not going to pray out here and embarrass anybody."

"You're the chaplain and you're not going to pray for this man? When he's *asked* for prayer?"

"Let's not get too foolish."

His words shocked and inflamed me. "Get over here and pray for this man!" I commanded. "Mister, if you don't start doing your job, you better just leave this position. You've got people in here who *need* you. You wear that collar so you better get out here and do it!"

My words took him by surprise. He prayed with the man, but I had gotten off to a bad start with him. I had always depended on Max Jones in Florida, but quickly realized I wouldn't be able to depend on this chaplain. In this prison, I would have only God's Word and the Holy Spirit.

At night, in my cell, I studied the Bible on my own. The Lord began to deal with me in many areas. I read where Jesus looked on the multitude and had compassion on them because they were like sheep without a shepherd. Many of the guys started seeking me out to ask questions about the Bible. They were like sheep without a shepherd. But I quickly realized how ignorant I was about the Word. Every time I was asked a question, I would write it down and go check out what God's Word had to say about it.

Before long, pressure came down from the Mexican Mafia, the Aryan Brotherhood, and the black brothers for everyone to join a work strike. Some of the Mexican Mafia came to my cell and told me not to go to work. I asked their reasons for the strike. They didn't have any real reasons. They just felt now was the time for a strike.

"I'll have to pray about it," I told them.

They laughed and told me I'd better pray real hard, then gave me a paper they wanted me to sign saying I wasn't going to work. That night I searched the Bible. I read in Romans how we should obey the authorities because they were ordained of God. I prayed about it and didn't have any peace about joining the strike. Most of the professing Christians were going to strike, but only because they were afraid of what would happen if they didn't. I told them we needed to stand up for our faith as Christians and go by what the Bible said.

The next morning, when the Mexican Mafia returned, I told them I wasn't going to strike. They didn't say much, because they were leery of my fighting ability, but while I was working that day, a note was placed in my cell that said it was going to be fire bombed if I didn't join the strike.

I went to the leaders of the Mexican Mafia and the Aryan Brotherhood and told both of them, "If anything happens to my cell, I don't care who does it, I'll fall out with you guys and personally give you your first karate lesson." Then I turned and walked away.

Prison is like a colony of baboons: the most dominant prisoners rule. If a person will fight, they'll give him a lot of room. I didn't have any trouble after that. Nobody bothered me and I continued to work. But the strike soon reached major proportions.

A few days later, I was in the main yard when a rifle shot echoed through the enclosure. A tower officer shot an inmate while he was stabbing another con. There was a rule that when any violence came down, the tower officers could shoot inmates in the yard. Everyone ran for cover. Fear ran through the prison like static electricity. Steel doors clanged and loud speakers blared for everyone to clear the area and return to their cells.

As the strike got very hot, there were more and more violent incidents. The cons tore the dormitories apart and even burned down several buildings. Anyone who didn't go along was clubbed or stabbed by other inmates. Eventually the officers stripped everyone and had them sleep outside on the athletic fields. Arizona State Prison was the most violent prison in the country at this time.

The striking inmates really picked on the Christians. Almost all of them checked into protective custody to avoid being stabbed or clubbed. Some of them stayed locked up for over a year. Only a few professing Christians stayed in population during the riots.

Bus loads of new prisoners were still coming in from the county jails. Because of the publicity the strike was receiving, most men were extremely paranoid when they arrived. More and more accepted Christ. The chaplain provided Bibles for everyone who trusted the Lord.

Each night I would go back into the isolation section where the new guys were housed and conduct a Bible study with those who had accepted Christ. We studied what the Bible says about obedience. All the people who had been greatly used by God were obedient servants.

The deeper I got into the Bible, the more I became convinced I was not living up to what God wanted me to do. The vision of that cross of lightning kept coming back to me. It impressed upon my mind that God was calling me into a deeper relationship with him.

Several of the officers came into my barber shop to talk. After two months in the prison, an officer trusted the Lord as a result of my witness. It really thrilled me that God had used me, a convict, to lead an officer to the Lord. The officer had been living with a woman whom he later married. The Lord pulled his life together.

I began talking to one of the counselors, a warm black man named Banks. He had made a decision for Christ at one time, but had fallen away. He rededicated his life to the Lord and I went into his office everyday to pray with him.

Seventeen new prisoners came in from the Phoenix County Jail right after that. I witnessed to them and three accepted Christ. I took the numbers of the men who had become Christians into Mr. Banks and all three ended up assigned to him—a minor miracle in itself. We prayed together in his office; then Banks went to their cells daily to make certain they didn't have any problems.

Because of the pressure, a great number of inmates became Christians. Of course, a lot of these men fell away from Christ, but many stayed true to the Lord. By the time the riots were over, we had a large group of Christians, who continued to ask questions. When they had problems they wrote me notes and we'd get together to read the Bible and pray.

After I had been in Arizona for six months, they transferred me out of the maximum security section to a medium security area called the Institution for Educational Rehabilitation.

The day of the transfer, I had all my gear and was standing in front of the yard office when out came several members of the motorcycle gang called Bad Company. They were all well-built weight lifters and each had large tattoos of two hands with handcuffs on them and the words "Bad Company" written underneath the symbol. I had heard about this group because they had been involved in several beatings, robberies, and even a murder or two.

The president, the warlord, and a few top members came up to me. Crowell, the president, ordered some of his members to pick up my stuff and carry it into the dorm. We shook hands and he introduced himself.

"I've heard all about you, Bob. I'd like to be friends." I didn't know what to make over this unusual display of friendship from such an obviously bad dude. He had his men take my stuff into the dormitory where he was living and made one of the guys move out of a bed so I could be in the upper tier of his bunk. His actions were humorous.

Most of the bikers spent their free hours lifting weights. It didn't take much to tell me what was on their minds. They wanted me to teach them karate.

"I can't do that. It's against prison regulations. And besides, I never let students choose me. I choose my own students." Even after I said no, they kept trying to talk me into it.

I knew most of the leaders of the "tough guy" groups and had won their respect because I would not take any intimidation. Whenever trouble came up—like a new inmate getting raped or an extortion plot—the guys would often ask me to talk to the leaders of the different sides. We stopped a lot of trouble before it started.

I came up for parole after I had been in Arizona about six months. The board went over every facet of my case. I admitted my guilt and told them exactly what happened and that I was extremely remorseful. They gave me a unanimous vote for parole. Their letter to the Florida parole board stated, "This man is extremely responsible and mature," which of course was saying they were ready to parole me whenever Florida was.

Florida said they wanted me to spend at least another year in prison. I was disappointed, but determined I would use that year to strengthen my walk with the Lord.

About this time, I received a letter from Jack Murphy. Norman and Phil, my two karate students, had been released from prison. Jack wrote, "Norman and Phil were in Chicago and tried to rob a residence. The man in the house was on the phone when they knocked on the door. The guy put down the phone and answered the door—to be met by Butch Cassidy and Sundance. The party listening on the other end of the phone figured out what was going down and called the cops.

"Phil tried to make it out the back door but was killed on the spot, shot in the chest. When Norman saw Phil killed, he knew he had a bad loser going for him: jail, prison, his wife. The whole mess was just too much so he 'went out smokin' and let them kill him. What a terrible waste. What a huge sadness for so many of us who loved him."

It seemed that either my friends became Christians or they threw away their lives. The news really blew my mind. Both of those guys had been so close to me.

I kept witnessing and leading guys to the Lord. Because there weren't any real Christian programs to go to, we got several guys together and started a prayer group. We also got a Christian Men's Fellowship started in that area of the prison. We met in the evening and talked the yard sergeant into letting us use a room to have our prayer circle. Soon the group was quite large.

I began to notice guys coming into our meetings who had occult and satanic tattoos. They would try to disrupt the Bible study portion of our meeting. I started studying more and more about demons and how Jesus cast them out. I remembered the deliverance ministry I had been through in Florida. I had done a study on the blood covenant and the power of the blood of Christ.

One night a group of occult people came into our group and tried to disrupt. I immediately started to pray aloud and they left. After we finished our meeting and walked out into the yard, a big 250-pound guy, the occult leader, came up to me. The Christian brothers had told me he was the high priest of the black occult and was in prison for cattle rustling (which he had sacrificed to Satan).

"I hate you!" he said forcefully. His eyes burned holes into me. For some reason I felt strongly led to ask him if he wanted to accept Christ.

"You want to be a Christian, don't you?"

He looked bewildered, but answered, "Yes."

"Do you believe that Jesus Christ is the Son of God?"

"Yeah, but I believe in the devil, too."

"I know you do, because you belong to him right now. Do you believe that Jesus died on the cross for your sins?"

"Yeah."

"Do you believe you're a sinner?"

"Yeah, but why are you trying to get me to pray out loud? I don't want to pray out loud."

Ignoring what he had said, I asked. "Do you want to accept Jesus Christ into your life as your Lord and Savior?"

"I can't do it! I can't do it!"

I stepped closer to him and put my hand on his shoulder. "You're name is Bill, isn't it?"

"Yeah."

"Bill, my name is Bob. Jesus Christ died for you, Bill."

"No, no. Don't talk stuff like that."

I started praying and he became very quiet. I motioned for other Christians to come up. "Put your hands on him and start praying with me." He didn't resist while we prayed.

I started leading Bill through the sinner's prayer. But when I asked him to claim the blood of Jesus Christ, he started to shudder violently. He pulled back his fist as if he were going to strike me. When I looked into his eyes I saw they were fixed in a glassy stare.

I told all the Christians to pray harder and started over with the sinner's prayer. But every time we got to the blood of Christ he could not confess it. After about five minutes, such a crowd of people had gathered to see what was going on that some officers came by to investigate.

Finally, I commanded, "Accept the blood of Jesus Christ in your life!"

He yelled out, "I accept the blood of Jesus Christ!" Bill's body stiffened, then relaxed and he broke down crying. "Thank you, Jesus! Thank you, Jesus! Praise God!"

Everyone standing around also started weeping. His conversion was quite emotional. We laid hands on Bill again and brought him into the Christian brotherhood.

Bill later told me he had been a master counselor in the occult for thirteen years. While we were having Bible studies he had sent several of his followers to try to put a hex on me—but he said it had no effect because of my strong faith. His conversion was a tremendous testimony to the power of God. He changed so dramatically the other inmates noticed quickly.

Several other cons who were into the occult received Christ soon after that. It was a difficult experience to go against the demonic forces, but God began to give us tremendous victories.

SIXTEEN
THE BROTHERHOOD

I had done a study on baptism. Mark 16:16 reads, "He that believeth, and is baptized, shall be saved." That had me worried. By this time I had led over a hundred men to the Lord and hadn't baptized any of them. I asked the chaplain if he could baptize the men. He told me the only thing he could do was take them into the bath tub and sprinkle some water on them. I felt that definitely wouldn't do.

Right after leading Bill, the occult leader, to the Lord, I told him I wanted to baptize him. I showed him several passages of Scripture on baptism and he was agreeable, but there was almost no available water in the prison.

Then we thought of the irrigation ditch in the prison yard next to the guard tower and we decided to baptize him there. This was shortly after his conversion and there was a large crowd around us.

While we were preparing for the baptism, the guard in the tower looked down and asked what we were doing. "We're going to baptize this man."

"I'll shoot you if you get in that water," he called down.

"I'm a Christian," I told him. "This man just accepted Christ. I've got to baptize him."

"I'll baptize you, *with this!*" he said holding out his rifle.

"God tells me in the Bible I should baptize this man. There's no other water out here but this. I've got to baptize him. Should I do what you say or should I do what God says?"

"What?" he said. "Ahhh, go ahead."

So I baptized Bill. Everybody standing around clapped, even the guys who weren't Christians. I'm certain some clapped because they felt it had been a victory over the guard, but most of the guys were really touched.

The next day I was called into the warden's office. "What kind of 'Christian mafia' are you trying to start in my prison?" There were all types of brotherhoods at the prison and he informed me very bluntly he wouldn't stand for another.

"What's this I hear about you baptizing someone in the irrigation ditch? There's no way I'm going to let you do that."

"Can we use the baptismal trailer that's been donated to the prison?"

The warden was an extremely godless man. He wouldn't let us use the trailer and whenever I talked about God, he began swearing violently. He threw things around and tried to intimidate me. I sat in front of his desk smiling.

"Warden," I told him quietly, "I'm praying for you."

That really upset him. He threw a book on the desk and said, "Get out of here with all that crap!" After I left, I ignored his orders and started baptizing the believers in the ditch. We must have baptized about seventy-five to 100 men in that irrigation ditch before they threatened to lock me up if I didn't stop.

We searched for another place to baptize the men. In front of the laundry there was a cleaning vat with running water. The vat was three feet deep, three feet wide and six feet long—it was perfect. Every Saturday we filled up the tank and baptized all the new Christians. I baptized many, many men in that vat. A lot of the prison's toughest guys were becoming Christians.

At one of our baptism services, the yard sergeant was so moved he got down on his knees in front of the inmates and officers alike and accepted Jesus Christ. He came to our Friday night meeting with Captain Turner. When I invited the captain up in front to speak, he praised the Christians and said, "Bob has me on the verge of accepting Jesus too, but I'm just not ready yet."

Captain Turner called me into his office. "Bob, everyone respects you. They all look up to your karate and what you did to those bikers when you first came in here. I know you don't owe me any favors but I've got a troublemaker, a real hardcore guy. Can I put this guy in your dormitory, in the bed next to you? I'd consider it a real favor."

"Captain, you keep putting all these hardcore inmates around me and I think you're overloading me a bit. You can put anybody next to me you want, but don't expect me to do your job."

The captain knew many of the hardened cons had become Christians and changed so positively there was a good chance this inmate could be helped, too. So he moved Fredrick "Midget" Reynolds into my dorm. Midget had been in the hole over a hundred times for rape, extortion, and fighting. He had been the warlord of Bad Company and was now its president.

For over a month, Midget watched me read my Bible and tell him about the Lord. He responded to the story of Zaccheus, a short man in the Bible who came to Christ. Midget was self-conscious about his size and had driven himself to be the weight-lifting champion.

I talked about the Bible in a way he found interesting. We talked about David and Goliath and how a small kid, who believed in God, had been able to wipe out a nine-foot giant.

I told Midget and many of the others how I had accepted Christ and how I pulled my appeal out of court because I wanted God to be the one who freed me. That really made a big impact on Midget and many of the other cons because no one else was doing ninety-nine years without appeal.

Midget couldn't understand why I wasn't bitter. "When I first went to prison, I'll tell you, I used to lie on my bunk and think about how I was gonna kill all the police officers who lied at my trial and the judge and the DA. I thought about killing them, their wives, their children, their cats, dogs, and canaries. I was very bitter. But when I received Christ, I started renewing my mind through the Bible. God took all the hatred and bitterness out of my system."

Midget accepted the Lord and every night we studied the Bible together for an hour. He really started getting into the Scriptures.

About this time, there was a murder in the dorm and we were all locked in, unable to go anywhere. We were crammed in like sardines. I was lying on my bed reading my Bible when a little mouse peeked his head around the corner. He was a cute fellow with meatball eyes. I took my towel and started to throw it over him so I could make a pet out of him, but he ran into our dorm and under a bunk.

"A mouse, let's get it!"

Everyone jumped up and started tearing the dorm apart, chasing after it. In a few moments our room was a shambles. We kicked boxes out from underneath the bunks while the little mouse ran from bed to bed. Guys were grabbing brooms and towels to try to capture the animal.

There was a new officer for our dormitory and, when he heard all the commotion, he thought something really bad was happening and locked himself into his cage.

Finally, Eric, a big weight lifter, cornered the rodent and yelled, "I've got it, I've got it!" Everybody was afraid of Eric because he was such a big dude. The mouse stood there looking up at him. It was a stand-off.

Eric slowly crept up on him, preparing to lunge for the creature, when suddenly, the mouse jumped straight up and squeaked at the big hulk in front of him. Eric jumped three feet in the air and screamed at the top of his lungs. Quickly the mouse hung a square corner, skidded sideways, and ran out the door.

Everybody roared. Guys were rolling on the floor. A two-inch mouse had bluffed out a 220-pound, muscle-bound weight lifter. The sergeant and the emergency squad came running into the dorm—which was a shambles, with boxes and beds lying everywhere.

"What's going on here!" barked the sergeant.

"You won't believe it, Sarge, but we were just attacked by a killer mouse!" somebody chirped. Everybody roared again.

But this was a serious situation because of the recent murder and we all knew the officers were anxious. The sergeant chewed us out and said he would completely lock us down and take away our food if we didn't settle down. "I don't want to hear another peep out of this dorm! You guys understand?!"

Nobody answered, but as soon as the officers had walked outside, somebody yelled out, "PEEEEEEP!" Everyone roared again. We were laughing so hard we were crying. It was hysterical.

I invited all the members of Bad Company to come to our Christian Men's Fellowship. In prison, respect is based on being a tough guy and I had to show them they didn't have to be weak to be a Christian. "Anybody you guys got that's a mean motorshooter, let's go out in the yard and see what they can do. *Anybody*, against me. And I'm telling you as a Christian." Nobody would take me up on it.

"Now, I've met you on your level, so meet me on mine. Come over and see what CMF is all about."

The guys took my challenge and the whole motorcycle club showed up with earrings dangling, muscles bulging and all kinds of tattoos showing. "Grizzly" was a 300-pounder and rightly nick-named. "Tumor" had a huge scar on his shaved head. "Dusty" was covered from head to toe with over 300 occult tattoos. They were a mean looking bunch.

That night, Richard Jackson, pastor of the largest church in Arizona, came down and preached. At the invitation, Eric and two of the other Bad Company members asked Christ into their hearts.

The next morning, all the remaining members of Bad Company, the ones who had not become Christians, killed another prisoner in the dorm and were immediately locked in max. They were later convicted of murder.

Our evening Bible studies in the dorm were starting to involve most of the men. Out of eighteen guys in the dorm, twelve came to our Bible study and prayer times. I began to teach on many different subjects like witnessing, obedience, baptism, being sensitive to God's voice, and so on.

One night when just Midget and I were doing a study, I felt a strong urge to stop. "Midget, something's not right. Let's take a break." It was 11:30 p.m. I got up and walked to the front of the dorm to get a drink.

The officer in the cage asked, "How ya doing tonight, Bob? How's the world treating ya?"

"The world's treating me bad, but Jesus is treating me good."

He laughed and said, "Well . . . I wish I knew the Lord."

I stepped up to the cage and began to talk to the officer. His name was Clarence Strohm and he was an older, but very good officer. He told me he had been a traditional Catholic but hadn't taken it seriously. We talked for a long time, and soon I was witnessing powerfully in the Holy Spirit. I went back to the dorm and got my Bible and talked to him about the blood covenant and why a person had to receive Jesus Christ into his life. I told him, "You never know when you're going to die. You could die tomorrow. If you don't know Jesus, you won't be ready to die."

When we had talked for twenty-five minutes, Clarence had tears in his eyes. He was having family problems and was drinking a lot. He told me he always wondered if he would go to heaven. "If you really and sincerely ask Christ into your life, there can be no doubt. You'll know you're going to heaven."

Several Christians came out and were listening to us talk. Clarence said he was ready to receive Christ. We prayed and laid hands on him. After we had prayed, we all hugged and he started laughing. He said he felt *so* good. It was really a touching conversion.

I turned to Midget and said, "Remember, we were talking about being obedient to the Spirit of God when he tugs on your heart? Well, God obviously wanted Clarence to become a Christian and that's why the Lord brought me out here."

"Man! Wow! That's really heavy." Midget was excited at how God had moved.

It was time for the shift change. We shook hands with Clarence and said, "Tell your wife hello."

"Hey, I'm going to go and tell my wife about Jesus."

Clarence left, and in about fifteen minutes another officer came in and said, "Some of the officers just got killed outside."

When I heard those words, I knew instantly. Clarence was dead. The knowledge went through me in a flash. God had me approach that man because he was calling for him. Clarence had no sooner pulled off the property than his car was hit head-on by a drunken driver. He and another officer were killed instantly.

All seventy-five of the men attending CMF voted to send flowers to the families of both officers. It cost us well over fifty dollars, and because the inmates made only ten cents an hour in prison, several went to the hospital to donate blood to pay for the flowers.

Clarence Strohm's death really sobered a lot of people. Midget was really upset when he heard the news. Midget had killed a bank guard in an armed robbery and had shot a bunch of police officers. He did time in Leavenworth and the guy he went to the joint with was soon stabbed to death.

"Midget, we throw our lives away, but God says, if we'll give our lives to him, he'll make our lives something beautiful. We took the keys and released that man to heaven; otherwise he would have gone to hell." Midget got so turned on he began to witness to everybody.

A few days later I came into the dorm and Midget and another Christian were witnessing to Richard Taylor, an officer. When they saw me, they immediately said, "Hey, Bob, he's got some questions we can't answer. Can you give us some help?"

I sat down and shared with Richard, and in twenty minutes this officer accepted Christ, too. Two days later, another officer became a Christian. The institution started thinking there was something wrong with Dorm Four. It seemed every inmate or officer they put in the dorm was getting converted. They started rotating the officers and stopped assigning them permanently to our dorm. But soon several of the officers were returning on their off-duty time to come to CMF and they even wanted to bring their wives in.

All of the sudden there was a real love between those officers and the Christian men. We would see them out in the yard and the Christians would go over and help them and say, "Hey, praise the Lord, I'm praying for you."

One of the head men in the Mexican Mafia became a Christian and he stopped doing heroin and started bringing a lot of his Mexican friends to our meetings. God started touching everybody's lives. It was the people you would never expect to be converted that started to respond to the Gospel. Many of the toughest guys in the prison were coming to Jesus.

The administration began to become paranoid about the Christian Men's Fellowship. They started losing a lot of the forms which the inmates had filled out so they could come to the meetings. They also began to turn away some of our outside visitors claiming the paperwork had never been done.

They had a limit of only 100 men in any club because of the past riots. We zoomed up to a 160 and 170 men regularly. So they called me in and told me I had to cut it off.

"You're telling me people can't become Christians? People can't come to CMF and hear the Word of God because you've got a limit? I'm not gonna do it."

We didn't have chapel services because our chaplain was liberal. CMF on Friday nights was our church. I studied the by-laws of CMF which had been established years earlier. As the duly-elected director, I had total power and could keep out whoever I wanted. So I wouldn't let cults like the Jehovah's Witnesses come into our meetings. I had the guys in the print shop do up stationery for us because the by-laws called for it. We began demanding the rights which the prison had already approved.

I told the other believers, "Be proud you're a Christian. When you get right down to it, the true Christian is gonna flourish when he's persecuted. What do you care what the administration does or what the other guys say? Would you rather serve the living God or bow to peer group pressure?"

The first time I preached at CMF, the Lord gave me a powerful message. "Lord," I prayed, "I'm here to do what you want me to. Give me the words and say what you want through me." Things came into my mind like fire; God really moved that night. Eighteen men came forward to receive Christ. I took them outside and baptized them on the spot.

One of the men who came forward was known as Bulldog. He was a big guy, with a devil tattooed right on his forehead. He too had been a high priest in the occult. He immediately turned on for Jesus and began growing rapidly.

About this time, several of the barbers were asked to go into the maximum security section. There is a stringent haircut code in prison, especially for those in solitary confinement. The authorities use it as punishment to take away that last bit of individuality an inmate has.

The barbers, of course, were afraid to go back into max, because the inmates were hostile and we never knew when we would have a violent incident. The last barber had been punched in the teeth. They asked me to go back.

"I'd rather not," I told them. "I'm an ex-cop; the guys yell threats at me, and I'd rather not put myself in a spot where I'm that vulnerable."

"Listen," the officer said, "they're afraid of you."

"Don't ask me to do your job. If I have any trouble back there, they can always get word into population and send somebody to stab me in the dorm. You're asking me to risk my life. I just don't want any part of it."

In spite of my complaints, they gave me a direct order to go back. They weren't giving me a choice. If I disobeyed, I would be written up. Disobeying a direct order in prison is like a felony on the outside. I would lose all my privileges and any chance to make parole.

Many of the guys are so bored in max they take any opportunity to start a fight just so they'll have something to talk about. And the kitchen is right over the cells, so many knives are lowered with string into the cells. We never knew what weapon a man was going to come out with.

One day after I had cut the hair of an inmate known as "Dirty Dennis," he asked to come back because he wanted a little more taken off. The officers knew he had just learned I was an ex-cop and was going to punch me out. On two different occasions, Dennis had killed other inmates and was waiting trial for murder.

Without saying anything, he fired on me and broke my lips open with his fist. I picked him up and body-slammed him to the floor. I had been praying about my physical aggressiveness and under normal circumstances, I would have gone berserk. But this time was different. I had complete control, even though I was bleeding freely.

"Listen, punk," I said, "I don't want to hurt you. I want you to know I'm giving you a break even though you don't deserve it. I'm gonna let you get up, but you better not do anything foolish!"

I could see Dennis was on acid or speed—his eyes were crazy looking. I let him get up, but he tried to kick me in the groin. When he did that, I immediately gave him a reverse punch to the forehead and, at the same time, I kicked him sideways in the stomach. The force of my kick made him double up like a boomerang and sent him to the floor a second time. I jumped on him and the officers started yelling.

"*Kill him! Kill that punk! Knock his teeth out! Break his neck!*" I stopped short. I looked at Dennis and then back at the screaming officers. Many of them had been attacked by Dennis and they were trying to use me to get their revenge. I saw Satan in them. They were telling me to go ahead and kill this man and nothing would happen to me. I backed off.

"I'm sorry I had to do that, Dennis." I turned to the guards, "This man has had enough. Take him back to his cell."

Dennis couldn't walk so they carried him back. Most of the guys in the other isolation cells began to yell threats to me. "We're gonna kill you, Erler! We're gonna kill you when you're sleepin'! We're gonna get you!"

I yelled back. "Anybody that wants a haircut, just tell the man to open your door and we'll see what you can do!"

Everyone suddenly got very quiet. I walked up and down the corridor and said, "I know there are a lot of mean dudes in here.

Anybody that wants his hair cut, show the rest of these guys what you're made of. Last chance now, anybody want to come out for a haircut?"

You could hear a fly buzz in the max cellblock. The officers laughed; they really thought it was funny. Nobody came out for a haircut, so I stepped out of the building to return to my section of the prison. As soon as I came into view from the max cell windows, they began to yell out threats again.

I turned and blew everyone a kiss. "I love you," I called back, "and I'll be back next week to cut the rest of you." Again, silence overtook the cellblock.

When the guys in my dorm saw I had obviously been in a fight they came up and asked what had happened. I said, "Praise God. The Lord really took away that old self." I wasn't mad. I wasn't in a rage. I knew Christ was purifying my life and taking away that old desire for retribution.

One of the guys who was in a max cell and saw the whole incident later got out of max and immediately came to CMF and became a Christian. He had been impressed at the way I had handled myself with Dennis.

I immediately found out all I could about Dennis from the other cons. Apparently Dennis had been assaulted and homosexually raped when he first came to the prison. Stripped of his masculinity, he turned a short sentence into a lengthy number of years by assaulting other inmates to prove his manhood. He had joined a gang both for protection and to prey on weaker cons. I couldn't help feeling compassion for him.

The following week, I went back to cut hair again. We cut hair in a little room off the cellblock. It had a big plate-glass window in it facing the cells. They brought out Booger Red, a captain in the Aryan Brotherhood, who was in max for several prison killings. After he sat down he asked the sergeant, "Are you gonna let me shower and rinse this hair off before I go back and lay my head on my pillow?"

"No, we've got too many men to cut because of the incident last week."

Booger Red jumped out of the chair. "Look, I'm doing a lot of time. Don't talk to me like a boy, I'm a man. I don't mind getting a haircut and going by your phony rules, but all I'm asking for is two minutes to rinse off in the shower."

"No, you're not gonna rinse off," the sergeant answered flatly.

Red picked up the barber chair and threw it on the floor. He grabbed a screwdriver out of my tool box and spun around. All the officers quickly fled and left me standing in the room with him. I feared Red would try to stab me so I dropped down into a fighting stance and said, "Let's go!"

"I'm not after you, Bob, this is between me and the officers."

"Well, take it away, Red." He slammed and barricaded the door and I just stood by the window. The officers ran up to the glass and motioned for me to jump on Red. I called out, "He's not endangering my life. This is your show. I'm not going to hurt an inmate for you."

The sergeant grabbed an axe handle, and without saying a word, shattered the window, sending glass crashing down on me, breaking on my head and face. The impact made me dizzy and in a moment my blood was everywhere. Red yelled, "I'll stab the first pig that comes in here!" He turned to me and said, "Bob, you better go. You're bleedin' bad."

"Booger, I don't want to leave 'cause they're gonna come in here and do a number on you. Why don't you just give it up? You've made your point."

"No," he said, "I've come this far; I'm going all the way with it." So I walked out and went to the hospital where they took all the glass out of me. Of course, they jumped on Red as soon as I left.

Almost every weekend there was an incident with me or one of the other barbers back in max. We all complained to the administration that it was too dangerous for inmates to cut hair in max. But in prison a man is just a number and he has to do what he's told to—whether or not it endangers his life. If he doesn't do what they say, he gets labeled as a radical or a troublemaker.

The officers came to me and said, "Look, Bob, we screwed up. That screwdriver wasn't supposed to be in your box. We told the captain there wasn't any screwdriver and we want you to agree with us."

"No, I'm not going to lie. If they ask me, I'm telling the truth about the screwdriver. I'm not going to lie for you."

That didn't make me too popular with the officers, but my unwillingness to take their side against Booger Red earned me a lot of respect with the inmates. Later I went to court to testify on his behalf at a hearing about the incident. All the prison groups respected me for being my own man. I wouldn't go for anyone's guff—I lived my life only for Christ.

A couple of weeks later, I asked Dirty Dennis to come out of his cell to let me cut his hair and told him there would be no problems. At first he refused, but later he came out and accepted a little New Testament from me. I told him I forgave him and was sorry the incident had to happen. I witnessed to him, but peer pressure was too strong for him to respond.

Dennis was trying to extort money and sexual favors from several other prisoners. Later, when another barber went over, they let out an inmate who had taken too much. Instead of getting a haircut, the man ran to Dennis' cell and shot and killed him. The assailant then ran to other gang members and shot and wounded "Wolf," "Sneaky Pete," and another convict before he ran out of bullets.

Some might find it amazing that a man could have a gun, but there are all kinds of weapons in prison. Guns are not as common, but they are certainly around; and this wasn't the first shooting that had taken place since I'd been in prison. After searching the cellblock, they found *three more* .25-caliber pistols and shells hidden in the room where we cut hair.

When Dennis was killed, the words of Christ flashed into my mind, "Those who live by the sword shall perish with the sword."

SEVENTEEN
SUDDEN CHANGES

A year had gone by and I was again brought before the parole board. I had accomplished much during that time period and didn't have a single write-up on my record. The captain called me in and showed me his report. He said it was the highest recommendation he had ever given any inmate in all the years he had been in corrections. Once again, the board unanimously recommended I be paroled. I was certain Florida would free me this time.

It was two and a half months before Florida responded with a "form letter." They said that due to the serious nature of my crime and the length of my sentence, they felt I should do more time in prison.

I must admit their response knocked the wind out of my sails. It really hurt. "Lord, what do I have to do? You know my heart. I've really been serving you." God knew how depressed I felt. He also knew he was sufficient for all my needs. He didn't owe me anything. With his strength I could make it.

I tried to live my Christian life naturally. If people can't see Christ in my life by the way I live it, then my life is in vain. A person doesn't have to act religious to be a Christian. In fact, religious-acting people turn me off.

I would often pray, "Lord, I want to make myself available." Then I would go out to the prison yard where all the guys congregate, and the Lord would lead me to different guys. One day I came out and saw an Indian who was known as "Crazy Tom" sitting on the lawn with his leg in a cast.

Tom stands six foot six. His father was Irish and his mother a full-blooded Indian. He grew up on the reservation and was constantly in and out of trouble. He had spent twenty-seven years in prison.

On that particular July day, the sun was burning down. I overheard him tell another inmate how thirsty he was. There was no drinking fountain in the yard and to get a drink we would have to walk way across the field. There was a can sitting there, so I picked it up, walked across the field, filled it up with cold water, and came back and handed it to Tom.

"Is that for me? Did you do that for me?" Tom was a little punch drunk and his head jerked as he talked.

"Yeah."

"Why?" he asked, not able to comprehend someone going out of their way to be nice.

"Because I'm a Christian." He looked at me, still not believing. Then he drank the water.

"I want to tell you something. I appreciate you doing that."

"That's okay, I know you'd do it for me," I said and started to walk away.

"Hey, what's your name?"

"Bob Erler."

"Yeah, yeah, I've heard about you. You're that cop, aren't you?"

"Well, I'd rather have you remember me as a Christian, Tom."

Every time I'd see him, almost every day, Tom would say, "Hey, I appreciate that drink of water." Apparently my small act of kindness had made a very big impression on him. But I was constantly tithing my time and money to the other guys. So many had no family, no friends, and no money. If I saw a man who needed a bag of coffee I would use some of my money to buy one and say, "Hey, I've got an extra bag of coffee you can have." I'd do this with soap or deodorant and never ask for anything back. After an act of kindness I'd usually say, "Hey, why don't you come to CMF. We'd love to have you."

Tom came to CMF with several other Indians. At the time, we didn't have any Indians in our fellowship because everyone stayed in cliques. I preached a very simple message designed for them.

"Tom," I said from the platform, "you remember, we were talking about how you were brought up on the reservation and heard about the 'Great Spirit in the sky'?"

"Yeah! Yeah! I believe in it!"

"Well, I want to tell you that Spirit's name. I'm going to show you who he is in the Bible. That Spirit is Jesus Christ." I gave a powerful testimony for Jesus Christ and how the Spirit had to come into one's life. All the Indians really picked up on the message, and when the invitation was given, twelve came forward to receive Christ, including Tom.

After that night, Tom never missed a meeting. He was not ashamed to tell anyone about the Lord. He would constantly walk around singing a Christian song or saying "Praise the Lord!"

One day when I was returning from my barber's job, the new warden of the section opened the door for me. "What are you so happy about today?"

"Well," I answered, "the Lord is really treating me good."

"What?"

"The Lord is really treating me good," I repeated. "Jesus Christ is really taking over my life."

"Yeah, yeah, okay," he replied quickly, trying to get off the subject. But my Bible was lying on top of all my barber tools and he picked it up.

"Warden, are you a Christian?"

"Well . . . ah, I'm Catholic."

"Warden, why don't you come over to the Christian Men's Fellowship and see for yourself what's going on. I know you're afraid of large crowds but we've never had any incidents."

"Well," he said, "I have to say I think you're doing a tremendous job there."

Right then, Crazy Tom came walking by, jerking his head and swinging his arms. "Hey, Tom, you coming to CMF tonight?"

"Praise the Lord! Praise the Lord!" Tom yelled. He grabbed the warden's hand and shook it. "Warden, I ain't never felt so —— —— good in all my life since I accepted Jesus!" Tom was so sincere, but he didn't know how to express himself without a few four-letter swear words.

The warden's eyes looked like fried eggs. He turned toward me and said, "I'll see you guys later," and took off.

I couldn't help but laugh at Tom's rough edges. "Tom, did you have to say it that way?"

"I ain't ------ you, Bob! It's true! I really love the Lord!"

I encouraged the Christians to get involved in every activity they could. It's not winning or losing, as most people think. It's getting out there and letting people know "I'm one of you. I think like you. I act like you. But inside I'm different."

As the Lord brought different men into CMF, I began to appoint them to positions where they could best serve Christ. Midget, who was only ten pounds off the world's record in weight lifting for his size, was appointed to Athletic Director.

We started a softball team called "the Angels" and challenged the officers to a game. It was the first major athletic contest after the strike. We fielded all-Christian teams in almost every sport and encouraged other inmates to play us. We would pray together and let them see we were not ashamed of the Gospel in our lives.

Jesus said he came not to call the righteous but sinners to repentance. Some of the guys who became Christians were the so-called "hopeless" cases. But there was a definite change in attitude and behavior on the part of these hardened cons. And it all came from Jesus Christ, not from a program, or because we had a good group to work with. It came when we realized we were sinners and that Jesus was the answer.

Every race came to our meetings. Ours was the only group the prison ever had with full unity from the different races. Everybody wanted to be with each other. But the more we grew, the more regulations we were hit with, and the more restrictive they became, the more our church flourished—just like the first century Christians.

Many members of CMF had cult or occult backgrounds, and were extremely discerning about false doctrine. If one of our outside speakers started to present a false message, they would jump up in the middle of the service and tell the guy to sit down. The guys spent hours in the Word and wouldn't let any "off-the-wall" teachings into our meetings.

I started a Christian newsletter and the print shop reproduced it. We sent them to people all over the country. There were no Christian services for the men on death row, max, and protective custody. I felt the Lord wanted us to change that, so I got the cons at the prison TV station to videotape our meetings and broadcast them over the prison channel.

The old jailhouse religion, where the inmate forgot about the Lord after being released, didn't apply to our men. Many got out and immediately became involved in local churches, some became missionaries, and several were ordained.

When I first came to Florence, my mother came to visit and looked at me with searching eyes. It was as if she was thinking, "He's been in prison so long now, he's gone off the deep end. He's just not the same anymore."

"Mom, don't look at me with those pleading eyes. I'm still the same guy. Only now I want to tell you about Jesus Christ."

My mother had been impressed by the banquet and other things the Lord had used me to do in Florida. "But Mother, all that wouldn't have been possible if I hadn't been a Christian. No matter how you look at it, the credit has to go to Jesus Christ."

"You " ..he agreed half-heartedly.

Every time Mom or the rest of my family came down to see me I encouraged them to go to church. Eventually Mom and my sister De De went to a large Baptist church in Phoenix and after a few weeks, God touched them.

I noticed the difference when they came to see me. They were smiling from ear to ear. Mom looked up brightly when I walked in the room. "Bob, we've got something to tell you."

"You don't have to tell me. You've already shown me. You're Christians! Praise the Lord!"

"Bob, how did you know?"

We prayed together and I started to teach them how to go to the Father on their own. I gave the analogy of a small prince, born to a king and queen. He doesn't realize the power he has until he grows up. So it is with Christians. We don't know how much power our heavenly Father will make available to us until we grow up spiritually.

Soon after that, De De's husband Chuck made a decision in the visiting park. Then my sister Bette and her two kids trusted the Lord and started going to church. Then my brother Jerry and his wife made decisions. Praise God, bit by bit, the whole family was beginning to come to Jesus!

After the members of my family became Christians, they were baptized at the North Phoenix Baptist Church during their morning telecast so I could watch it on TV. It was exciting to see them trust the Lord.

After I had been in Arizona for a while, I received word I had a special visitor. The only person in the visiting park was Dave Koelsch, the officer to whom I had surrendered. There were three guards standing in the corner.

I broke into a smile and stuck out my hand. "Dave, how ya doing? It's been a long time."

We shook hands and he said, "I'm doing fine, Butch. How you doing?" As we sat down, he kept a wary eye on me.

"I got your letter," he said. I wrote to him after he told Mom he was afraid I'd get out of prison someday and come after him.

"Good. How come you haven't come down before now?"

"Well, I've been real busy." He still seemed nervous. We small talked for a while, then he said, "You know, Butch, I did advise you of your rights. You remember that, don't you?" He had sworn in court he'd advised me of my rights.

"Dave, it doesn't really make any difference if you did or didn't." He kept staring at me. "You know, for a long time I was really bitter against you."

"I know. There's a lot of us, about six people, that think the first thing you'll do when you get out of prison is kill us."

I looked right in his eyes. "You really think that?"

"I really do."

"Dave, I became a Christian four years ago. I gave my life to Christ and I've been serving him since then."

"Well, I don't know anything about religion, I'm not religious. But I know you."

"No, I don't think you do. You know the old me, Dave. At one time I lay in my cell and thought about you and all the people who lied to get me convicted for ninety-nine years, and I thought about killing all of you. But if our roles had been reversed, and you had been on trial and I had been in your shoes, I probably would have done what you did."

He tilted his head slightly. "Do you really mean that?"

"Yes. And I want you to know something. I am really and truly sorry all this happened. I hurt those people, because I'm guilty." He didn't know how to handle my words. "I can tell you're feeling guilty over what happened." He shrugged his shoulders trying to act unaffected. "I forgive you, Dave, for anything you've ever done in thought or deed against me. I'd like to be your friend. I don't want to spend the rest of my life in prison, and when I'm out, I'd like to be your friend, not your enemy."

"You're really sincere, aren't you?"

"I'm telling you from the bottom of my heart, I'm sorry I've caused all this harm . . . Now I want to ask you something. Can you forgive me for all I've done?" I held out my hand.

He stared at me for one long moment, then reached out and shook my hand. "Butch, I do forgive you."

We decided to have an annual CMF Christmas party. We had almost 200 in attendance including a lot of outside guests. Dr. Richard Jackson, my pastor from North Phoenix Baptist, was also there. As the meeting started, a con called Missouri Red came into the party. Red was known for carrying a knife; he kept it in his pocket and made certain everyone could see the handle, almost as a status symbol.

Red was constantly high on drugs and usually watched me like a hawk. He would come up and say "I'm not afraid of you and that karate." I went out of my way to be friendly to him, trying to win him over.

At the Christmas party, Red was really high on drugs. I approached him. "You're not authorized to come in here when you're high. You know that. You know better than to cause trouble for us."

"How 'bout lettin' me stay for the party. Promise I won't cause no trouble."

"One man could spoil everything for 200 people."

"Man, I give my word. No trouble. Just let me eat some cake and ice cream and I'll listen to the message."

"All right," I said.

After Red sat down, I asked a couple of brothers to keep an eye on him. After the meeting, I was standing next to Dr. Jackson and some of the other outside guests, when Red walked up with his hand in his pocket. He tapped me on the shoulder and I turned to him. "I'm gonna stab you in the heart and kill you," he threatened ominously.

Dr. Jackson jumped. I took a step backward and said, "Nobody tells me they're gonna stab me. Nobody. If you take your hand out of your pocket, I'm gonna do a number on you right here."

He just looked at me, trying to stare me down. "Red, the smartest thing you can do is back up and walk out of here—while you still can."

He continued to try to stare me down. "This is the last time I'm gonna tell you, back up and leave." Finally he took a couple of steps backwards, turned and walked out.

After the meeting we had a time of prayer with Dr. Jackson. He was moved by how much God had been able to accomplish in spite of the threat of violence under which we all lived.

Later Red said he was sorry to me and wrote a letter to Dr. Jackson apologizing. I restricted him from coming to any meetings for thirty days, but he pleaded to come to CMF. He seemed to be coming around, so I dropped his restriction to a week.

I was recommended for outside trusty; the classification committee gave me a unanimous approval for the change. Outside trusties were classified as minimum security. I had already been asked to speak at a number of national conventions for such organizations as the Gideons but because of my status, the prison had been unwilling to let me out.

The security committee gave me the same recommendation. While in the security office they called the trusty warden and told him they wanted to send me outside. The telephone had a room speaker so I could hear his voice.

"You're not sending Bob Erler out here. He's much too powerful an inmate and he's not gonna run my prison. Get him out of here." I smiled at his comment, but was certain his decision would end any attempt to move me to outside trusty.

I went to the new chaplain's office and was going over some policies about CMF. He felt I was too powerful. The administration was disturbed because I had so much influence over the guys' lives.

"Yes, but it's all positive."

"It makes the administration uneasy. If you ever turned against them, you'd be a powerful force to reckon with."

The telephone rang in the chaplain's office. It was the yard sergeant. "Erler, I want you back in your dorm. And pack up, you're leaving for Fort Grant."

I thought he was joking. Fort Grant was a minimum security prison, considered even better than outside trusty. It was supposed to be the next step to the street. "Fort Grant? Are you serious?"

"I wouldn't joke to you about that, Bob. Pack up, they're waiting for you."

"They're waiting for me?"

"Yeah, the bus is there waiting on you right now."

"Wow!" I immediately returned to the dorm and packed up my stuff. While I did, I told everybody they were moving me to Fort Grant. We called all the Christians together quickly and had prayer. I appointed one of them temporary director of CMF, then carted my stuff outside.

The bus was waiting inside the main prison walls. I walked up to the sergeant and held out my hands for cuffs. He grinned. "We don't handcuff anybody for Fort Grant, Bob."

It was difficult to imagine not being handcuffed. Once on the bus I noticed none of the guards had weapons. My heart was pumping furiously. I was afraid someone would run out and say, "This is a mistake. You've got to come back."

We pulled out of the prison and headed south toward Tucson. Before long we stopped while the officers got some coffee. They left one officer at the door—with no gun. Any of us could easily have overpowered him and escaped. I couldn't believe the lax security.

I didn't want to talk to anyone; my eyes were glued to the window. I wanted to absorb as much scenery as possible. It was fun trying to guess the make of a car by its looks. Most people have no idea how sheltered a man feels when separated from the rest of the world for so long.

We stopped in the desert so everyone could go to the bathroom. The sergeant looked at me and laughed. "What's the matter, Erler? You look like you're in a stupor."

"I can't believe it. I just can't believe it."

"Hey, we know you're not gonna run. You know you're going home soon when they send you to Fort Grant."

After a long drive, we pulled up to the prison. Fort Grant was in the middle of nowhere. It was situated at the foot of a small range of mountains and the elevation made it much colder than Florence. The scenery looked beautiful to me.

There were no gun turrets, no walls, and no armed guards. Every night after the 8:30 head count we could go anywhere—out in the desert or up on the side of the mountain—as long as we were back at the dorm by 10:30. Even the food in the mess halls was better.

The Fort had a little restaurant and telephones the inmates could use.

There were very few fights as any violation was an excuse to send a prisoner back to Florence. Most inmates desperately wanted to keep away from the main prison. In the history of the institution only one man had ever been murdered—quite a change from Florence.

Still, I found myself constantly looking over my shoulder, waiting for something to happen. I was at Fort Grant for a couple of weeks before I finally began to feel at home. It took getting used to.

I put in to have my teeth cleaned and because the prison has no dentist, they take the men to the city. At 5:00 in the morning, several of us were loaded into a station wagon with one unarmed guard and we drove forty miles to the town of Willcox.

After my teeth were cleaned, the transporting officer told me to go outside. I walked out and stood on the corner at a fairly busy intersection. A woman pulled up in a United Parcel truck. I'd never seen a woman truckdriver before. I felt like a stranger in a strange land.

Nobody was watching me. I could have run off so easily. "Wow, Lord, this is fantastic. Lord, you're moving that mountain for me."

A guy walked up and asked for directions. I had to tell him I didn't know. He commented on what a nice day it was and I asked, "Are you a Christian?"

"Well, I think so."

I started witnessing to him when some of the other guys came out of the dentist's office. The man I was talking to excused himself and walked away.

"Lord, here I am doing a ninety-nine-year prison sentence, walking around without a guard—and witnessing on the street. That guy didn't even know I was a convict."

Fort Grant has an outside visiting park. Unlike the stringent two-hour visits at Florence, a family can come for the whole day and have a picnic, complete with a barbecue. I was not rushed in and out on visits and it was a much better atmosphere for building family relationships.

My brother Paul and his wife came to see me right after he won a big contest as Pacific Stereo's top salesman in the country. I reminded Paul his testimony had convicted me to become a

Christian. Both he and his wife rededicated their lives and they moved back from Texas to Phoenix.

I wasn't at Fort Grant very long before I started to receive phone calls from different newspapers. A reporter from the large Tucson newspaper, *The Arizona Daily Star*, called and asked for an interview. I prayed before granting it because I had received so much bad publicity.

His article appeared right on the front page and had a six-column headline reading: "Churchmen Betting on Killer Cop Because He's Macho for God." Although the article was somewhat sensationalistic, it was basically positive. The story was immediately picked up by Associated Press and went to newspapers all over the country.

Then *The Arizona Republic*, the state's largest paper, came down to do an interview and gave me a big positive spread in their Sunday forum section. Their article was titled: "From Prison to Pulpit— A Convict's Dream" and it was quite positive. A photographer from *People Magazine* came in and shot over 100 photographs of me.

The prison administration became increasingly leery of me. I could tell all the writers and newspaper people worried them. Having access to the press makes an inmate both powerful and dangerous to them.

EIGHTEEN
THE SYNAGOGUE
OF SATAN

At Fort Grant, I was assigned to teach school and help the men receive their high school diplomas. I worked hard with all the men and spent many extra hours teaching them after regular school hours were over.

One day, one of my supervisors called me into his office and gave me some literature from his church. I took it back to the dorm to study.

When I compared it to the Bible, I realized it disagreed with the Word. I returned the literature explaining I felt it was contrary to what the Bible taught.

Soon I was called in to see one of the most disliked assistant wardens in the prison system. He is six-foot-four, weighs about 240 pounds, and has an intimidating air about him. When I entered his office he immediately grabbed my shirt collar and started to lift me up. I thought he was joking, but he held me up for ten seconds and glared at me like a wolf. I had to push his hands away and tell him not to touch me.

"Erler, we've just had another telephone call from the newspapers and they want to come up and interview you again. Are you going to accept or deny this interview?"

I explained I was witnessing Christ in my life. I told him the Bible commanded me to be ready to give an answer to anyone who asked about my faith, but he wasn't really interested in my answer.

"You and I are going to get something straight right now, Erler. What I do or say to you is no one's business! I really don't care if you tell anyone what I say to you because, if you're foolish enough to say anything to anyone, you can take your old Bible and swear on it, then I'll take a stack of Bibles and swear you're a liar! And who do you think they'll believe?"

I looked at him in disbelief. "You, of course."

He laughed. "So now we understand one another. You're in my country and I'm a very religious person. This administration doesn't appreciate you focusing attention on the prison because we don't want people snooping around here. Do you understand what I'm saying?"

"Sir, I don't want any trouble with you or the administration. I'm a Christian and I'm trying my best to make parole and. . ."

He interrupted and told me he didn't want any more games from me. If I didn't straighten up he would change my security status and ship me back to the main prison. That would automatically block any chance for parole.

After leaving his office, I spoke to several of the men about what he had said. They all agreed the administration was corrupt and would probably try to set me up because I was a threat to them.

Many of the men I had led to the Lord in Florence had been transferred to Fort Grant, and they were eager to begin a Bible study. We started a study in the library and about 25 men came up every night. But soon several officers arrested me for an "unlawful assembly". Regulations stated no more than three men were supposed to gather together on the prison grounds.

We decided to meet with one of the school teachers who was a Christian. I would go up to where his class met, teach him the Bible, and he would let the other men sit in. Our meeting then became a legal gathering. God continued to add new brothers to our church every week.

While behind the prison walls at Florence, a tax-exempt ministry was turned over to me from some people in California. But the ministry had no funds. I felt I would probably never be released from prison after being denied parole over 20 times already, so I gave it away. The ministry was given back to me three times. After a lot of prayer, I realized God must want me to keep it.

Not knowing how to run a tax-exempt ministry, and with no money to incorporate, I shared the problem at our Christian Men's Fellowship meeting. Over 100 of the inmates that I had personally led to the Lord Jesus went over to the prison hospital and donated their blood, and then donated the money from their blood to the International Rock Ministries (I Cor. 10:4). That really touched me deeply to see this kind of dedication. I believe International Rock Ministries is the only ministry in the world which was set up behind prison walls on the blood of Christian convicts.

So many men had accepted Christ at Fort Grant, we decided to ask Christians in the Phoenix area to come up under the auspices of International Rock and visit the new brothers. Several of these inmates had not had a visitor in six or seven years. But this activity brought down another warning from the assistant warden.

One of the officers spoke to me about his church in the dorm. He suggested it would certainly be good to have his church behind me with my upcoming parole hearing. As a member, I could do a lot for their church, and they would probably allow me to go out and speak. When the parole board saw that, it would enhance my possibilities for release.

I told the officer I couldn't accept the doctrine of his church, as it was against the teachings of the Holy Bible. I felt it was false doctrine and I simply could not embrace it. To do so would be to deny Christ, and I would be a complete hypocrite.

Piles of their church literature began to appear under my pillow each night. I asked the inmates who was putting it there and they said it was the officers. I threw it away and complained to a sergeant, but the literature kept coming. Somehow, Chaplain Jones was finally able to stop it.

One day, as I was waiting in line for a telephone, a Christian inmate came out of the counselor's office extremely upset. Through his tears, I learned the man's wife had just been killed. Quickly I took him to one side and began to pray. Several of the other brothers came over and we formed a prayer circle.

In the middle of our prayer, some of the officers arrested me for causing an unlawful assembly. When I tried to explain about the man's problem they said, "Listen, Erler, we don't care what the problem is. You're no one special. You have to obey the rules just like everyone else." But they didn't write up anyone else.

Clyde Roberts, a Christian newspaper publisher, wanted to do a series of articles telling my story. He published several small weekly newspapers in the area and I knew the cult members would see it, but I felt the Lord wanted me to go ahead and give my testimony this way.

When the articles appeared, I was again called into the assistant warden's office. He said they were very upset with me. They didn't appreciate what I was doing and said, "You're cutting your own throat." When I returned to my dorm that night, two officers strip-searched me and went through my locker looking for anything that could be used against me.

Another officer warned me to be careful. He said the administration "hated my guts." Because they were so corrupt, they would probably set me up and bust me on false charges.

When the date arrived for Arizona to have my courtesy parole hearing, over 30 people showed up, including Dr. Richard Jackson, my attorney, my family, Jim Gibson who is a member of the Gideons, and a number of Christian friends. The warden and his assistant seemed upset with the number of people who had come on my behalf.

They informed us only some of the visitors could come into the parole hearing. Then they said my lawyer could not represent me. Finally a phone call was placed to Florida, and it was discovered Florida had enacted new parole laws. My hearing was then cancelled until the state decided how it was going to administer their new laws.

We started to walk down to the visiting area when Dr. Jackson called everyone together for prayer. The warden and his assistant were watching through the picture window in the administration building. They sent a lieutenant down to get me. He screamed for me to get into the bathroom.

"I want you to tell Dr. Jackson and the rest of those Christians they have exactly five minutes to get their rear ends off state property or I'm putting you in the hole!"

"Lieutenant, I have a free-visit day. These people have taken off from work and spent all this money to come out here. They've brought food for a picnic. We only have two hours. . ."

"You have exactly four and a half minutes left! Now you go out there and tell them what I said!"

"You want me to tell them that, lieutenant?"

"Now!" he demanded.

I walked out to Dr. Jackson id pointed to the lieutenant. In a loud voice I said, "Dr. Jackson, that lieutenant told me to tell you,

'Tell Dr. Jackson and the rest of those Christians they've got five minutes to get their rear ends off state property or else he's going to put me in the hole." The lieutenant looked at me in disbelief then stomped off.

Dr. Jackson was shocked. "What was that all about, Bob?"

"These are cult members up here and they don't appreciate Christians."

"Listen, Bob, we don't want to cause trouble for you, so we'll just do what they say." So my family and friends picked up their belongings from the visiting area and left on the 200-mile journey home. When he returned to Phoenix, Dr. Jackson preached a message about the "synagogue of satan," and mentioned the problems at Fort Grant.

We continued our Bible studies and one of the officers came up to listen. I started witnessing to him and discovered he and his wife were members of this religious cult, but God was really dealing with the man's heart. He gave his life to Christ and both he and his wife withdrew from the cult church. Before long he was forced to resign by the administration.

The officer's conversion brought a great deal of persecution down on me. They began to wake me in the middle of the night with a flashlight in my eyes so they could ask me trivial questions such as what my name was. They constantly invented new rules that didn't apply to anyone but me.

One of the inmates who worked downtown told me several employees from the institution were talking about me because of the articles in the papers. They were taking up a petition and started a letter campaign to write to the parole board stating that they never wanted to see me released. All this was based on my Christian activity and the fact they didn't believe a murderer could be saved. Several others checked for me and agreed the cult members were soliciting people to write in against me.

One Sunday morning, right in the middle of the regular chapel service, two officers walked in and arrested me. When I asked if I had done anything wrong, they said, "You'll find out soon enough. Are you refusing to come?"

"No, sir, I'm going to do whatever you say."

They took me down to my dorm, strip-searched me, and then checked my locker. Of course they found only commentaries and Bibles. One of the officers seemed to be trying to provoke me. "You don't mind if we do this, do you, Mr. Erler?" he kept saying, more as an accusation than a question.

"Well no, sir. You're officers and I'm an inmate."

"Well, we hope this meets with your approval."

"Yes, sir. I appreciate these shake downs as they show you how clean I am. Tell me, you seem to be trying to provoke me into an incident. Can I ask what this is all about?"

"You know what it's about. Don't try to play games with us." And with that, they left.

I went back to the chapel and told Chaplain Jones what had happened. He was quite upset. No inmate had ever been arrested during a church service for no reason. On Monday he complained to some of the officials. Tuesday morning I was called into the assistant warden's office. He was smiling.

"Erler, you're going back to Florence."

"Yes, sir," I said. "Is there any reason for it?"

"Yeah. You tell your preacher he can shake his Bible at you down there. And you can make parole from Florence, that is, if you make it."

"Sir, sending me back like this, at this crucial time, is gonna look bad. It certainly isn't going to help me make parole."

He grinned. "You said that right, Erler."

Two officers were waiting outside the door. The assistant warden said, "Take this punk to isolation. We're shipping him back to Florence."

They marched me down to an isolation cell and took away my possessions and my clothes. When I asked why they took my clothes, they said it was routine procedure. I asked for a Bible but was told they didn't have one. The officers told me I couldn't take any belongings back to Florence. Everything would have to be sent out and I would have to pay the postage.

I laid back in the cell and prayed. I was in that cell for three days. When the chaplain brought me a Bible I asked him if he thought this transfer would hurt my chances for parole.

"I think that's what it's designed for, Bob."

On Thursday afternoon, three officers came and put handcuffs on me, a restraining chain and belt, and shackled my legs together for the walk down to the administration building. Once in front of the committee, I was informed they were reclassifying me to maximum security as part of my transfer back to Florence. I asked what the charge was.

"Due to your prior escape, we feel you're an escape risk."

"All of you knew about my record before I was ever classified to come here. I've been here five months with no trouble. I've even talked men out of escaping (which was in my records). So this is what I'm being punished for?"

Nobody answered. They took me back to my cell to await transfer early the next morning. At 10:30 that evening, after I had gone to sleep, the assistant warden took the keys and ran them over the bars of the cell. He opened my door and told the officer guarding me to leave.

"Get up, tough guy. I want to talk to you."

"What's all this about, sir?"

The assistant warden just stared at me. "Erler, God is going to destroy you for what you've done!"

"What?"

"I told you I'm a very religious man. I've never missed a Sunday service in my life." As he began to relate his history as a member of his church, I looked into his eyes and saw he was spaced out. He had the padlock wrapped around his middle finger and kept socking it into his other hand in a threatening manner. I had the feeling he might try to hit me with it. "You know what? I think they should have castrated you. They should have drawn and quartered you in the streets for what you did."

His words shocked me. He seemed to be changing into a madman. "Sir, Christ died on the cross for me. He has taken my place. I've accepted Christ and the forgiveness He's given me."

"I don't want to hear all that garbage, Erler." He told me I was wrong. The Bible had been mistranslated. There was no redemption for murder. No murderer could be saved.

"What do you do with Moses then? He killed an Egyptian. Are you telling me that he couldn't be saved and used by God?" He just looked at me. "What about King David? He killed Uriah, Bathsheba's husband. Are you telling me that God won't save his soul? And what about the Apostle Paul? He killed Christians. Can't he be saved and forgiven?"

He just stared at me. "I don't know about all that. But I do know that God is going to destroy you for what you've done."

"You seem to be getting very personally involved with my case. That's kind of unusual for a warden, isn't it?"

"You're darn right I'm personally involved, Erler. When you get down to it, I'm your god, because I tell you when you can get up, when you can eat, what you can wear, and where you can go."

I jumped up. "You're not my God! Jesus Christ is my God! You're of the devil! You are a devil!" He started laughing. He seemed to be working himself into a rage. I felt completely helpless. If he tried to hit me and I had to protect myself, I knew I would be the loser.

I got down on my knees in front of the bunk and started praying aloud. "Father, in the name of Jesus Christ, and through the blood he shed for my crimes and sins, please help me, Lord! Father, I forgive this man for what he's doing to me because he's lost. I pray that Jesus will touch his life and save him." I prayed one of the most sincere prayers of my life.

After about three minutes, I stood and told the assistant warden I had forgiven him. I told him I knew he didn't really know what he was doing.

"Erler, I don't really know if you're sincere or not. You could be. But I want you to know, as far as I'm concerned, you're a religious fanatic!" With that he walked out, slamming the door behind him.

I stuck my head to the bars and yelled, "Well praise the Lord for that!"

The next morning, officers entered my cell and put me in shackles and chains. I was then shipped back to Florence.

I found out that the administration at Fort Grant had done a few other things to keep me from making parole. They called the newspapers in Florida and informed them that I had been sent back to maximum security because I was a "security risk". They also called and wrote the Arizona Department of Corrections and said I was acting in a "bizarre manner" concerning my religion and was "mentally unbalanced". I learned later they even had a staff psychologist, also a member of their religious cult, "doctor up" my prison jacket, claiming I was extremely dangerous and a real threat to everyone because of my dedication to the martial arts.

A few days after arriving at Florence, I was transferred to the state hospital in Phoenix, Arizona. There I was placed on the criminally insane ward along with all of the mental patients who had either killed other inmates in prison or committed another act of violence. They were all awaiting psychiatric evaluations to determine if they were sane enough to be tried for their crimes in a court of law.

Trussed in a straightjacket and chains on the mental ward of the state hospital, I was scared to death; especially with all these extremely dangerous mental patients who were freely walking around the ward. I remember one big guy, filthy and badly in need of a shave, who came up to me in a rage, saying, "Hey, buddy, ya got a cigarette?" His putrid breath and nicotine-stained teeth were just a few inches from my face. I had never felt so helpless in all my life.

After observing me for several hours, some officers and the head psychiatrist came out on the ward and took me into an office. They spoke with me for a while before they finally took off my chains and straightjacket.

The psychiatrist looked at me and said, "Robert, I want you to tell me all about your religious experience."

I looked at him and responded with, "Yes, sir. Are you a Christian?"

He glanced at one of the officers, then back to me, and said in a negative tone, "No, I'm not!"

Instantly, fear knifed through me as I realized I was sitting eyeball-to-eyeball with a secular humanist who was about to make a final decision on my sanity—a final decision on the sanity of a man known as the "Catch Me Killer" serving a 99½-year sentence and already labeled as a religious fanatic.

A Bible verse popped into my mind that went: "For God hath not given us the spirit of fear; but of power, and of love, and of sound mind" (II Timothy 1:7). This was one of those little memory verses I had memorized in my isolation cell at the Florida State Prison.

God was saying to me, through His Word, that I was not crazy. He was in control of the situation, even though it didn't seem like it to me, and I was to share my faith in Christ with this man of authority.

I began by saying I wasn't a religious fanatic because I had baptized all those men in the irrigation ditches at the Florence prison. I was simply a believer priest, ordained by God through His Word, and commanded to act upon what He says to us in the Bible.

The psychiatrist just stared at me for a moment and then jotted down several notes on a pad. He glanced up at me and said, "Go on, Robert."

I testified to him about how I felt only God could forgive me for what had happened; that I believed Jesus Christ is God in the flesh. He came into this world about 2,000 years ago, through the virgin birth He was born to Mary, and later died upon a cross for Bob

Erler.

The psychiatrist's eyes looked like fried eggs as he stared at me a moment before jotting down more notes on his pad. He then looked up at me and said, "Continue on, Robert."

I figured I might as well let it all hang out then, so I said, "I believe that Jesus Christ rose from the dead to prove He was God. And I believe when I was on the phone, crying out to the authorities to 'please catch me', that in truth it was my lost soul crying out to God for salvation! I believe when I asked Christ to come into my heart that He did, and not only forgave me, but He divorced me from being half a police officer, and divorced me from being half a convict, and made me a whole Christian—born again in the spirit, by the Word of God."

The officers and psychiatrist just stared at me for a while before the psychiatrist finally said, "Robert, we need to observe you for at least ninety days in order to make a complete evaluation of your case. You may go back out on the ward now."

It was not until many months later that I realized Dr. Baker, the head psychiatrist, was convinced from all his tests on me that I was not crazy. He felt it was highly unlikely I would ever commit a crime again. Both he and Hal Carden, head of the diagnostic department at the hospital, felt Florida should examine me closely and seriously consider giving me an opportunity to prove myself on parole.

As a result of a telephone call from my mother to the Department of Corrections, an investigator came and taped my version of all the problems that had occurred at Fort Grant.

Soon after the preliminary investigation, an attractive woman walked up to me at the hospital and said, "Hello, Robert." I had seen her picture in the newspaper and recognized her as Camille Graham, the deputy director of the prison system. An officer led us to a room where Ms. Graham began to interview me about my testimony of the corruption at Fort Grant.

We talked for several hours as I went over every detail about the abusive treatment I received at Fort Grant. I told her how the administration at Fort Grant was stealing from the warehouse and blaming it on the convicts. I explained how many of the inmates were being extorted by the administration, how cattle were being stolen, and detailed many other corrupt practices. Ms. Graham wrote down everything in great detail. She was extremely professional and quite cordial to me.

Because my psychic evaluation was good, she decided I had no mental problems. And because I didn't have a single disciplinary report or warning ticket for over ten years, she wanted to investigate my case completely. She told me if I was completely truthful with her, it would all go well. But if I lied—even a little—she would be very disappointed and I would never get any help from her in the future. She asked if I was willing to take a polygraph test to prove the truth of my statement.

"You know I'm telling the truth. I'm going down there to take that polygraph and I'll pass it a hundred percent on everything I've said. I haven't lied or exaggerated. I want to take that test."

She smiled and said, "Let's go. If you're as right as I believe you are, Robert, I assure you your record will be cleared and I will return you to minimum security as you deserve."

At the Arizona Department of Public Safety, I was questioned by the lie detector examiner. He told me the machine was so sensitive it would pick up any trace of a lie. He asked me questions about the details of my testimony, then concluded with several overall questions. "Did you lie to Ms. Graham in anything you told her?" "Did the assistant warden physically grab you?" "Did he enter your cell and tell you that you should have been castrated and drawn and quartered?" "Have you exaggerated anything in any way to try and hurt the assistant warden?" He even asked me to tell the details of my crime. I passed everything.

After three and a half hours on the polygraph and six different tests, the examiner shook his head and said, "Mr. Erler, I believe you are telling the truth. I don't think you lied at all to Ms. Graham."

I was taken back to the state hospital and Ms. Graham called the next day. "Bob, I want to thank you for telling me the truth. I'm flying up to Fort Grant this weekend with Mr. MacDougall (director of corrections in Arizona) to talk with the people you suggested." Their surprise visit made the front page headlines in the *Phoenix Gazette* the following Tuesday. It read: Fort Grant Warden Resigns.

Apparently they found so much corruption they forced the warden to resign and transferred the assistant warden. Later, as the investigation continued, they fired him from the system instead of letting him resign. They also fired another assistant warden.

The deputy director wrote a letter to the Florida Parole Board clearing my record. She told the board to disregard the results of any articles that appeared in Florida newspapers concerning me being returned as a "security risk" because they had done much housecleaning at Fort Grant.

Hal Carden, my supervisor at the hospital where I had been made a trusty, began to look over my records. He held a staff meeting where they recommended unanimously that I be placed in a halfway house in Phoenix. I was told to call my family and tell them I was going to a halfway house and would be able to come home on pass every weekend. Of course I was thrilled by their decision.

I was instructed to pack all my belongings and the captain walked outside to get his personal car to take me to the halfway house in Phoenix. I had all my belongings on a cart by the door when the staff psychologist and all the counselors called me to come down the hallway. I figured they wanted to say good-bye.

When I walked down to them, they said, "Bob, we want you to prepare yourself for some real bad news." Immediately I figured they had changed their minds about sending me to the halfway house. I sat down and they told me they had been notified by Florida I would have to serve 25 years before I could be considered for parole. I couldn't believe their words. I was numb.

"How are you taking it, Bob?" one of the men asked.

"All I can say is praise the Lord. I'm a Christian and I'll have to do my time, one day at a time, for Christ."

"What did you say? I can't believe you're taking it like that."

"Listen, I'm hurting deep inside, but what can I say? I believe in Christ and I know He knows what's best for me."

Dr. Baker looked at me anxiously. "Bob, are you going to commit suicide over this? Are you depressed?"

"I'm a Christian and I'm not going to hurt myself or anyone else. I might cry a little bit inside, but I'm just going to pray about it and see what the Lord is going to do."

That night, back in my cell, an officer came down and asked how things were going. "Well, Joe, I'm gonna have to do another 15 years before I'm considered for parole."

"I heard about that. They put a suicide watch on you." He showed me a card instructing him to keep a close eye on me.

I just laughed. "You don't need that."

"I didn't think I did, but everybody said this would really be a big test for your faith."

"Do you want to pray with me?" I asked.

He winked and tore up the card. "Listen, most of the people here are behind you one hundred percent. We all feel you should be freed. I think you know that."

The next day the investigator came down to see me. "Listen, Bob, you're a political prisoner. Arizona wants to put you on the street; your problem is with Florida." I was concerned for my family. I called them and we all cried together over the phone.

After two weeks, I was notified that the extra 15 years I was going to have to serve was not final. They hadn't approved it yet. Because I couldn't be taken to Florida to represent myself, my family and I decided to send my attorney, Stanton Bloom, down to the hearing to represent me. Florida changed my hearing date and didn't tell my lawyer. He learned of the date from a reporter for *People Magazine* who had just finished his story on me. My attorney was certain they were trying to close all doors to keep me in prison. They were making everything difficult. It took him almost a year just to get a copy of my trial transcript.

They televised my parole hearing in Florida. Six parole commissioners were present out of seven. Three of them voted to release me in 1985 or earlier and three voted to keep me in until 1994. It was a deadlock. The seventh parole commissioner would cast the deciding vote.

The missing parole commissioner had followed my progress through the system and believed in me. He was in favor of voting not for 1985 but for an even shorter date of 1981. Another parole commissioner was apparently upset because the seventh had voted for 1981, so he switched his vote to 1994. That made it four to three against me.

Camille Graham came down to see me. "Bob, if I put you back in minimum security with all this time, would you escape?"

"I've committed my life to serving Christ. What would I escape to? Florida?"

She laughed. "Bob, we're putting you back in minimum security because we know you are not a danger or threat to anyone. As long as you are in the state of Arizona and conduct yourself like you have, you'll be minimum security." So in a few days they transferred me back to Fort Grant.

Upon my return to Fort Grant, Chaplain Earl Jones had me assigned as his chapel clerk. My duties included teaching a college-level class on the history of the Christian church and another class on Christian discipleship. I was elected president of the Fort

Grant Christian Men's Fellowship. Dr. Richard Jackson paid for me to take a two-year course from the Moody Bible Institute in Chicago. I spent hundreds of hours learning the Word of God and teaching what I learned to the other prisoners.

After a few years, the North Phoenix Baptist Church was able to have me brought to Phoenix and Dr. Richard Jackson baptized and licensed me as a minister. It was overwhelming to me that a church with over 16,000 members believed in the gifts and callings of God in my life. A little over a year later, I was taken back to the church and ordained by Dr. Jackson and the members of the church as a Southern Baptist minister. My mother and the rest of my family were able to be in the ordination service and witness this miracle that was taking place in my life.

One day, in the chapel at Fort Grant, as I was getting ready for our Bible study class, a fist fight broke out between two inmates. I immediately jumped in between them, separating the two, and made one go outside the chapel to cool off while the other one stayed inside.

When I went back to the chaplain's office, the inmate I had sent outside came back in and became very abusive to me, screaming profanities and yelling, "I'm not afraid of all that karate you know. You don't scare me a bit!"

He had his nose touching mine as I tried to calm him down. He became so enraged that he shoved me. I grabbed him and spun him around, bending his arm behind him as I wrapped my other arm around his neck. Refusing to listen to me when I asked him to calm down, he stomped on my foot. I blew my cool.

I said, "If you insist on acting like a complete jerk, then I'm going to treat you like one."

Chaplain Jones was really upset and pleading, "Bob, please don't hurt him," as I marched the guy out of the chaplain's office and into the restroom where I forced his head into the toilet bowl and flushed the toilet! By this time I realized satan had won over me, so I just walked over to the punishment lockup cells and checked in, telling the officer in charge they would be looking for me shortly.

A few hours later, they had a shift change in the isolation section. The new officer on duty, who disliked me intensely because he was a member of the local cult church, cupped his hands like a megaphone and yelled out into the middle of the cellblock, "Hey, you guys, did you hear about the great revival in the chapel?" Into the ensuing silence he bellowed, "The 'Right Reverend' Bob Erler held a baptismal service in the chapel toilet bowl today!"

All the men in the entire cellblock broke out in hysterics. The officer then yelled, "How about it, Erler. I thought you loved Jesus!" The hardcore convicts roared over this.

Upset over his heckling, I yelled, "I do love Jesus, but I happen to be a mean Christian that God isn't through with yet!"

The cellblock rocked with laughter for about five minutes. I felt terrible about the situation as I had been a bad witness. I asked God to really forgive me for acting so impulsively and so unlike the Christian witness I was trying to be.

I received ten days in lockup because of the incident. When I was released, I went back over to the chapel. The inmate who was involved in the fight came over to me and apologized for his part in the incident. As a joke at our next Bible study class, I issued him a baptismal certificate.

NINETEEN
LADY AND
THE TRAMP

Having been in prison for so many years, I finally realized just how lonely I really was. My mother and family would come to visit me as often as they could, yet I still had a deep void within me.

As I was studying the creation of the universe one day, I kept reading Genesis 2:18: "And the Lord said, 'It is not good that the man should be alone; I will make him an help meet for him.' "

About this time there was a great controversy going around in the Christian Men's Fellowship about just which Bible verses a Christian could claim and which ones he couldn't. I personally believed that the whole Bible is the very Word of God so I started claiming Genesis 2:18.

When I mentioned this at a Bible study, most of the men thought it was quite foolish of me to ask God for a Christian wife when I had little or no hope of ever getting out of prison—especially since I was serving a 99½-year sentence. Still, I became more persistent in my prayer life. This went on for about two years.

One day, I received a surprise visit from a minister who was somehow able to get permission from one of the captains to visit me. This was very unusual since the captain in question had a great dislike for me.

When I entered the visiting area, I was greeted by Jerry O. Green, a pastor from Tucson. I shook hands with him and sat down at a table and queried, "How were you able to just walk into the prison to visit me without being on my visiting list?"

Jerry responded, "Bob, I feel God opened this door for me to visit with you. I read an article about you in a Tucson newspaper and really felt impressed to drive up here to Fort Grant to meet you, talk with you and pray with you."

We quickly became friends, and several times in the months ahead, Jerry drove the 130 miles from Tucson to Fort Grant to visit with me.

On one occasion, he mentioned that he had a daughter who was working on her degree at a university in California and was also a gospel singer. Jerry had sent her a copy of my testimony on cassette and she had been quite impressed with my ministry in the prisons. I asked him if she would care to correspond with me.

Several months later, Debra came home to visit her family and was able to come to Fort Grant with her mother and father to visit with me. Debra was very beautiful with large hazel eyes and auburn hair that hung down to her waist. She was tall, well dressed and very proper. She had a real cute smile that I liked immediately. Within a few months, she moved back to Tucson so we could visit each weekend and on holidays in the visiting park.

During this time, I was studying the Bible many hours a day. Chaplain Jones told me about many requests that were coming in from pastors all over Arizona and from different organizations who were interested in having me come and share my testimony or preach. I smiled when Chaplain Jones mentioned this to me, not believing the prison system would ever allow the "Catch Me Killer" to go out of prison just to speak to these various groups.

Chaplain Jones asked me how I could have so much faith in so many other parts of Scripture and not in Revelation 3:7,8. I went back to my bunk and read both verses. "These things saith he that is holy, he that is true, he that hath the key of David, he that openeth, and no man shutteth; and shutteth and no man openeth; I know thy works: behold, I have set before thee an open door, and no man can shut it: for thou hast a little strength, and hast kept my word, and hast not denied my name."

A group of people from the city of Douglas, Arizona, located on the Mexican border, came to visit Chaplain Jones and me in the chapel. They were concerned about the street gangs which were dividing the city and causing many problems. They requested that I be allowed to travel with Chaplain Jones to Douglas to speak to the street kids at the local Catholic center. They felt sure that with my background, I would have a positive effect on the gangs.

The man in charge of the group was the chief psychologist for the Behavior Health Clinic in Douglas. He had brought several problem kids to talk with me in the chapel. I talked their language and we got along well, but I never thought the institution would allow me to travel to their town to speak to the other street kids.

In order to obtain permission for me to travel around the state, Chaplain Jones really put his job on the line. He believed in me and told the new warden he would accept full responsibility if I escaped or anything else went wrong.

A few weeks later he showed me the papers, signed by the warden, which would enable me to travel. I just couldn't believe this new warden would take a chance on me after all the problems I had with the old administration.

The very next day, I was called into the warden's office. Mr. Hargett told me to sit down so I did. He began by saying, "Bob, many times I have to make tough decisions on people and I really don't like saying 'no'. In your case, with all the national publicity on you, it would be a very easy thing for most officials to simply say 'no' in order to be on the safe side as far as their careers went in corrections. I'm sure you understand what I mean."

I nodded my head and he went on.

"I've read your jacket and spoken with a lot of my staff who have known you for many years. I want to have an understanding with you." My heart started pounding as I felt he had reconsidered my case and would have to deny me. He said, "If I allow you to travel outside the institution on speaking trips, am I going to be foolish?" He just stared at me from across the table for a minute.

In a state of shock, I looked directly into his eyes and said, "Mr. Hargett, if I am allowed to travel outside the institution, I promise you I will never escape or cause any problems for the Department of Corrections."

He stared at me for a moment longer before his eyes dropped down to a Bible on his desk. "Douglas, Arizona, is on the Mexican border, Bob. When that van comes back from Douglas, I want to see you on it."

My heart skipped a beat and I wanted to thank him for his trust in me, but he put up his hand to stop me. He said, "I don't go around publicly, in my position, telling people this, but I believe in what you are doing as I serve the same God you do."

He then got up, came around the desk and put his hand on my

shoulder as he prayed with me. We shook hands and he told me his door was always open to me if I ever had a problem. I walked out of the same office from which, only a few years earlier, I had been led out in shackles and chains.

When I got back to the chapel, the shock of what had happened had worn off. I broke down weeping, thinking how great God really is.

We drove down to Douglas in a prison van without any guards. The Catholic Civic Center was packed that night! The whole town was excited about our program.

When I gave my testimony and an altar call afterwards, over 50 people came forward to receive the Lord, including the head psychologist who had invited us down there to speak. I was so excited about what God was doing, I jumped off the stage and hugged all the new converts.

This trip, and the positive response from the community, opened the way for Chaplain Jones to take several of us from the Christian Men's Fellowship around the state of Arizona for various speaking engagements over 50 times.

Debra and I had been visiting for about two years now and we had become very serious about each other. Her mother and father would bring her to several of the churches I spoke in and she and I would spend all day in the visiting park on weekends. We prayed about it and decided to get married. Almost everyone in the Department of Corrections was against it and they refused to allow me to get married.

I was then a state-wide driver and allowed to drive the prison van whenever we went out on speaking trips. I decided to put in for a three-day home furlough which the prison had recently adopted.

I was granted a home furlough for 72 hours. I visited my family in Phoenix and then went to Tucson to visit Debra and her family. We discussed marriage with both of our families and everyone was in agreement. Since I would now be allowed a 72-hour furlough every ninety days, we planned to get married on my next one.

On April 20, 1981, I went on a three-day furlough and was married to Debra by her father in Tucson, Arizona. The wedding was attended by my family and Debra's.

For getting married while on furlough, I lost my furloughs for one year. After six months passed, Camille Graham gave them back to me! Debra and I spent each weekend in the visiting park. Several of the men from the Christian Men's Fellowship would tease me about one aspect of our visits. Debra would always bring me baskets of food that I had never been able to get in prison. One guy told the Christian Men's Fellowship, "I saw Bob and Debra in the visiting park today. Debra set her food basket on the table and was walking across the yard to meet Bob when Bob suddenly came through the gate and ran right past Debra to look into the food basket before even giving her a hug or a kiss."

Chaplain Jones said, "I don't know how such a big, ugly, beat up old convict like you ever got a pretty lady like Debra to marry you."

I said, "You've heard about the 'Lady and the Tramp' haven't you?" Everyone got a kick out of that.

The prison system has just recently adopted a new policy to allow telephone booths to be installed on the prison yard. A prisoner who was off duty could use the phone between certain hours although every call had to be made collect.

After coming back from preaching at a local church one night, I found an empty phone booth and called Debra. I was excited about several new decisions for Christ which were made at the service and I wanted to share this with her. This particular phone booth was in a dark area of the prison yard and someone had broken the light out of the booth.

As we were speaking, I didn't notice the twelve convicts who had surrounded the booth in an attempt to murder me. One of them hit me over the head with a 15-pound pipe, crushing my skull! I dropped the phone and my knees buckled as blood spurted all over the phone booth. Somehow I was able to come out of that booth and fight for my life on pure instinct!

Within a minute or so, I was able to run off all the men who were assaulting me. I went back inside the phone booth and grabbed the receiver. Debra was absolutely terrified as she heard the phone drop and then the noise of the fighting. I told her, "Debra, I'm hurt really bad, honey. I've been hit over the head with something and I'm bleeding all over the place."

I felt sick to my stomach and was very dizzy as I tried to stop the bleeding. I told her, "If I don't make it, darling, just remember I love you."

I hung up the phone and turned to try and make it to the medical building. Several of the convicts had come back with big rocks and were throwing them at me. They ran off as I tried to fight with them. As I tried to make it to the clinic through a little alley way behind the gym, I fell to my knees a couple of times. Stumbling to my feet, I glimpsed one of the attackers following me with a knife in his hand. I was so enraged at this that I charged at him and losing his courage, he fled.

I knew if I passed out in the alley, I would either be killed by the gang who attacked me or die from loss of blood. I finally realized I would never make it to the clinic, so seeing the control room across from the gym, I made my way to the door.

Captain Hughes was on duty that night and his eyes widened as I staggered into the control room, soaked in blood from head to toe.

He exclaimed in shock, "Oh my God, Bob! What happened!"

I said, "I've got an Excedrin headache, captain, and I need to get to the clinic right now."

He tried to get me to lay on the floor as they called the clinic for emergency help, but I felt I would die before the medical staff could get all the way down to the control room to give me treatment. I started back out the door but the officers grabbed me to restrain me. Then they helped me to a truck and rushed me up the hill to the clinic.

I remember collapsing on the floor as they helped me in the door. They put me on a table and I could hear everything perfectly clear, although I was semi-conscious by then. They started tearing my jacket and other clothing off as the doctor took a straight razor and shaved off my hair.

I felt the doctor applying pressure all over my skull and saying, "Oh no! I think his skull is crushed and the bone has gone into the brain!"

I could hardly breathe as my nose and mouth were full of blood. They were putting pressure bandages on my head to try to stop the bleeding.

They were in a panic as they put me in the prison ambulance and started out across the desert with the red lights flashing and the siren blowing. We were enroute to the emergency room of the hospital in Willcox, Arizona, about 35 miles away from Fort Grant.

One officer held the pressure bandage on my head while the doctor used a blood pressure cup trying to get my blood pressure. I felt a calmness and peace about it all, believing I was in the process of physical death and going to be with the Lord.

The doctor was yelling at the driver as he took my blood pressure, "We're losing him! We're losing him!" He started beating on my chest as I had just about stopped breathing.

I felt like I was drifting in a twilight zone. The doctor, no longer able to get my blood pressure or pulse, said to the officer in the front seat, "This man has expired!" I could clearly hear everything he said, yet I was unable to respond at all to let them know I was still alive.

They turned off the red lights and siren and I heard the doctor call back to the prison on the radio and say, "Inmate Erler has expired enroute to the hospital emergency room." There was silence all the way to the hospital.

As they were carrying me into the emergency room hallway, I heard someone exclaim, "What is that bloody mess?"

Someone else replied, "It's Bob Erler. He died enroute to the hospital."

A nurse in the emergency room who had heard me speak in her local church, ran over to me and ripping the bloody bandages off my head, cupped her hands to my ear and yelled, "What is the meaning of Romans 8:28?"

I instantly felt like hot electricity shot through my body. I opened my eyes and said out loud, "And we know that all things work together for good to them that love God, to them who are the called according to his purpose." I looked around the emergency room and saw all the prison officials staring at me with eyes that looked like fried eggs.

The warden came over to me in the emergency room and said, "Bob, you're hurt pretty bad, son. Don't be moving around and causing more bleeding. I need you to tell me who assaulted you."

I looked up at him and said, "I know I've been hurt real bad, sir, and that I might even die from this. But if I do die, I know I am saved and washed in the blood of Jesus. I was fighting so many people and was hit so hard that I don't know who it was."

He looked at me a minute and said, "Bob, if you know who hit you, and I think you do, would you even tell me?"

I said, "Warden, you know I can't do that."

He replied, "You need to know you might not make it through this and I need to know who did it."

I said, "I can't remember anything, sir." And they wheeled me into the x-ray room.

I learned later that on the night I was assaulted, the warden had every convict awakened at 1:00 a.m. He told the prison staff, "Anybody who got into a fight with Erler has got to have some physical telltale marks on them." He instructed the whole staff of officers to go to each area and wake up every inmate so they could strip search them and look for any visible injuries.

They found seven convicts, all belonging to one of the notorious prison gangs, who had injuries which none of them could explain. One had a broken finger, another had teeth missing and still another had broken ribs and black eyes.

They locked up these seven inmates in isolation. They soon told on one another and a total of twelve convicts, who were involved in the attempt on my life, were locked up that night. All of them were shipped back to Florence.

When I returned to Fort Grant from the hospital, I was escorted into the warden's office. The warden, assistant warden, and three captains and officers were having a special hearing on me. They did not know what to do with me.

One captain who disliked me very much said, "Robert, we have no other choice but to put you in protective custody and keep you in isolation from now on. This attempt on your life was so serious we have to protect you as well as the administration. . ."

He hadn't finished speaking when I jumped up and said, "Captain, in all the years I have been in prison, I have never been in protective custody nor will I ever be. Yes, many people have tried to kill me, but this has been going on for all the years I've been locked up."

I told the committee, "If you ever locked me up in protective custody, it would amount to the death sentence for me since all the convicts would believe I was a coward." I went on to say, "I know prison life and convicts. I do not want any protective custody now or ever. I accept responsibility for myself."

The captain stared at me for a moment, then said, "Are you saying that you want us to allow you to go right back out to the general population after a serious attempt was made to kill you?"

I said, "Yes, I do. If you don't allow that to happen, you will be responsible for getting me killed by a convict looking for a reputation whenever you finally let me out of protective custody. Please just let me go back out to my same job, bunk and work area. Then all the other convicts will respect me for being a man."

The captain said, "You know we found the pipe they hit you with. It was covered with bloody fingerprints and hair. We intend to try these inmates for attempted murder and you have to testify against them."

I looked at him straight in the eyes and said, "Captain, I am serving a 99½-year prison sentence and I might never make parole. I am the only one who is doing this sentence. Not you or anyone else. I will not testify against anyone, regardless of whether they tried to kill me or not. I demand to be allowed to go back out in the prison population and serve my time as a man. I will not hide in a prison isolation cell for the rest of my life! If someone kills me, I release the prison from any responsibility concerning the matter. It is my decision and choice to live as best I can inside the general prison population, sir."

The captain looked at me a minute, then glanced around the room at all the other officials and said, "Will you sign a paper releasing the prison from any responsibility if you are harmed or killed?"

I said, "Yes, sir, I will."

Everyone nodded in agreement and I was given a release form which I signed, saying that neither I nor any member of my family had a right to file a lawsuit or complaint against the prison administration if I was assaulted or killed by other inmates.

I thanked the committee and walked back out onto the prison yard. All the other convicts were staring at me since my head was shaved and all stitched up.

Since I had been "rolled up" and had lost my position in the chapel as clerk during my stay at the hospital, they reassigned me to work on heavy duty equipment. The real reason for my new work assignment was the administration wanted me out of the chapel since they felt I had become too powerful in my position.

They put me on a bulldozer out in the middle of the desert, pushing up piles of dirt all day. I remember praying one day while I was out in the desert, saying, "God, I realize I asked you to use my life to move mountains for your kingdom, but this really wasn't what I had in mind."

I saw a truck speeding across the desert, driven by the officer who conducted the daily count of the inmates on their jobs. He pulled up to my bulldozer and yelled at me to get in the truck.

I asked if there was a problem and he simply said, "Get in the truck, Erler," which I speedily did.

The officer drove me to the classification office. I felt sick to my stomach thinking they were going to reassign me to a different job.

He ordered me to go to my classification officer immediately, and not knowing what to expect, I walked into his office. He simply said, "You made parole, Erler. You're going home."

UPDATE:

Bob Erler walked out of the Department of Corrections in the state of Arizona on July 19, 1983. He is on a lifetime parole and currently lives in Dallas, Texas, with his wife, Debra, and their little toy poodle named Killer.

Bob's son, Bobby, came to live with Bob and Debra when a federal judge granted Bob full custody of his son. Bobby was 17 at that time. He completed high school, was recently married, and is now serving in the United States Army.

Since his release from prison, Bob has spoken well over 700 times on national television and radio, and in high schools, county jails, state and federal prisons, and mental wards across America.

If you would care to have Bob as a guest speaker, write or call him at:

Bob Erler, Director
International Rock Ministries, Inc.
P.O. Box 901907
Dallas, Texas 75390-1907
(214) 272-8999

Above: Bob's baptism by Dr. Richard Jackson of the North Phoenix Baptist Church, March 26, 1980.

Above: April 20, 1981—Bob's mother, Winifred Erler, Bob & Debra, Debra's parents, Audrey and Jerry Green.

Left: Alligators in the prison's moat that Bob swam through to escape.

Bob Erler, Jr., 19 years old.

Bob on the yard at Angola State Prison, Louisiana, during one of his many speaking engagements since his parole.

Above: Police car driven by Bob in high-speed chase when he was a member of the Hollywood Police Department in 1968.
Below: Car hit at an intersection at 100 m.p.h. during that chase.

Debra Erler

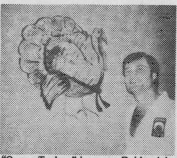

"Super Turkey" became Bob's nick-name after winning a karate fight. This was painted on the wall of Bob's cell by an inmate.